THE
PUNA
KAHUNA

Other Ben McMillen Hawaiian Mysteries
by Mark Brown

Game Face
Yellowfin

THE PUNA KAHUNA

A Ben McMillen Hawaiian Mystery

MARK BROWN

OX BOW PRESS • WOODBRIDGE, CONNECTICUT

Published by
OX BOW PRESS
P.O. Box 4045
Woodbridge, Connecticut 06525

Printed in the United States of America

Library of Congress Cataloging-in-Publication data

Brown, Mark, 1947 -
    The Puna Kahuna : a Ben McMillen Hawaiian Mystery /
Mark Brown.
        p.   cm.
    ISBN 1-881987-02-7   (hardcover :   alk. paper)
    1. McMillen, Ben (Fictitious character)—Fiction. 2. Police—
Hawaii—Fiction. 3. Hawaii—Fiction. I. Title.
    PS3552.R6942P86   1993
    813'.54—dc20   93-24262
                                                                    CIP

The paper in this book meets the guidelines for permanence
and durability of the Committee on Production Guidelines
for Book Longevity of the Council on Library Resources.

For those with a lifelong commitment to the land

Aloha 'aina

Aloha and *mahalo* to—

Jim Albertini
Eileen D'arujo
Palikapu Dedman
Jean Greenwell
Alyson Hagy
Nelson Ho
Carol K. Hollenshead
Mary Lassiter
Margaret McGuire
Lucille Morowitz
Annie Szvetecz
Rasin Tek
Anne Wheelock

and ...

Kona Historical Society
Pele Defense Fund
Big Island Rainforest Action Group
Sierra Club—Big Island Chapter
Rainforest Action Network

... for making this book possible

All characters in this novel are a figment of my imagination, but the geothermal drilling in the Wao Kele O Puna is not.

Cover illustration and design— L. C. Mac III
Author photo— Zelda Brown

Double-hulled outriggers crossing the uncharted ocean. Polynesians, sailing by the stars, following their goddess Pele to a new homeland.

They came with their children. They brought chickens and pigs, and carefully wrapped taro plants, sprouted coconuts, and shoots of banana. They planned to stay a long time.

As they neared the shore of Hawai'i, ribbons of fish turned the cobalt water silver. On land they found rich soil and tropical rain forests and flowing mountain streams choked with clear rainwater. They found the new home of Pele.

They divided the island into *ahupua'a*—strips of land that stretched from the sea to the top of the great volcano—so there was equal opportunity, so each would have access to the ocean, the grasslands, the forest, and the fiery mountain.

They invented aquaculture when they built fish ponds. They never took two adjacent *koa* trees for building canoes. Conservation was a way of life. When they made a ceremonial cape of '*ō'ō* and '*i'iwi* feathers, it was the contribution of many birds—a few feathers from each. Their *mele* and prayers, their gods and goddesses, their religion and folklore were based on the gifts of nature. Their own personal guardian spirits—'*aumākua*—were owls and sharks and lizards.

They respected the land and the goddess who lived in the mountain and spewed fire and smoke, reminding them of her power …

... generations later their descendants are faced with fished-out waters. Their *'aumākua* are endangered. In fact, more than a third of the earth's endangered species call Hawai'i home. Exotic plants and grasses are strangling the native plants and herbs that for centuries have provided medicinal cures. There are not enough *'ō'ō* to make a single feathered anklet ... let alone a glorious cape. The forests are shrinking. The land is eroding at an alarming rate.

And in their most precious forest, the Wao Kele O Puna, there are human predators. Clearing the land, constructing drilling platforms, filling the air with toxins, contaminating the precious drinking water, killing the *'ōhi'a* and its bodyguard, the *hāpu'u* fern, endangering the happy face spider and *'io*, the great Hawaiian hawk.

Now, they cannot leave, these descendants of the Polynesian sailors ... there is no place for them to go.

They must stay and fight for the land ... and for the beliefs of their ancestors.

Chapter One

January 1985

SWIRLING PURPLE CLOUDS were building in the western sky above Grand Teton National Park. A few miles east in Jackson Hole the sun still shone brightly, but it would only be a matter of hours before the region was another foot closer to a record seasonal snowfall.

Massive snowdrifts crusted with frozen rain sparkled in the sunlight as if someone had decorated them with millions of diamonds. Hardly a footprint, human or animal, marred this glacial ocean. The wind, which had been negligible at dawn, was now gusting, scattering loose ice crystals across the high desert plateau. At the western edge of town seventy-foot evergreens—blue spruce planted as a windbreak many years before—rocked back and forth, shedding clumps of trapped snow. Limbs had torn free, jagged depressions in the snow the only trace of their plunge to earth.

The midmorning temperature had reached a balmy forty degrees, but the approaching Arctic front, laden with moisture from the Pacific northwest, sent the temperature falling throughout the noon hour, and now, the mercury hovered just above freezing.

The corporate campus seemed forsaken. The main parking facility was less than one-tenth full. The only vehicles left were Jeeps, a variety of 4x4s, and several Bearcat snowmobiles. Wet blowing snow was turning them into sleek cocoons.

Parked in the circular drive by the main entrance was a super-stretch limo, whiter than white, with its engine purring, and a stiff-figured driver hopelessly scraping at the windows with a piece of yellow plastic.

And inside—inside the silvery glass edifice, headquarters of Jackson Hole Geothermal—the remaining employees thought about tire chains, frozen door locks, and the arduous trek home. And for some, the men seated in the boardroom, the scene brought the vision of an airport that wouldn't remain open past two-thirty.

This was a prestigious group. You could trace their board directorships, land holdings, and energy leases into every sector of American business. They had met in the morning to deliberate the firm's most visible endeavor—the geothermal project in Hawai'i. After much discussion, the meeting had ended at eleven, concluding to their mutual satisfaction—a political solution, the panacea of the wealthy. Catered lunch followed. Then back to the boardroom for one last meeting.

The board rarely met on Fridays, let alone on a Friday afternoon in the middle of the Wyoming winter. The lack of enthusiasm was evident in their expressions. So now they waited for the chairman's signal indicating that the meeting could begin. But actually their interest was focused on the approaching winter blizzard and concern over the prospect of being stranded many miles from the warmth of their mistresses.

A few stared out the expanse of glass at the bleak winter scene. Others tapped eraser ends on the mahogany conference table while impatiently shifting back and forth in their leather chairs. Jackson

Hole's chairman was in character—a perpetual frown. In board meetings he concentrated on tweezing his eyebrows with his fingers. He was a dour man. Never smiled. Never a kind word. Some postulated that he had been the recipient of a charisma bypass operation.

The chairman waved his hand.

With that Geddes cleared his throat. He turned to the man at the back of the boardroom who was leaning against the large whiteboard. "Let's get on with it, Konanui," Geddes implored. Geddes sat grim-faced with brooding dark eyes, shaking his head slightly to indicate that he thought this was going to be a waste of everyone's time. "We'd all like to leave," he tapped the face of his Rolex, "and beat this shit outside."

Nohea Konanui took a deep breath as he pushed himself away from the wall. He approached the conference table, legal-sized army-green folder tucked under one arm, the fingers of his right hand running through his wavy black hair. With his approach, each man seated around the table folded his hands in front of him, seeming prepared to listen, but just as likely each could have been praying for the meeting to end quickly. Nohea eyed the chairman, noting the old man's expression. It was anything but supportive. As for the rest of the board, there were no smiles. Not a glimmer of interest, just the muted sound of shuffling feet beneath the large table. Apparently, this meeting was just a polite political exercise in deference to him, the senior engineer—the man who was supposed to make them richer than any of them had a right to imagine.

But Nohea was determined. He would show them.

"I'll get right to the point." Nohea held up the large folder that contained nine copies of his report. He flipped open the folder and handed all nine sets to Geddes, his boss. Geddes kept one and passed the others along. Nohea assumed the posture of an instructor, clasping his hands behind his back. He took a deep breath. "The lava flows have added more than three hundred feet of base material to our drilling site. Reports from the U.S. Geological Survey indicate the seismic activity in the East Rift Zone is more intense than ever before... and probably will continue for several years."

"Years?" The speaker was the firm's finance man, an overweight Wharton graduate, who had stated many times that the project was too risky. He had been Nohea's only sympathetic ear.

"Years," repeated Nohea. "We simply can't drill in Kahauale'a any longer ... and ... the land swap ... " he glanced around the table, "... is unconscionable."

A few board members shifted in their seats but none offered a comment.

"The Puna Reserve is ceded land ... it belongs to the Hawaiian people. The law states that tenants within an *ahupua'a* ... an *ahupua'a* is a land division that extends from the uplands to the sea ... that these people have access to the land in perpetuity. We can't keep them out and we can't get drilling permits if outsiders are free to roam about the drilling site."

"That won't be a problem." This time it was the firm's attorney speaking, a man with a persistent wry smile, whose bright eyes hid behind tinted glasses.

Nohea started to glare at the lawyer, caught himself, then formed a polite smile and nodded. Right now Nohea didn't need another battle with Andrew Takehiro, a small, trim man of Japanese and Hawaiian descent. He and Takehiro were both from the Big Island, but as different as the ancient fisherman who used a simple fishhook made from a shell and the ocean fishing factory unfurling mile after mile of netting.

Nohea wet his lips and continued. "The plan you have before you," he gestured to the three-page handout, "is a viable alternative to geothermal."

That got their attention—at least they were looking at him now.

"It converts the Big Island's non-peak electrical output into a re-usable source ... super-charged, highly compressed air." His chest expanded as he inhaled deeply. "We have a unique situation in Hawai'i.

The water is extremely deep just a short distance from shore. We can use off-peak power ... say from eleven p.m. to six a.m. ... to compress air. We store it a mile or two offshore in a domed container anchored to the ocean floor. The water is a few thousand feet deep just two miles out, so the intense pressure will keep the air compressed. Later, when we need it, at six in the morning, we reverse the process, extracting the compressed air to drive a turbine and then a generator and we have electricity. The costs are much lower using super-charged air. It enables us to use smaller turbines and, therefore, less fuel. I think we can reduce the cost of producing power by at least a third. It doesn't damage the environment as the rain forest project would or interfere with native Hawaiian practices. We're clear of major seismic activity, and ... in terms of construction savings ... we have equipment near the airport at Keāhole Point that we can retrofit, *and*, a HELCO substation close by. There are production facilities of exactly this type in Europe." Nohea grinned. How could they refuse? He felt the tingle of confidence in his cheeks.

"The construction costs compared to geothermal are significantly lower. We can place several of these facilities near larger cities on each Island and do away with the construction expense and maintenance costs of cross-island towers and undersea cables connecting the geothermal site with O'ahu." He looked around the boardroom. He felt a frown replace his optimistic smile. He knew the color was melting from his face. He expected questions: What were the costs? How long would it take? Instead, they were glaring. The board members of Jackson Hole Geothermal looked as if he had asked them to vote Democratic. No one uttered a word. Then, in unison, their heads turned toward Geddes, who was making a soft clucking sound with his tongue. Geddes eyes shifted for a second to the chairman, whose stony expression said 'deal with this without *us*.'

Immediately, Geddes stood. He took two paces away from Nohea. Then he turned and simply said, "We'll take it under advisement."

With that they all got up smiling, shook hands, patted each other on the back, and headed for the large, double doors. No one made eye contact with Nohea again. No one even shot him a sarcastic look. The good old boys just filed out, including the finance man whose head was awkwardly turned away, purposely avoiding Nohea's pleading stare.

And on the boardroom table, left behind, were nine copies of his plan. None of them creased near the upper left corner staple. They hadn't even turned to the second page.

Geddes remained for a few moments, shaking his head, and then he too, walked out.

Red-faced, Nohea followed Geddes into his office and slammed the door behind them.

Ten minutes later, completely frustrated, both men took pause from their argument. Geddes simply leaned back in his chair, scowling. Nohea, agitated and feeling a clammy sweat on his forehead and neck, stood, crossed the large office, and faced the window, observing the broad expanse of the bleak plateau that bordered the eastern edge of Jackson Hole. Nohea closed his eyes, blocking out the winter scene, thinking instead of the lush rain forest halfway across the Pacific next to his hometown of Pāhoa on the Big Island. A warm, soothing feeling passed over him. He pictured himself as a small boy walking the forest trails with his father, careful of the deep fissures in the earth, listening to the sounds of the Wao Kele O Puna, mud caking on his bare feet, a seemingly endless canopy of *ōhi'a* branches above his head. Hardly any sunlight filtered through. Midday seemed like dusk, and it was humid, yet cool. After many miles, they came upon a taro patch that Nohea's grandfather had planted long ago. His father explained that it provided food on long hunting trips. Your first time into the forest you brought provisions and taro shoots. The next time your food was already there.

A large drilling platform and tower forced its way into Nohea's reverie. Suddenly, he felt cold again.

His adversary remained seated, locked behind the fortress that was his desk. Nohea could sense that he, too, was thinking about the rain forest. Or at least what was underneath it.

The two men were very different. The man standing by the window was Hawaiian. Eleven-sixteenths pure. The rest was a confusing mixture of Portuguese, Irish, Scottish, and Australian. After receiving his undergraduate degree at USC, he'd earned a master's and doctorate from the University of Wyoming in chemical and petroleum engineering, respectively. He was thirty-one years old and highly paid by Jackson Hole Geothermal, Ltd. Usually, he sported a broad smile— brilliant white teeth against his dark Hawaiian skin. But now his face was filled with anger and his deep tan held a reddish tint.

Jeffrey Parsons Geddes got up, went to his liquor cabinet, poured some Scotch and added some ice. After twirling the amber tonic, he held it up to the light for a few seconds, watching the spin of the fine granules of charcoal. With a satisfied sigh he lowered the glass and took a sip. Then he returned to his desk, sat, and clasped his large, weathered hands behind his head.

He was forty-five, had served a tour in Vietnam in the late sixties, then found his way into the oil business in Louisiana when his year was up. After twenty years in the deserts and gulfs of the world, Jackson Hole had hired him away from a California competitor and put him in charge of the Puna Project—a massive geothermal project designed, when fully operational, to produce 500 megawatts of power. Unlike his Hawaiian *friend*, he only knew a little about geothermal energy. His expertise was drilling. Oil, people—it didn't matter which. His tactics were questionable, but he always produced results—a bottom line as black as oil. Geddes could count his friends on one hand. He'd have to be a millipede to count his enemies.

He swallowed some more Scotch before he cleared his throat.

When Nohea heard Geddes clear his throat, he decided to give his plan one more try. He turned and faced his supervisor, a forced smile on his face, but *'you sunnufabitch'* ready to spill out of his mouth. "The Wao Kele O Puna rain forest is ceded land and an important source of the herbs and plants my people use for healing medicine. My people hunt there … they practice religion … "

"Your people!" Geddes sounded indignant. "That 'your people' shit ended when we kicked Queen what's-her-face out of the palace. You're an American now … not some Polynesian medicine man."

Softly, lowering his head slightly, Nohea mumbled, "Another disciple of Custer, just what we … "

"What'd you say?"

"Nothing … " A deliberate sigh. For a few moments, Nohea's attention was captured by a framed map of the drilling site hanging on the wall. With the absence of the sun, he could easily see the reflection of his face in the glass. The lines of frustration around his mouth and a weary look in his eyes were clearly evident. Nohea knew where this was going. And where it would end. "Look … " he exhaled slowly through his nose, "we took the risks and drilled in Kahauale'a and now lava's covered most of it. We're trying to pull a fast one, swapping our land for the people's rain forest. As soon as we do, we'll ruin part of the rain forest with our roads and platforms. Eventually, we'll ruin the rest of it with toxic by-products, to say nothing of the weeds we'd introduce into the ecosystem, which will eventually destroy the native plants. It's all ridiculous."

"I don't control the flow of lava," Geddes retorted. "We have a contract to tap into the geothermal energy and that's what we're going to do." He swung around in his chair and faced the window. The wind had stopped but heavy snow had begun to fall. Geddes glanced at his watch.

"That's exactly my point. Madam Pele controls the lava and the energy, and when she sees someone destroying her land, she … "

Geddes spun around. "Don't give me that crap. You're an educated man. There's no God and there surely aren't any goddesses.

Jesus." He rubbed his forehead with his left hand. The right one was clenched.

Nohea walked over to the conference table and unrolled a tube of drafting paper. "Do me a favor, just take a look at this. It's a detail drawing of … "

Geddes pointed toward the boardroom. "I heard it all in there. We're a drilling company. We make money selling what we bring to the surface. We're not in the retrofitting business. We're not looking to reduce the short-term costs, we're interested in becoming the main supplier. Ridding ourselves of those Arab bastards once and for all."

Nohea narrowed his eyes. "You didn't let me finish. This is another plan. Not one I'm thrilled with, but it may spare a large part of the forest."

"C'mon, Konanui. Forget it. Why can't you just do your job? We certainly pay you enough."

"Just hear me out. I re-drew the plans last night. We can drill all the wells we need in Kahauale'a if we build a berm around the northwest perimeter. It should divert any future lava flows around our drilling sites. We won't have to go near the rain forest. We won't need the land swap."

"You know how long building a berm out of lava will take … let alone the cost? This is ridiculous. If you'd spent more time working on the venting problem, like we asked, then maybe we'd be on time."

Nohea scowled at Geddes. "The cost of destroying the last lowland rain forest in America is a lot more than the cost of a few bulldozers."

Geddes stood. "That's it."

"Whaddaya mean, that's it?"

"Get out!"

"What?!"

"Get the fuck out! I'm not wasting any more time with you. Either do your job or hand in your resignation. I've had enough of this rain forest shit! You've worked on drilling projects all over the world.

There isn't one that hasn't screwed up the environment in some way. You didn't complain about those. The cost of relying on those fuckin' Arabs for oil is much higher than isolated problems with the environment. Now we got one small Hawaiian rain forest ... Shit! I shouldn't have to explain this to a bright guy like you." Geddes's face was red and he was grinding his teeth. "Why do you think you were chosen for this project? Huh? C'mon, Konanui, think about it." Geddes snorted. "Because we wanted a Hawaiian on our side. You're our token Hawaiian, Konanui. You're our Hawaiian symbol ... our advertisement that everything we're doing is okay." Smirking again, he placed his hands defiantly on his hips. "How about it, Konanui; you gonna get in line or not? Huh? You oughta be more like Takehiro. Now, there's a company man."

At the mention of the wiry attorney Nohea's stomach filled with fire. His lips quivered.

"We can get another engineer anytime. We don't need *you*, what we need is a Hawaiian!"

"I quit."

"What? Fine. Fine. We'll have you replaced in no time. This time with a Hawaiian who'll appreciate the opportunity."

"I want you to know you're making a big mistake, Geddes. If you and the other assholes in this company think I'm going to let this die, you're wrong. You're dead wrong! Some how, some way, I'm going to stop you and this damn project. And soon. Damn soon! There are a lot of people on my side. You'll see." Nohea grabbed his plan and headed for the door, rolling up the drafting paper as he walked. At the doorway, he spun around and shouted, "And you can send my pay check to the Pele Defense Fund!"

Geddes stood there with a big grin on his face, nodding.

The force of the slammed door knocked the map of the Puna drilling site from the wall, shattering the glass.

Geddes laughed. "The Pele Defense Fund ... " he took another sip of scotch, then shrugged and finished the rest in one swallow ... "now there's a bunch of losers."

Chapter Two

March 1986

THE HEAT WAS OPPRESSIVE and the sharp stench of sulfur permeated the air, but the beautiful woman who was sitting among the steaming rocks didn't seem to mind at all. In fact, she appeared to be enjoying herself.

She had just awakened and was thinking of her lover, a god who lived in a high mountain cave on Kaua'i. Instinctively, she turned toward the west and caught his fading image as it disappeared into the misty Pacific. She yawned, and stretched carefully, not wanting to wake the people in the southern villages just yet. Except for a few fishermen who lived near Ka Lae, no one began the day before her.

Up above, a rare pair of '*ō'ū*—Hawaiian honeycreeper—were putting the finishing touches on their fragile nest, high in an '*ōhi'a* tree, one of the few left standing near the new lava flow. It would eventually help re-seed the devastated forest.

To the east, morning sunlight wavered across large expanses of *pāhoehoe* lava, smooth rippling waves of frozen black magma that appeared suspended in time. Although a heavy downpour had bathed the area during the night, only a scattering of puddles remained in the larger depressions of the lava field. It had been a dry winter and rainwater disappeared quickly, even in the seemingly nonporous lava. Much of the *pili* grass was tipped brown and yellow. Many shrubs were brown as well. Ground cover and food for the animals were at a premium.

Down below, in the deepest recesses of Kīlauea crater, the beautiful woman began eating *'ōhelo* berries, brought to her by her sister from a special place east of Kalapana, *kapu*, off limits, to the villagers. Surrounding the woman in the fiery pit was a flower *lei*, once moist and fresh with fragrance and color, now dried and shriveled and brown. And there were rocks wrapped in ti leaves, offerings from her devoted worshipers. She stretched and yawned again, this time with little concern for her people. The tremors of her movements were felt for miles around. It was time for her subjects to rise. The trembling sent the *'ō'ū* to flight.

And so the day started for Madam Pele, the mystical architect of the Hawaiian Islands.

Fifteen miles to the east was the Wao Kele O Puna Forest Reserve, the last remaining lowland rain forest in the United States. It was Pele's favorite place. The one area she was determined to protect forever—a refuge of what life was like in days gone by. A symbol of how things should be. The forest was covered by a majestic canopy of *'ōhi'a* leaves, and beneath were *'awa* shrubs, glorious *hāpu'u* ferns, carpets of moss, and patches of taro planted in cleared areas by local hunters. It was a vibrant garden of life that had provided her subjects with medicinal plants and food, as well as the essence of their religion ever since they had followed her from the South Pacific to Hawai'i. She was proud of the rain forest, and proud of the people who frequented it. Native Hawaiians, people who respected the land. People who took only what they needed to survive. People who believed in her power.

A Hawaiian hawk—'*io*—wings fully extended, soared effortlessly above the forest canopy. She had returned to her favorite hunting ground after a week's absence.

As she dived toward a preoccupied field mouse, there was a violent explosion that shook the forest. Hydrogen sulfide gas filled the air. The hawk veered sharply, prey forgotten, and she flew away, not wanting to look back. Unfortunately, '*io* could not see the color-less cloud of gas that blocked her retreat.

Her two little ones would go hungry.

The woman in the caldera bolted upright at the sound of the ex-plosion, then floated to the rim of Kīlauea, disguising herself as she rose in black tapa. Her hair crackled fire and her eyes became glow-ing embers. As she emerged from the pit, she sensed the invisible cloud of poison slowly drifting downslope. It passed over her head and rolled on toward the Ka'ū district. The intrusion made her furi-ous and she hurried toward the rain forest to discover the offender. From her vantage point far above the trees, she could see a new clear-ing in the '*ōhi'a*, and finally, Madam Pele, known affectionately and respectfully to her people as Tūtū Pele, spied a tall stack belching smoke and ash. Surrounding it were wires and pipes, and just be-yond the network of pipes a large pond filled with brine and silica, and everywhere the smell of rotting eggs. She thought she had ended this nightmare, covering a similar-looking structure with lava two years before. But it seemed as if the strangers who had come to vio-late her land had moved to the downslope and started over. This time they had chosen her favorite rain forest.

Fury filled her darkened face. Her eyes glowed with vengeance as she streaked away, back to her home, back to Kīlauea. There was work to be done. More work than ever before. These strangers who drilled deep into her soul and were ruining her rain forest would have to be taught a lesson.

Soon the earth shook and a steam vent opened. Then a new fissure was exposed in the East Rift Zone, waiting to accept the wanton thrust of the goddess's hips and the torrent of lava that would soon follow.

She would teach them.

And then the lava started to flow.

It has flowed every day since. It is a symbol of her promise to the people. People with a lifelong commitment to the land.

Ua mau ke ea o ka 'āina i ka pono.

In theory, the motto of Hawai'i—
"The life of the land is preserved in righteousness."

But what law do these people live by who desecrate my land?
She thrust her hips again and again. And the lava flowed and flowed.

Then she thought of the man who lived in the simple farmhouse at the edge of her forest. The man buried in the cane fields of Pāhoa. She knew he had only recently returned. She wondered if she could trust him.

Chapter Three

Present day

A T MIDNIGHT in the Wao Kele O Puna rain forest under a thickly clouded sky, a dark, caped figure approached the Jackson Hole well. He walked quietly near the edge of the road, careful of the fissures that lined the forest floor, some dropping a hundred feet into the underground labyrinth from which he had emerged fifteen minutes before. He carried with him two *ki'i kālai'ia*. Each was crafted from *'ōhi'a*. Each idol was about twelve inches long and four inches in diameter. Angry faces had been carved into the wood.

Headlights! Two sets.

The *kahuna* ducked behind a tree. He hadn't expected anyone on the road this late. The security guards should have changed shifts an hour before. His heart pounded and perspiration beaded on his brow. He swallowed and wet his lips. The lights illuminated the blacktop, surging forward and spreading out into the brush like a tide of flowing lava. As the vehicles approached, the *kahuna* saw the silhouettes of two men in the first car. He could make out their hard hats. He wondered why there were well workers around at this hour. When one man lighted a cigarette the *kahuna* saw that their faces were streaked with dark lines. Maybe it was oil or lubricant. Maybe there had been a problem. Maybe this was the repair crew. He shifted his gaze to the second car, which was driven by a security guard. The *kahuna* recognized his peaked cap. The guard was supposed to be stationed at the gate, two miles back down the road. Maybe his help had been required and he was headed back to his post, escorting the repair crew to the exit. The *kahuna* knew that usually no one was stationed at the rig itself. But he'd have to be careful. There might be another repair team, or another guard, still up there.

After the cars passed, the *kahuna* stepped back onto the roadway and watched the red taillights retreat into the night. He breathed a sigh of relief and moved on, walking briskly. He covered the remaining mile in under ten minutes.

Now he was standing before the drilling rig, which rose a hundred and fifty feet into the starless sky. It was well-lighted—blinking red lights—a safety precaution for low-flying aircraft. Sometimes, when Kīlauea was particularly active at night, tourists paid extra to get a glimpse of the fiery display against the black backdrop. Then the sky filled with helicopters.

The *kahuna* had witnessed a nighttime eruption only once, many years ago, with his grandfather, as they trudged up the mountainside to pray to the family guardian—Pele—their *'aumakua*. Not many families claimed Pele as their protector, but the family of this particular *kahuna* did, for one night, long ago, an ancient ancestor was saved by Madam Pele. The ancestor had been hunting wild pig in the forest when his foot became caught in a tight crevice and he fell to the ground. The impact knocked his spear from his grasp. It landed out of reach. He struggled to free himself, but couldn't; his ankle had already swelled. And then the wind shifted, and his scent reached the snout of the pig he had been stalking. Usually *pua'a* ran from the scent of a man. But this one seemed to sense that the hunter was harmless. The three-hundred-pound *pua'a* came to investigate.

The pig moved into the clearing, snorting, raking its tusks across the ground. The hunter was helpless. The pig prepared to charge. But just then, there was a loud rumbling, and the earth shook, and several huge boulders fell from the sky. Mauna Loa was erupting and Madam Pele hurled boulder after boulder into the forest. One killed the pig. Soon, the fissure in the ground that trapped the hunter widened, and he was free.

The pig made a fine feast. And from that day forth, the Keahilihau family were devoted to the fire goddess.

As he approached the rig, the *kahuna* started to worry. He knew he was breaking the law, and if captured, he had a lot more to fear than a summons for trespassing once they discovered who he was and what he was doing. He wiped his hands on his *malo*, mixing dirt into the streaks of gray that already soiled the loincloth. He licked his lips again, but they remained dry.

―――――――

A few miles away at the entrance gate, the guard resumed his watch from the front seat of his car. He had just let the repair crew out and relocked the swinging iron barrier. The gate blocked the road. The rugged brush and clinkery *'a'ā* lava blocked access on either side of the gate. No vehicle, not even a four-wheeler, could make it around. And at night the entire forest was nearly pitch-black; most moonlight and starlight was cut off by the canopy of *'ōhi'a*. Besides, the invisible fissures in the lava floor made it foolhardy to try to enter the geothermal site by way of the forest. The only safe way was the road. And the guard wasn't about to let anyone sneak by him. He needed this second job desperately. Otherwise, he wouldn't be working for the drilling company. He wasn't a devout environmentalist, but he knew the drilling was dangerous. He had listened to the protesters. He knew the project was no good.

The car radio was tuned to an all-night 'oldies' broadcast from Hilo. He had it up loud, partially to keep him awake, partially to warn the teenagers from Pāhoa High School that he was there, awake and armed. He was tired of their pranks. A month before, he had fallen asleep. He awoke and realized that he was a bit lower to the ground—all four tires had been slashed. A few days later, with another car, he had fallen asleep again. The kids had spray-painted the car windows black, then sneaked by on their dirt bikes and made it all the way to the rig. Luckily for him, they had only tied tree ferns and ti leaves around the base of the well. He was spared his job, but he had been warned—the next time he was gone. The only reason he'd lasted this long was because not many Hawaiians would work for Jackson Hole Geothermal, and no *haole* would work for minimum wage.

He smiled to himself. That gave him some comfort.

Maybe they won't fire me no matter what.

Sitting before the great rig with his legs beneath him, the *kahuna's* eyes were closed and he prepared himself for the *pule kāhea*—the calling prayer. A chant for Pele to come and help in this crisis. To rid the forest of the steel tower and the men who labored on it. Before him was an old placemat made from tapa—bark of the *wauke* tree pounded thin into fabric, just like his *malo* and cape. Carefully placed on the weathered material were fresh *'awa* roots, an offering to Pele.

The *kahuna* began to chant with sharp intonation …

Eia ka 'ai, e ke akua,
He 'ai lani wale nō.
Inu a ke kama …

… his voice softened and his mind drifted upland to Kīlauea, to

Pele. He chanted for a long time and when he finished, he stood and walked quietly away, back down the road, leaving the tapa mat and *'awa* roots and the two angry images behind.

At two a.m. the guard started his car, put it into reverse, swung around, and, shifting quickly through the gears, headed up the road. Every two hours he drove the three-mile road, making sure it was clear and that there was no one by the well. For weeks now there had been no one. In the past many trespassers had been jailed, but lately, hardly any came. Maybe the novelty had worn off. The Pele Defense people and BIRAG—Big Island Rainforest Action Group—still protested at the drilling site entrance and in Hilo at the State and County Office buildings, but they didn't enter the drilling zone any longer. The guard smiled to himself. Except for one guy just last week. He had darted by a surprised worker in broad daylight, climbed the rig, and attached a banner to the top of the structure. Then, as he descended, the banner neatly unfurled out of his backpack. Of course, by prior agreement, a small plane flew by and a photographer got the shot. The cover of the next day's *Hawaii Tribune-Herald* showed Jackson Hole's rig draped with a banner deploring the drilling project.

ALOHA 'AINA

LOVE THE LAND   STOP THE DRILLING

Halfway up the road the guard's smile disappeared when he thought he saw something moving in the short grass next to the asphalt. It could be a wild pig. He'd seen a few. The pigs were smart. They followed human trails when no humans were about. They knew the deep fissures could accommodate both man and beast. The guard stepped on the accelerator.

The *kahuna* saw the approaching headlights and began to run. His cape billowed behind him, giving him the appearance of a giant bat as he dashed for a large *'ōhi'a* tree fifty yards in front of him—the one with a bright yellow reflecting ribbon tied around its trunk. The car was speeding now, only a hundred yards away. He was afraid to go any deeper into the forest. There were deep fissures all around, but none with stone steps like the one he had used to surface only two hours before. He decided not to hide in the forest. He wanted to leave the cape—it slowed him down—but it had been made by his great-great-grandmother long ago. He had to make it to the tree.

The car was upon him, his eyes temporarily blinded by the head-lights. The *kahuna* reached the *'ōhi'a*, ripped off the yellow plastic ribbon that he had secured around its trunk, and disappeared into the earth. He stuffed the yellow marker into a crevice next to the stone stairs and rushed down to the cave floor. He pressed against the slick wall, holding his hand over his heart. The *kahuna* heard the car door open. He hoped the guard hadn't been close enough to see him enter the fissure. If he had, he could follow and a secret portion of the underground network of lava tubes would be revealed. In the time that the geothermal well had been in the forest, many people had used the tubes to bypass the guards and the workers. Jackson Hole officials knew of the tubes, but they didn't know which ones were part of the Wao Kele underground network. It had taken years to find the passages and to discover which led to safety and which did not. Discovery of the underground entrance by the geothermal people would ruin his plans. Then there'd be no safe entry into the forest under the cover of night.

He edged slightly deeper into the lava tube, then stopped and listened. There was no noise except the trickle of rain water. If the guard came down, should he surrender? Was his disguise good enough? The gray in his hair? His bent back? If he was arrested, would they undress him? Should he fight? Should he run? Suddenly, he heard heavy rain. If he made no noise and the rain kept up, maybe the guard wouldn't discover the crude steps by the base of the tree. Maybe he'd leave. Maybe he wasn't sure he'd seen a man.

Maybe he thought it had been an animal.

So the *kahuna* waited.

Five minutes passed. Several times he heard footsteps near the cave opening. But no one came down the steps. Finally, he heard the car door slam. The engine roared and there was a crunch of gravel. Then both sounds disappeared.

The *kahuna* came forward and peered out of the hole. His breathing slowed. The sound of running water increased. He could hear the wind whistling across the mouth of the entrance. He removed his cape, folded it, tucked it under his arm, and then disappeared into the darkness of the ancient underground passageway.

The next morning the first workers found the idols and the *'awa* roots. They all felt a little uneasy.

Chapter Four

THE SUN WAS LOW in the sky, maybe an hour away from the shimmering horizon. It was hot for October and Ben couldn't remember a more grueling race. He checked his watch. Strong pace—seven-and-a-half-minute miles. He pressed another button. Eight hours, forty-seven minutes, twenty-two seconds. Where was he? He stared ahead. On his left—*makai*— was Keāhole control tower. The turn-around was just ahead, a little beyond the airport. That meant ten miles more to the finish line. Quickly, Ben calculated what he needed to do to break ten hours. He had to improve by fifteen seconds per mile, not an easy chore, but within his reach. For years now, he had dreamed of finishing the Ironman in under ten hours. Now he was too close to let it slip away. He increased his pace. He still felt good, but he wished he was twenty-one, not thirty-one.

He noticed there were more women than before. When he first started racing triathlons, his goal had been to stay with the top women. He hadn't realized that their goal was to stay with the top men. He smiled and then shifted his concentration back to his goal. Ten hours— no, nine hours, fifty-nine minutes, and fifty-nine seconds. That was all he cared about. Ben pumped his arms a little faster. His legs seemed to follow.

Someone handed him a huge yellow sponge. Squeezing it over his head and holding it against the back of his neck refreshed him. A second hand reached out with an orange cup of Exceed. Most splashed over his chest, but he managed a few gulps, tossed the cup aside, and quickened his pace a bit more, assuming he had lost a few seconds. In the background, he could hear the cheering crowd, much denser here than on the lonely stretch of the Kohala coast where most of the bike segment had taken place. Soon he would be at Honokōhau Harbor, then the sprint toward Kailua, and the last downhill leg to the finish line on Aliʻi Drive.

"Woo, woo, woo!" The crowd cheered and shouted encouragement, raised fists pumping in the air.

When Ben McMillen wasn't swimming, biking, or running, he was either fishing, hiking, or investigating a crime. Ben was a Kona detective. This was his second stint as a cop, after a two-year go at retail that had ended when his surf shop on Maui burned to the ground. His first stint ended when his mentor, a Japanese-Hawaiian, was passed over for the Captain's position, a promotion he had earned. The job had been given to a *haole*. So when Tobi Otaki resigned, so had Ben. Now they were both back. Tobi as Captain, and Ben as Detective Sergeant, and Ben not too far from Lieutenant, although he wasn't sure if he wanted to disappear inside with the paperwork.

Triathlon training kept his body in tune. At five-ten and one-eighty, dark-skinned—his Hawaiian heritage—he caught the eye of many women. But one, Lisa Scott, who was waiting with Tobi at the finish line, seemed to be the one in his future. Their relationship had been anything but smooth. Recently, there had been a separation when he returned to the Big Island after *Swift Benny's* had been consumed by fire. But now Lisa was entertaining thoughts of a transfer to the Hyatt Waikoloa. Maybe things would work out. Lisa seemed more respectful of his need to be alone at times, and more and more, he'd been thinking of a long-term relationship. In fact, he had promised himself that he was going to suggest they live together if she transferred. And he was going to be careful not to make it sound like a trial arrangement.

A small knot formed in his right calf. Instinctively, he glanced down. If it got much bigger, breaking ten hours was out of the question because he'd either have to slow his pace and make sure the knotted muscle didn't tighten more, or he'd have to stop and massage it for a minute or two before he could continue. Either way, hopes of achieving his goal would be dashed. Trying to relax, yet maintaining his pace, Ben forged ahead, keeping his mind on gliding, breathing evenly, and not thinking about the pain. He pushed all of his concentration away from his leg. He envisioned Lisa's face. Her shiny black hair, recently cut short. Her big brown eyes. The seductive way she smiled at him. The muscle in his leg seemed to be cooperating.

Eight miles to go, but only an hour until the ten-hour mark.

Twenty minutes later, Ben saw the throng of spectators by the entrance to Honokōhau Harbor, where most of Kona's charter fishing fleet docked. His mind sent him back a few days, when he was relaxing in a deck chair, sipping a cold Beck's and watching off the stern as four squid lures bounced in the wake of Danny Mitchell's Hattaras. They had been two miles out, off Kealakekua, a few miles south of Kailua, when the whine of the line had gotten their attention. Retreating with breathtaking speed was a deep blue sail, racing like mad with the bright yellow lure. Ben had jumped up, grasped the rod, and waited until it felt just right before he jerked it back, firmly but smoothly, setting the hook in the blue marlin. Danny threw the twin engines into reverse and followed the fish, which now headed into a steep dive, thrashing its head, trying to cut the line with its powerful sharp bill.

In unison there were more, "Woo, woo, woo," the newly adopted Ironman chant. The cheering crowd brought him back. With lips pressed together, breathing evenly through his nose, Ben increased his pace a little more. His leg cramp was gone. But it was replaced by light-headedness. He hadn't been concentrating on his breathing. The blue marlin, which had actually weighed in at 467, had consumed his thoughts. For the last mile, he had been running on memory, a dangerous scenario in any race. When that happened, you weren't aware of every step, and could stumble. You weren't controlling your breathing, you could become dizzy, and most times it was hard to regain your concentration. It always screwed up your pace. Ten hours was a long time to focus on anything. Not concentrating felt too good. The temptation to 'just finish' the race began to overwhelm the desire for a personal best.

His guttural scream startled the crowd, which became strangely silent for a few seconds, until they realized he wasn't hurt. He just needed to get back on track, and screaming was the only thing he could think of, outside of asking someone to slap him in the face.

The black lava gave way to rocky hillsides and housing developments nestled into the valleys. Plumeria covered the sides of the road and the town of Kailua came into view in the distance. Now people lined the entire route—some waving Ironman programs, some American flags, a few with yellow bows still attached to their tops.

Just ahead, Ben spotted the woman who had had the tenth best women's time two years before. He had run with her in a warm-up just the other day. Her name was Greta and she had been a West German Olympic swimmer in '84. She, too, was aiming for the ten-hour mark. They had planned to race together but were separated during the swim segment, which Ben thought of as the equivalent of a foot-wide stream filled with determined salmon, where only the winner gets to spawn. Apparently, Greta had swum much faster than he, for this was the first time he had caught sight of her since his first frantic strokes in Kailua Bay.

He ran a little faster until he was at her side. She glanced over and smiled at him. "Stay with me," she puffed, "you'll make it."

And he did, but just barely. 9:59:17. Greta gave him a kiss and a hug, then trotted off to her husband. Ben leaned against a road barrier, breathing hard, but thrilled with his accomplishment. Then he felt a pair of arms around him and soft lips on his neck.

"You did it!" exclaimed Lisa. "You did it, you old fart!"

They hugged. Ben tried not to stand too close, trying to keep his sweating body from her, but she didn't seem to mind and pressed him closer. Soon they were kissing full on the lips. Ben's throat was parched and he found it hard to breathe, but Lisa wasn't about to let go. Opening his eyes, Ben saw Tobi approaching. All smiles. Obviously proud of his detective. And for once, it didn't seem as if there was anything hidden behind his smile, as there often was when the thrill of accomplishment was tempered by the introduction of another puzzling case.

Tobi simply said, "Time to celebrate." Then he frowned for a second as he looked at them. "That is … after you both shower."

Pleasant idea. Ben knew Lisa was thinking the same as he.

Merriman's had become Tobi's favorite restaurant. Like his past favorites, it would only remain on top for three months or so, then it would be time to find something new. But while it occupied the top rung, the restaurant would be a weekly ritual.

Located in Opelo Plaza in the town of Waimea, Merriman's was only a ten-minute drive from Tobi's house. The haute cuisine menu featured American and European creations, all made with local ingredients: Kohala lamb, Parker Ranch beef, and, of course, the local catch. The sauces had a local flair as well—papaya, mango, and a raspberry puree. Tobi's favorite entree was a new addition to the Hawaiian fish markets—opah, a West African moonfish. Merriman's prepared it by wrapping a succulent filet in philo dough with snappy, fresh vegetables. Tobi had gotten in a rut. He had had opah on each of his last three visits.

The interior was painted light gray and there was a beautiful flower mural by the reception area, but the highlight of the restaurant was the airy domed ceiling, trimmed with an aquamarine border, and below that, at the top of the walls, was a wide strip of wallpaper with a tropical floral print. Tall palms separated a few of the tables. The kitchen was in full view with an up-beat lavender wall as backdrop. Chefs and wait persons were busy, almost frenzied, but organized and smiling.

And for an outdoorsy touch, two large white umbrellas provided a quaint canopy in the center eating area.

They were seated in white wicker chairs, amply cushioned, separated from the two adjacent tables by the areca palms. The large frond that floated just above Ben's head resembled a feathery fan, like the kind that might have cooled the royalty of the old Hawaiian court. Tobi sat demurely, his eyes subtly shifting back and forth between Ben and Lisa. He stroked his gray wispy beard a few times as if he were planning how to get them to realize they were ready to make a commitment to one another. Ben knew what Tobi was thinking— that he and Lisa were different personalities, both stubborn, both a little lost and afraid to admit it. Ben wasn't sure what he should do with *his* life, let alone someone else's. Lisa feared she was a threat to Ben's sense of freedom.

Lisa was studying the menu. Ben was studying her. He liked her hair cut short. He liked that she kept makeup to a minimum—lipstick, mascara, and eyeliner. There was always a sparkle in her eyes, but now it seemed brighter. For the first time she seemed happy about the prospect of moving to the Big Island.

Three years before, when Ben had resigned from the Kona Police Force, he had moved to Maui and opened a surf shop called *Swift Benny's*. After a year and a half of weekend romances, Ben had met Lisa. He'd been sitting at the bar in Longhi's in Lahaina, nursing a cold Beck's, when he spotted her crossing the street. Impulsively, he slapped a five on the bar and dashed out, catching the flash of her tropical wrap-around just as she turned into Kimo's, a restaurant half a block farther down Front Street. He found her seated at the bar, obviously waiting for someone. He took a seat on the veranda, facing the bar, and ordered another beer. When she had looked at her watch for the fifth time, frowned, and eyed the entrance, Ben made his move. He remembered sifting through all his come-ons. None seemed right and a slight sense of panic struck him because this time it seemed important.

He smiled to himself now, thinking back on how he had sat next to her and cleared his throat, telling her that he'd followed her since he first laid eyes on her on the mainland. She had smiled and responded that he must be a very patient man, because she'd been on Maui for nearly two years.

But she had accepted his dinner invitation.

Without asking, the waiter said, "There's no opah tonight, sir."

Tobi wrinkled his face, inflating his cheeks.

"But we have something else you might like … *pāpio*, baby *ulua*. The chef, *himself*, caught several this morning. Very tasty, and if you'd like, we can prepare it just like the opah."

"That will be fine," Tobi said with a grin. "Lisa?"

"I'll have the poached salmon and a small Caesar salad."

"Sir, I forgot, a salad or an appetizer for you?"

Tobi chose steamed mussels.

"And you, sir?" he asked, facing Ben.

Ben hadn't decided. Eight entrees and he hadn't eliminated one.

"How about a slight variation? I'd like the *pāpio* as well, but poached, and a spinach salad with house."

"Very well. May I show you the wine list?"

Tobi spoke. "Alderbrook Chardonnay ... '86, if you still have a bottle."

"I'm sure we do. Thank you." The waiter departed.

"Well, how does it feel to make your goal?" asked Tobi.

Ben beamed. "Absolutely great. I was worried there for awhile ... I had a leg cramp right around the nine-hour mark. It went away, though." Ben smiled and shook his head. "I knew I'd be close, but if I'd come in at 10:00:01, I would have felt like I'd failed."

Lisa shook her head. "Because of one second?"

Ben smirked slightly. "A goal is a goal."

"And next year?" she asked.

"Nine-thirty."

Tobi raised his water glass. "To nine-thirty."

While they ate, the conversation focused on Lisa's move. She told them she had been offered the opportunity to transfer, but first the Hyatt had to find a replacement.

"That can't be too hard."

"Thanks a lot, Ben."

He laughed. "I didn't mean it like that. I meant, how tough can it be to offer someone a transfer to Maui. Wouldn't any mainlander jump at the chance?"

"It's not so simple. Most of the people qualified for my position are married. They have spouses with jobs. Kids in school. And the pay doesn't make up for the higher cost of living. If you're single, being in paradise can make up for the fact that you have to live in a small apartment. But if you've got a family of four, minimum housing over here is kind of expensive."

Ben folded his arms across his chest. "What about someone who's already here ... can't they promote someone?"

"Touchy subject. I recommended my assistant, Mailelani. The Sales Manager, Joe ... *you know* Joe ... " Ben nodded, " ... he sort of stammered through an explanation about how she didn't have enough experience. Hell, she was there four years before I was. To put it politely, I think they want a mainlander from one of the other resort properties."

Tobi looked pained, but he didn't say anything.

Ben shrugged his shoulders. "I empathize, but ... "

Lisa patted his hand. "I know, you can't solve the world's problems all by yourself. Eat, enjoy. Forget it. We're supposed to be celebrating, remember?"

Tobi raised his wine glass. "To your transfer and Mailelani's well-deserved promotion."

Lisa raised her wine glass. "I wish."

After dropping Tobi at his home and declining an invitation to come inside, they left. Ben was beat. He was surprised that he hadn't fallen asleep at dinner. He had trained exceptionally hard during the last month. It had been a good thing that no tough cases had come up during that time. There had been two burglaries. He and Detective Cooper had wrapped them up in a few days. Same story and it was starting to wear on Ben—a teenager with a fifty-dollar-a-day 'ice' habit. Prejudice aside, that was the problem he wanted to put an end to.

As they came to Waikoloa, Lisa asked if he wanted to spend the night. Ben thought for a second and then accepted. The fifty-minute drive south to his small house didn't appeal to him, and besides, he didn't have to be at work at seven. He'd arranged to take two vacation days, which gave him the next three off counting tomorrow, Sunday. He planned to visit a friend who lived in Pāhoa on Monday. The thought of sleeping late, then lounging around the Hyatt after gorging on the Sunday buffet, compliments of Lisa's job, seemed like a reward richly deserved.

Shit ... under ten hours. Old fart, my ass!

Lisa snapped her fingers.

Ben looked up. He didn't remember turning off Highway 19, but here he was, parked in front of the Hyatt, and the parking attendant was waiting for him to get out of the car. He *was* tired.

Lisa leaned over and kissed him on the cheek and whispered, "Let's make love on the beach."

"You know a spot?" he asked, not tired any longer. "A safe spot?"

"I know the *exact* spot ... but it's only safe if you wear protection."

Chapter Five

O n MONDAY, THE OCEAN was just beginning to reflect the first rays of the morning sun. The waterfowl, up early as usual, glided across the placid bay in search of breakfast. Brown noddies and wedge-tailed shearwaters skimmed just above the surface, sharp eyes looking for flashes of silver or yellow. 'Ewa'ewa—sooty terns—always present in vast numbers—hovered over the water, peering down, only moving when a gust of wind altered their position. Always ready to dive and strike. But regardless of their tactics, each of these seabirds was searching for small fish, usually mullet, or tasty baby squid.

Ben watched this scene most mornings. Sleeping late was impossible for him. Some friends told him that later on, when he'd lived by the ocean for awhile, the pounding surf and the seabirds wouldn't wake him, but for now, he woke at the first glimmer of dawn.

Although he planned to take a month off from training—no biking or running—he had decided to swim a little, but only for the exercise. And he'd still follow his routine of stretching, sit-ups, and push-ups, ending with a series of arm and shoulder exercises using a heavy-duty piece of surgical tubing wrapped around one of the posts on his *lānai*.

Ben's house was small—the realtor had called it cozy. Ben had ended up with only a small portion of the settlement after *Swift Benny's* burned down. Most of the money went to the bank to cover the floating loan on his inventory. After the conclusion of the homicide case that had brought him back to the Kona force, he'd bought a new Jeep Wrangler for $12,000—$2,000 up front and $195 per month. He paid $7,000 down on the 'cozy' two-bedroom house, with a mortgage payment of around $550. Then there was clothing, furniture, and appliances, which left him with just over $5,000 in the bank. With an annual salary of $32,500, he just made it every month—unless Lisa moved in. After making love on the beach two nights before, they had gone back to her room and laid awake for hours, talking about living together. Cutting the bills in half seemed like winning the lottery to him, although that was hardly his motive.

The house sat fifty feet from the edge of Moku'ōhai Bay, which was just south of Kealakekua Bay and the town of Nāpō'opo'o. His property was less than a third of an acre, but since no one lived closer than a few hundred yards, Ben felt as if he was on a five-acre spread. Being close to the water was important to him. No matter how rocky the beach was—actually, there was no beach, it was *pāhoehoe* lava and big brown boulders—Ben would have been willing to crawl, if he had to, to get to the sea. He swam almost every day.

The weathered gray cottage needed lots of work. One day each weekend, usually Saturday—most Sundays were set aside for game fishing—Ben took on a project. For the last month he had been repairing the *lānai*. All it lacked now was a coat of waterproofing. That could wait until next week. He needed a rest from the Ironman. Right now, he didn't have the energy to open the can of sealer.

The narrow kitchen with a small window not quite centered over the sink was his next project. New cabinets and a bigger window. Much bigger. There was a small dining room and a tiny bathroom. After the kitchen, he planned to enlarge the bathroom, especially if he was going to share it.

Ben came inside and checked the coffee. Another minute more. He went to the front door, opened it to improve the cross ventilation, saw yesterday's paper on the coffee table, scooped it up, and headed back to the kitchen. He thumbed through the first few pages, pausing to read Big Island Briefs. Nineteen DUIs netted in a trap on the Hilo side. A Hāmākua man was being held for an alleged knife attack on his brother-in-law in a Hilo bar. The Four Seasons Resort construction project had been put on hold—financing problems.

The sports section held his interest for a few minutes as he reached over the counter and poured a cup of coffee, splitting his view between the newspaper and the mug he was trying to fill. A sip. Hot, but good and strong. He put down the mug and went to the refrigerator for skim milk. The first sip of coffee each morning was straight black. Then he added skim milk and a teaspoon of raw brown sugar. But only in the first cup. All the rest were with milk and sugar from the start.

The first sports page had a wrap-up of the Ironman and a feature on the father-and-son team from Massachusetts, a man who competed pushing and pulling his son, a victim of cerebral palsy. Ben remembered the first time he had witnessed their finish. There hadn't been a dry eye. An exhausted but beaming father, grease-pencil numbers melted with perspiration, and his son, a courageous young man proudly holding his wobbling head and frail arms high. That, to Ben, was worth more than his ten-hour finish, more than winning. What an experience for them to share.

His eyes glazed and he turned the page.

The Dodgers won. Beat the Braves 11-7. *Shit! … three errors, two by the infield, and five unearned runs … almost blew a 10-1 lead! When are you guys ever going to get an infield that can field … and a bullpen? Hey, Tommy, how about an Ultra Slim Fast bullpen? Still … we're in first. But we should be eight up instead of only four.*

Tossing the newspaper onto a stool that served as his recycle pile,

Ben grabbed his mug and headed for the bathroom. A shave, shower, breakfast, and then off to the other side of the Island to visit his friend from USC, a photographer named Nohea, who spent more time protesting the geothermal drilling than making a living.

———

The Wrangler roared to life and Ben shifted into four-wheel drive as he headed slowly up the rocky road that connected his house with the road to Nāpō'opo'o. At the junction of the crushed lava road and 160, Ben turned right, following the coastline, Nāpō'opo'o to his rear. Ten minutes later the uphill climb connected with Highway 11 and Ben headed south toward Ka'ū and then Puna, beyond to the east. Highway 11 was called the Māmalahoa Highway. For the longest time Ben had thought it had been named after a great Hawaiian chiefess. He later found out that it was the name of a law of Kamehameha the Great, a decree that guaranteed safe passage on the highways for all. It was said that the law was formulated after Kamehameha had come ashore in Puna to chase two fishermen. He slipped and his foot became lodged in a crevice. One of the fishermen, trying to seize the advantage, struck Kamehameha over the head with a paddle, which broke apart. Kamehameha escaped but the entire episode made a lasting impression on him. He created the law of the highway—*the law of the splintered paddle*—so that the kind of unfortunate circumstance he had experienced would not happen to helpless travelers. *Māmala*, splintered, and *hoe*, paddle. *Hoa*—friendship—has replaced *hoe*.

Makai, the view was magnificent. Ben was at an elevation of a thousand feet and the vast Pacific stretched out so far that Ben believed he could see the curvature of the earth. Upslope, *mauka*, lush foliage covered the steep mountainside. Banana trees became emerald green shadows, wet leaves shining with early morning dew. Spider webs, each coated with a film of water, looked like patches of the galaxy bathed in tiny rainbows. A wet hazy mist covered the cliffs. Muted sunlight pierced the shadows and slanted across the roadway, only to disappear right before his eyes as the sun finally edged above the tree line and evaporated the dreary haze.

Ben liked the winding drive to the volcano. Early, there was little traffic heading toward Ka'ū. You set your own pace and didn't worry about straddling the yellow line. There was plenty of time to think while the beautiful landscape framed your thoughts. First, he thought about Lisa. He was happy at the prospect of living with her. The separation of four months had shown him just how much she meant to him. He sensed he had crossed some sort of hurdle. He wasn't quite sure when that passage had taken place, but he felt he had a much different perspective about himself and what he wanted. He was more willing to compromise. A little more sure of his goals. Feeling good about being a Kona detective. Time had healed some old wounds.

Lisa seemed different, too. She was willing to leave work at work. Even when it wasn't work it used to drive her crazy if they weren't doing something. Eating out, visiting friends, shopping. Recently, she told Ben, she had been staying home more. Cooking dinner, even though it was for one. She read more, a novel each week. And she found that she was becoming more interested in Hawaiian culture. Ben had asked her if her new job would require more work time, not less. She said it wouldn't if she didn't let it. What about her career with the hotel? She said that wasn't necessarily the most important thing in her life any longer.

Living together. Ben wondered if they would keep it that way. Act married, live married, but not get married.

He slowed to pass a swamper—an old wooden flatbed truck loaded with bags of coffee berries. Ben waved to the driver as he passed and caught a wide, white smile in his rear-view mirror.

Soon, the foliage retreated and the gray lava flows from the turn of the century appeared. Visible were new *'ōhi'a* guarded by patches of tiny tree ferns. *Pūkiawe* and *māmaki* shrubs dotted the hillside. Above, a solitary hawk glided in the thermals. And the road curved gently east.

Farther on, the grasslands of Ka'ū bordered the highway. Ka Lae, South Point, was visible in the distance, eleven miles south. Ka Lae was where the ancestors landed after a three-thousand-mile voyage across the uncharted Pacific, from the Marquesas Islands below the Equator to a new home in Hawai'i. Ben was reminded of a story his grandmother had told him about Ka Lae. Although she was from Maui, Ka Lae was well known to her. Until the spread of Christianity by the missionaries in the nineteenth century, each Island had its leaping point—*leina-a-ka-'uhane*—a place where a person's spirit would come when its body was about to die. A place where the soul would unite with the others who had died before by leaping from a cliff into the sea, joining the world of spirits and gods. Ka Lae was such a place.

She told him that her great, great uncle, who had lived near Nā'ālehu on the Big Island, had gotten very old. And one day while he fished by the shore, he slipped on a wet rock and fell and hit his head. One of the younger men who had been fishing nearby found the old fisherman unconscious and carried him home, where he remained asleep for many days. Miraculously, he awakened, just when everyone had given him up for dead. And he told a story of watching his soul leave his body and make the final journey to the leaping point at Ka Lae. When his spirit arrived at the cliff by the sea, the surf was rough and the tide was high. It was said that when you journeyed to the leaping point your *'aumakua* would lead the way. Because the family *'aumakua* was the spinner dolphin, a dolphin would greet the spirit at water's edge and encourage it to jump and join the gods of the nether world. But on this day when the uncle's spirit came to the edge of the lava cliff, the spinner dolphin came near shore and gestured with its nose in the direction of the uncle's village. It was not time to die.

Ben's grandmother told him that this uncle lived another seven years. When Ben asked, 'When he died, did the dolphin appear and urge him to leap?' his grandmother had furrowed her brow, looking at him with a hint of scorn, and answered, 'Of course. Otherwise, he would not have died.'

I miss you, kupuna wahine.

An hour later he reached Hawaii Volcanoes National Park and instead of continuing east on Highway 11, Ben took the southern leg around Kīlauea and headed down the Chain of Craters Road. He drove past the seven craters to where the road had been completely covered by the recent lava flows, where the town of Kalapana had stood. He'd heard that some locals now called it Devil's Throat. But even though he'd have to retrace his path to reach Pāhoa, there was someone he wanted to visit before meeting his old friend Nohea.

Ben pulled his Jeep to a stop in the midst of a grove of palms. The shore was fifty yards away. To the east he could see plumes of steam rising into the sky where the flow from Kīlauea's eastern vent reached the water. He got out and closed the door quietly, respectfully, for the man whose funeral ceremony had taken place here a few months before. He walked across the coarse black sand, heading for a spot that jutted out into the ocean a few hundred feet away. When he reached the six-month-old flow, now hardened and already supporting a few forms of moss, he dropped to one knee and closed his eyes, envisioning the ceremony. Ahi's funeral. Remembering the man's written words.

... scatter half my ashes there

The Puna Kahuna

for there I shall start anew ...

Ben stood and looked around, thinking for a second that maybe he'd find some of Ahi's remains. Soon he laughed at himself, realizing how foolish that was. The wind and the rain had scattered Ahi's dust over the entire flow. Although invisible, it was there at his feet. And there, over by the palms. It was in the tiny mosses that struggled to survive.

Then his gaze focused on the sea and the rest of the poem floated into his head.

... cast my remaining ashes into the sea
for I wish to travel the earth forever ...

Ben wondered what it would be like to sail the seas forever. Death itself, he reasoned, was nothing to fear. There was no pain. The problems of life were for someone else to deal with. There really was nothing to fear as long as someone remembered you, as he was remembering old Ahi, a man he never met in life, but a man he felt he knew very well. It would be terrible to die and know that no one would remember you.

What he really feared about death was not knowing what would happen after his passing. If he had children, what would they do? Whom would they marry? Where would they live and what would they believe in? *Will they embrace their heritage?* And the same for his friends. What would become of them?

How would things turn out? Would there be a cure for cancer? World peace? Food for the hungry? When would the human race run out of energy?

Will I really join my ancestors? Are they watching me now?
What will happen to the Hawaiian culture?

Ben remembered a saying of his grandmother's. 'Gone on the road from which there is no returning.' The first time she used the expression, she had quickly sensed his worry. She had patted him on the head and added, 'One day you will not be able to return here, but you will be able to follow the road that leads elsewhere. Your time on earth is but a small part of what you will experience.'

He felt his eyes glazing over. He stood. Time to go.

I'll be back, Ahi. And maybe one day … I'll join you.

Retracing his route, Ben headed back up the Chain of Craters Road, then east once again on Highway 11. Thirty minutes later he reached the junction of 11, which swung up to Hilo, and Highway 130, a nicely paved two-laner that dipped south to Pāhoa. Ben took 130.

As the green forest that flanked the road zipped by, Ben's thoughts turned to Nohea, a fraternity brother at USC. Ben had joined ADφ during his freshman year. The fraternity was not an animal house, nor was it a haven for nerds. It was a cross section of jocks, engineering students, and liberal arts majors. It was also the fraternity of all the Hawaiians. Between beer parties, there were community fundraisers. Between pranks—like the time they stuffed cow manure down the neighboring sorority's kitchen vent—they served as Big Brothers to small boys from broken homes, raised money for the Ronald McDonald House, and adopted a few families, for whom they sought donations of food at Thanksgiving and Christmas.

Nohea had been a senior engineering student and the frat's math tutor. Ben, struggling with a required calculus course, needed help. They spent many nights working into the morning hours, trying to keep Ben from drowning in a sea of triple integrals. And Nohea, who turned out to be a reasonable athlete, soon began to follow sports, and, with Ben's urging, played on the fraternity's intramural football team. Same position as Ben—tailback.

Ben had lost track of Nohea until recently when he had read an article about a series of arrests at a protest in the Puna district. The activists were protesting the geothermal drilling project in the rain forest. Ben knew a little about it. Some said it was a violation of their religious beliefs—defilement of their goddess, Pele, who ruled the land and lived in the volcano. Others, environmentalists, talked about endangered species, the venting of hydrogen sulfide gas into the air, brine pools containing other toxic substances that would ruin the drinking water. But most of all there was the destruction of the rain forest. And on Hawaiian ceded lands, no less. Clearly, it was illegal. At least Ben thought so. And so did his friend Nohea Konanui, who was quoted extensively in the newspaper article. Nohea, as it turned out, was a member of the Pele Defense Fund. Ben smiled. From chemical engineer and veteran of many drilling projects to spokesperson for a cause dedicated to stopping a drilling project in his backyard.

But what Ben remembered most about Nohea was how comforting he had been when Ben's grandmother passed away.

A week before, Nohea had received Ben's call with great enthusiasm until he found out that Ben was now a detective. He had been friendly, but his tone had cooled somewhat. Ben realized that their friendship needed some reconstruction, some mortar between the cracks that time and ideology had put there.

Pāhoa was an old town trying to become a new one. A simple two-lane street, lined with leaning telephone poles and covered with a maze of overhead wires, cut through the center of the village. The storefronts were quaint; mostly they housed produce stands of locally grown vegetables and fruit. A raised platform boardwalk connected many of the stores. Much of it needed repairing. A bank, a post office, an old Dairy Queen, a small print shop, a few small restaurants, and a pre-fab police station. And of course, the vintage landmark, the Akebono Theater, which, when restored, was to show classic films. Classics to the rest of the world—probably first-run features to the people of Pāhoa. But Ben found nothing wrong with that.

From Tobi's description of the town, Ben knew the people were friendly and happy to live there. He had said the children had per-petual smiles etched into their faces. Another detective had added—'Even the marijuana growers,' who slipped into town in mud-cov-ered pickups, 'smile. I wouldn't describe them as perpetual, though.'

Nohea lived in a sugarcane field in a ramshackle farmhouse a mile and a half behind Pāhoa High School. The house had belonged to his parents. Both were dead. He was an only child.

The paved road that ran past the school turned to packed dirt just past the athletic fields. And a short distance after that the sugar-cane started, obscuring the view. Tall stalks were everywhere. Nohea's directions were very specific and he had emphasized following them exactly—otherwise, he warned Ben, 'you'll drive around for hours following your own tire tracks.'

Ben shifted his eyes between the dirt road and the directions he had scribbled in his notepad. 'Second left. Pass two crossing dirt roads. Keep going straight.' He remembered Nohea adding— '*Makai, mauka*, north, south, east, and west have no meaning back here.'

And since it was cloudy, the position of the sun wouldn't reveal much either.

'Then a right and a quick left. Keep going straight. Careful through a big puddle, but don't worry, it's only two feet deep. Unless, of course, it's raining when you come, then try to keep two wheels in the cane field. You'll come to a green house on the right. That's not it, but at least you're not lost. Next left. Go a half mile and turn into a narrow drive. Follow that until it ends and get out. Follow the trail to the right. The left one will get you into stuff as bad as quicksand. Walk the right trail for a hundred yards. Don't act intimidated when the dogs start barking or they'll come after you.'

What the fuck am I doing here?

When he finally arrived, a faded, light orange Karmann Ghia coupe blocked the end of the narrow drive. Ben hadn't seen one of those in a long time.

"A detective, huh?"

Ben gave Nohea a sheepish grin. "Doesn't mean I'm not an environmentalist."

"Doesn't mean you wouldn't arrest me for trespassing."

"When did you get out of jail?" Ben asked.

"Which time?" He chuckled. "Last week. We didn't want to leave, but they've only got room for fifty-one prisoners in Hilo and we had a hundred people taken in. Actually, I don't think they wanted to feed us any longer. Have a seat, Ben. How 'bout something to eat?"

"Actually, I'm starved. Whaddya got?"

"A lot of vegetables. How about a veggie omelet, bruddah?"

Ben nodded. "Still speak pidgin? I remember you when you first joined the frat. Only the other Hawaiians understood you." He laughed.

Nohea let a small grin slip onto his lips. "We spoke it when we were homesick. Now, I throw in a few *bruddahs* and some *howzits* every once in a while … that's about it."

"Say … where are the dogs?"

Nohea swept his arm toward the forest in back of the house. "Probably chasing something. They'll be back."

Ben wondered—Nohea had almost said it as a warning.

Nohea went to the refrigerator, a small model, dormitory size. As he busied himself scrambling six eggs and dicing mushrooms, onions, and red peppers, Ben looked around the farmhouse. The kitchen blended into an eating area and then into a large living room. There was a door to what he guessed was Nohea's bedroom. He wasn't sure if the house had indoor plumbing. But there was a telephone and electricity. Ben knew many of the homes off the beaten path had no electricity and no running water. People bought bottled water for drinking and employed a series of catchment barrels for bathing water and for washing dishes and clothes.

He walked over to a window that overlooked the back yard, a

small patch of land with one large *ʻōhiʻa* and a nice-sized vegetable garden. At each end of the house were two large redwood catchment barrels. He spotted the ends of half-pipe that funneled rainwater from the roof into the barrels. An empty clothesline danced in the breeze. Looking down, he saw a 4-kw Honda generator under the eaves. It was humming, although it was remarkably quiet. Turning around, Ben noticed there was one other door, which led to a room behind the kitchen. He observed it was the only door with a keyhole. Although he was curious, he didn't ask about it. He remembered Nohea being described in the newspaper as a free-lance photographer. Maybe it was his dark room.

"This must be a big change from what an engineer is used to."

Nohea laughed. "If you saw some of the holes I've lived in, you'd think this was the Ritz."

"No shit?"

"Don't get me wrong. Some of the quarters on the platforms are pretty nice. But when you go drilling in Indonesia or in some of the jungles of South America, it's as third-world as it gets."

"That's some tree out back."

Nohea smiled proudly. "That's my tree."

Ben eyes narrowed.

"You don't know about that custom, do you?" asked Nohea.

Ben shook his head.

"When a Hawaiian child is about a week old and the stump from his umbilical cord falls off, the parents take it along with a seedling and plant them together. It is said that as the tree grows, so does the child. It becomes the child's 'tree for life.' "

"I like that."

"Were you born here? I forgot."

"No. And my grandmother never spoke to me about a tree." A small sigh escaped Ben's lips. "Maybe it's something I can do for my children someday."

Nohea nodded for a few moments, before returning his attention to the cooking. He began to whistle. After pushing the eggs around, he folded the omelet until the edges met, pressed the top a couple of times with his spatula, and slid his creation onto a plate. "Here you go. There's hot coffee." He pointed to the aluminum pot on the back burner of the stove. "No toast, but I think there's a roll or two in the refrigerator."

Ben said he would skip the roll.

"Well, slice up one of those papayas and we'll share it."

"Okay."

As he was looking for a knife and Nohea was pouring more beaten egg into the pan, Ben asked, "How'd you get interested in these geothermal protests?"

"Long story, bruddah. Long story."

"Well, you invited me to spend the night ... so let's hear it, ... bruddah."

Nohea grinned.

As they were eating, and Nohea was warming to his old friend, he explained what he'd done with himself since they had last seen each other.

After quickly describing graduate school, Nohea said he had endured three boring jobs with three major oil companies before going to work for Jackson Hole Geothermal.

"You mean you actually worked for the people who are drilling right here?"

"Uh huh. That's when my life as an engineer fell apart. I guess I'd finally had it. The Hawaiian in me told me it was wrong for a lot of reasons. But funny thing is, it makes no sense economically. I've seen drilling projects abandoned that were a lot less risky and had much better potential return. This is crazy. It's about power and politics. I developed several alternatives. One has a lot of merit, but those assholes at Jackson Hole aren't interested in reducing costs and protecting the environment. They're not interested in energy conservation. They want control. They hate the Arabs. Shit, ten years from now they're gonna make the Arabs look like *bruddahs* ... like ... like ... "

"Easy. I doubt the Arabs are ever going to be our buddies."

"Easy, you say! Okay, Ben. Forget the environment, forget the endangered species and the violation of Pele, and the fact that we ... that you! ... no longer have access to ceded lands." He paused to catch his breath. "Forget all that. Which way did you come?"

"Huh?"

"Saddle Road or around."

"Eleven, around," Ben answered.

"Okay. When was the last time you were in Hilo?"

"A few months ago."

"And before that?"

"Same thing."

"And before that?"

"Shit. I don't know. Maybe two ... two and a half years."

"Okay, good. Three years ago you remember crossing the Wailoa Bridge?"

"Yeah, I guess so."

"Was it under construction?"

Ben smiled. "It's always been under construction."

Nohea jumped to his feet, knocking his fork to the floor. "See! There it is! They've been building that dumb bridge for four years now. Do you know what the plan is for geothermal?"

Ben shook his head.

"They want to create 500 megawatts of power." Nohea's voice was loud.

"That's a lot."

"You bet it is. It's much more than we need on the Big Island. What they plan to do is to generate enough electrical power to feed *all* the Islands."

"All?"

"All. You know how?" Nohea had a doubting look on his face. He didn't wait for Ben to respond. "They plan to build a series of eighty-seven-foot towers clear across the Big Island from here to 'Upolu Point. Then an undersea cable to Maui. Then more towers across Maui. Then another cable through the channel between Lāna'i and Moloka'i to O'ahu. And then, another set of towers to a plant on Foldagger Estate property. Forget the cost. It's a fifty-year project, man. Shit, they can't even build a simple two-hundred-foot bridge." Nohea was perspiring.

Ben, eyebrows raised, said, "So if you really believe they'll never be able to finish the project, what are you worrying about?"

"Hey, Ben. You don't have to understand calculus to figure it out. They'll destroy the rain forest long before they're ready to give up. We've got to put a stop to it now! We don't want an apology ten years from now when the forest looks like a prairie!"

Later, after cleaning up, they went outside and sat on the grass under Nohea's tree. After ten minutes reminiscing about college, while Ben was reflecting on why he and Nohea had been reunited, there was a rustling noise and then much commotion in the forest. Before Ben could get to his feet, two dark shadows pinned his shoulders back against the *'ōhi'a* tree. The next thing he felt was two wet tongues licking his cheeks.

Nohea's vicious dogs had returned from their romp in the rain forest.

Nohea smiled and said, "At least *they* have free access to the Wao Kele O Puna, bruddah. No one's jailed my dogs ... so far."

Chapter Six

CURTIS LYMAN HAD LIVED on the Big Island all his life. On his father's side he was descended from a Nantucket whaling man who had traveled a good part of a year to reach Hawai'i to seek his fortune. Three times the whaling man had come to Lahaina. The third time he decided to stay. Curtis's mother was descended from a New England missionary family who had made the trip in the 1830s. Both parents had died in a boating accident when Curtis was eight, and he, an only child, was taken in by a Hawaiian family from the uplands just west of Hilo. During his youth and the years that followed, enough Hawaiiana had filtered into his life that he thought of himself as Hawaiian. And so he was.

In 1983 he sold his small, struggling construction company and went to work for Jackson Hole Geothermal. Until a year ago, he had never regretted that decision.

But for some time now, the concentration of hydrogen sulfide in the air around Pāhoa had been alarmingly high. The situation was being investigated internally, but no one except a handful of Jackson Hole employees understood the severity of the problem. The latest venting had been the worst. The rotten-egg odor had been unbear-

able. The residents of the Hawaiian Acres subdivision on the southern boundary of the drilling site had to be evacuated for three days.
Many complained of headaches, sore throats, and eyes that wouldn't
stop tearing. The Pele Defense Fund had staged a demonstration in
Hilo. No one was arrested, but there had been much pushing and
shoving and the daughter of a PDF member required six stitches to
close a wound above her eye. That was being investigated, too.

So finally Curtis Lyman had had enough. He no longer wanted
to be part of the geothermal project. What he was about to do would
surely get him fired by noon. That hardly bothered him. At sixty, it
was time to retire anyway. Maybe he'd grow a few crops. Or orchids.
He loved orchids.

It had just gotten dark. Curtis explained to the guard that he was
going to take some air quality measurements. The guard unlocked
the gate, walked it open far enough so Curtis's late-model Toyota
pickup had room to pass, and then walked it back.

Curtis waved into the rear-view mirror and proceeded down the
long black road. He drove slowly, windows down, wanting to inhale
the smells of the forest. But even though it had rained most of the
day, the night breeze was coming from Ka'ū, and he could still detect
a hint of hydrogen sulfide in the air.

For him, working for Jackson Hole had presented many conflicts.
He knew how much the Islands depended upon tourism. It was the
number one industry. Both of his adoptive parents had worked at
resort hotels. But the hotels used a great deal of electricity. Each day
the Hyatt Waikoloa alone consumed somewhere between four and
eight percent of the entire Island's output. Something had to be done.
There had been occasional building moratoriums, but they simply
slowed the pace of construction; they didn't put an end to it. Curtis
believed energy conservation would have to be part of the long-term
solution. And solar energy would eventually become more afford-
able. But the Hawai'i Electric Company, HECO, believed that solar,

conservation, and all the other alternatives were just stop-gap measures, and conservation was impossible to enforce. A HECO spokesperson said a long-term solution was needed. Geothermal energy was the natural solution. Curtis could envision the next wave of PR material where the electric company underlined the word 'natural' in front of the word 'geothermal.'

But most important to Curtis was that his 'second' parents had raised him Hawaiian. They believed in the gods and goddesses of the Islands. And Pele was the strongest. Pele was the one who was violated each time a slant well was drilled into Kīlauea's East Rift Zone. Also, there was the environment. He had been taught to respect nature, to use it carefully so that it always had a chance to replenish itself. If you needed to make two canoes, then you cut down two trees that were far removed from one another. If you were a fisherman, you only caught what your *'ohana* needed for food. And you fished many waters so as not to deplete a particular area or species. There were religious practices that required certain plants and bird feathers, but you didn't kill a bird for its feathers. You trapped it and took a few, making sure it could still fly and that there were no bald spots exposed to the tropical sun and parasites. Finally, there was the threat to the drinking water. The water table had been infiltrated with concentrated silica and the toxic minerals it carried from the brine ponds, a nasty by-product of the drilling effort. The people of Pāhoa were in danger. He envisioned crippled and deformed children. It made him sick.

In the Wao Kele O Puna rain forest there were endangered species. The hawk—*'io*. *'Ōū* the Hawaiian honeycreeper. And his favorite, the happy face spider—*lanalana*—whose body markings resembled a smiling face. Who knew what other remarkable endemic species were yet to be discovered.

Those were the negatives. In Curtis's mind they far outweighed the need for geothermal power.

The Puna Kahuna

A flash of lightning illuminated the northern sky. The ominous shape of the fifteen-story drilling rig was silhouetted for a split second. It seemed horribly out of place among the *'ōhi'a*. Curtis frowned, but inside he was pleased with his decision.

As he drew closer to the well he let out a long, slow breath and shook his head. "What idiots." Shaking his head, he thought— *Even if all the negatives are put aside, how can a cost-effective connection to O'ahu ever be accomplished? Ninety miles of towers? An undersea cable through one of the most seismic ocean floors in the world? Another sixty miles of towers across Maui? Another cable? And then the final leg to a power plant on the other side of Honolulu?*

Jesus Christ! What the fuck are they smoking? Puna butter?

But it would end tomorrow. Curtis Lyman had all the data. The air quality. The water table. Recent seismic activity had put a huge crack in the platform foundation, a fact that had been kept from the public. He was going to tear off the camouflage and expose the truth. He shook his head.

Shit, the cement patches on the rig base are probably still wet!

Another flash of lightning and another eerie picture of the steel intruder in the Wao Kele O Puna.

He parked his pickup near the edge of the forest behind the rig and got out. He wasn't sure what had possessed him to return. That afternoon, when the rains came, they had all left early. The other workers headed for their favorite Pāhoa bar. Curtis had thought about joining them, but on the way out, a double rainbow had filled the sky above the well. It was then that he made up his mind. He had told himself he'd never return, only later he realized he needed to come back just one more time. He had to say farewell to the rain forest he loved. Maybe it was also a test of his character, because for the last week he had thought about blowing up the platform. How hard would it be? He had two dozen sticks of dynamite in his pickup.

That would be enough. He knew just where to place them. He'd be caught. But it would buy the activists some more time. It would draw attention to their plight.

Damn!

So he stood there now before Well #1 knowing he shouldn't blow it up. His Hawaiian parents had done a better job of raising him than that. Curtis smiled and turned his gaze to the bed of his pickup. In the corner was a stainless steel container. And inside …

I have to fight this with data … not with dynamite.

He walked past the rig toward the brine ponds. He wanted to be reminded how bad they looked.

A shadowy figure, hidden from view by a tool shed, dressed in a flowing tapa cape and a tapa *malo* with red markings, watched Curtis as he walked from the rig to the silica ponds. At the man's side was a carved image similar to the ones left a few nights before. The face carved into the *ki'i akua* was angry, scowling. In his right hand the man held a long staff made from *koa*. On the end, affixed with cord, was a sharp spearhead made of stone, chiseled by time, but honed to razor sharpness on a electric grinding wheel. Flecks of crystal on the stone's edges sparkled in the darkness. And as Curtis Lyman's figure disappeared into the night, the man dressed as a *kahuna* rose from his haunches and quietly started to follow, bare feet silent in the finely crushed lava rock. The scowl on his face mirrored that of the idol.

A few feet from the brine pond Curtis tripped over something. He regained his balance just before the slippery incline. He wondered if he *had* fallen into the pond whether he would have been able to get out. It wasn't very deep, only four or five feet, but he wondered if he might have become overcome by the toxins in the pond. As he righted himself, he turned to see what he had stumbled over. He took a few steps back, then knelt as his eyes focused upon a dark object on the ground. He reached out and his fingers touched something round and stiff. His eyes widened and he quickly backed off, repulsed. A dead hawk. Curtis's breathing became more pronounced—he was incensed, angry. "That damned well!" Just as he uttered those words, he heard a small sound, like pebbles tumbling down a hill. He peered into the darkness in the direction of the rig. He saw nothing but the cross-hatch of shadows from the large tower.

Softly, he said, "Just a mouse." He turned and headed back toward the tool shed in search of something to hold the dead hawk. He knew he should carry it to the sea and cast it into the ocean so its spirit could join those of its ancestors. That's what his Hawaiian parents had taught him. That's what he would do.

The man dressed in ancient garb watched as Curtis Lyman left the brine pond and made his way back to the drilling platform. He crouched near a small patch of tree ferns that had shared the space for many years with a venerable *ʻōhiʻa* until the sacred tree had been cut down to make room for the drilling site. The man wearing the cape knew Curtis Lyman and watched as the inspector rummaged through a pile of burlap bags that had been stacked next to the tool shed. He had learned not to trust Lyman. Once he had thought they were on the same side, but it was obvious to him that that was no longer the case.

He watched the inspector select a large bag and then walk back to the brine ponds. The man waited until Lyman had passed before he slowly got to his feet and followed, careful not to trip over his flowing cape.

Every burlap bag, except one, had been slit open at both ends. They were coffee bags, hundred-pounders, and the well workers used them to clean drill bits and other tools that had become encrusted with dirt and debris.

Curtis found some small consolation in the fact that the burlap bag resembled the sennit coffins the old Hawaiians had used to wrap the bones of their dead for burial. Sennit—*'aha*—was a braided cord made from coconut husks, human hair, and animal intestines. The rope served many purposes. It was used for the strings on musical instruments and to form the outline of a new *hale* so the posts could be properly placed. And it was woven into caskets for the dead.

Curtis lighted a match. It flared in the dark. He examined the dead bird. The hawk appeared to be a fine specimen. There were no marks on its plumage that Curtis could see. It had not met with an accident or been shot. He guessed it had simply flown too close to the venting and had been exposed to a lethal dose of hydrogen sulfide gas. He doubted it had taken a drink from the brine pond. *'Io* was too smart for that. He scooped it into the bag, somewhat surprised at how heavy it was. Then he stood and looked past the silica pits to the forest beyond. Tears flowed down his cheeks. He stood there for a long time, wishing the drilling project had never started, for already many native plants and herbs had been eliminated by the introduction of alien weeds, carried from other construction projects by the huge rubber tires of the earth-movers that had cleared the roadway into the Wao Kele O Puna. And those native plants that remained, he had been told by a friend, were not of high quality. You had to go deeper into the forest for those.

He bent, hoisted the burlap bag over his shoulder, and turned to leave, to go to his small house on Kapoho Bay at the eastern tip of the Big Island. To send the hawk soaring on its final flight. *'Io* had ancestors, too.

Curtis heard a 'whoosh.' But that was all. The spear pierced his aorta and blood poured out of his heart and filled his chest cavity. He was dead before he hit the ground, landing on his back, sliding down until his head was partially submerged in the brine pond, the burlap bag still tightly clenched in his fist.

A few minutes passed before the man in *kahuna* clothing approached. Kneeling next to the body, he placed the *ki'i akua* in the pool of blood. He stood over Curtis Lyman, his eyes frozen on the pulsing chest wound. He took a deep breath and brought his left hand to his face, covering his nose and mouth. But nothing like what he expected happened. He wasn't even perspiring. Nausea and guilt didn't consume him as they had the first time. It was easier after the first, and Curtis Lyman was now the fourth person connected with the geothermal project that he had killed. The others he had hidden. Their bodies had not yet been discovered, and probably, they never would be. And even if they were, it would all be very confusing. *Kāhuna* were clever people—high priests, respected for their wisdom and their power. The power to cure. The power to make death.

But this murder needed to be different. Things were getting worse. Time was running out. He had much at stake. This body would have to be found. Right where it was, near the well, with a fishing spear connecting Lyman's heart with the heavens, reaching upward into the darkness of the second night of the lunar month. The night when ghosts—*hoaka*—cast shadows to keep the fish away.

And like a ghost, he disappeared into the night.

Chapter Seven

"I'M NOT SURE this is a good idea."

Nohea turned and smiled and then continued walking. From over his shoulder he said, "C'mon ... it's about time you found out just how much Hawaiian you are."

This was wrong. Whether he was on Nohea's side or not—and he believed he was—he was a detective. He was supposed to uphold the law. Now, as he followed his old fraternity brother, he was about to break it. Not just trespassing. This was real, visible trespassing— illegal entry. The kind of thing that made the front page and forced superiors into handing out suspensions. He wondered what the penalty *would* be if they were discovered. Suspension without pay? What if they fired him? He knew he was letting Tobi down.

"Nohea, wait a second. I'm not sure I should go with you."

"Ben." Nohea stopped and took a deep breath. It seemed as if he was trying to inhale some patience. His hands went to his hips. "We're not going to get caught. This is something you should see. Every Hawaiian should see it. They've cut through the middle of the rain forest. There are silica ponds infiltrating the water table. The smell of hydrogen sulfide fills the air. And this is but one of dozens of planned wells with pipes running through the forest connecting them with a half dozen power plants. More brine ponds, more hydrogen sulfide, more roadways … to say nothing of Pele. They are murdering our goddess, Ben. Raping her repeatedly. To me this is no different than desecrating the Vatican and defiling the Pope." He gave Ben a dumb smile as if he were lecturing an idiot. When Ben remained silent, Nohea said, "Okay, Mister Detective, let's go!"

Nohea increased his pace and Ben followed, his lips pressed tightly together. Anxious, but resigned, and praying they wouldn't get caught. He liked it better when Nohea called him *bruddah*.

They had parked Ben's Jeep at the end of Pikake Street in the Hawaiian Acres subdivision. Then they walked across fairly flat land toward the edge of the rain forest. Both of them were dressed similarly—khaki hiking shorts, hiking boots, and simple cotton shirts with long sleeves. Nohea had a canteen of water. Both had flashlights. There were a few houses in the subdivision, but most of the lots were empty. There were several large subdivisions on the Big Island, the result of an advertising blitz in the sixties. Buy 'a slice of Paradise.' The land was described 'with ocean views, giant native trees, sloping grasslands, and beautiful weather,' and all of that was collectively true. But not every lot had trees and not every lot sloped gradually. For the most part, grasslands meant lava covered with sparse patches of dried weeds. Nevertheless, for a few thousand dollars, many people bought a parcel, usually sight unseen. But few built. The roads were coarse gravel. There was no electricity, no water, and no telephone service in the majority of the subdivisions. For a few owners, generators, catchment barrels, and the lack of outside communication were just the thing. But for the rest, well, they owned 'a slice of Paradise.'

Nohea slowed his pace and raised his hand in warning. Up ahead, a man sat on a rock, facing east, looking like a one-man greeting party for the sunrise, which was only minutes away. Nohea cocked his head and squinted. Then he turned toward Ben and smiled. "Kalima. He's a friend."

When they were within thirty yards of the man, Nohea shouted, "Kalima … aloha!"

Kalima turned and waved. He was nodding at the same time, and smiling, showing he knew where they were going, showing he approved.

To Ben's relief they went no closer to Kalima. Ben was worried that Nohea, outspoken as he was, would introduce him as a Kona detective, deriving pleasure from the fact that he had convinced one of the enemy to break the law. But those thoughts soon passed as the sun pressed its yellow crown above the horizon and inched its way out of the dark Pacific. It was a beautiful sight.

They stopped. Standing on the lava slopes, without a hint of civilization in any direction, it seemed as if they were witnessing the birth of more than just a new day. It was a feeling Ben had experienced many times before but only in the Islands, never on the mainland. Standing on the cliffs of Malibu Canyon, or north on the high ridges near Simi Valley, hadn't been the same. The sunrise in those places did not come from the ocean, but inland, where evidence of man's attempted dominance of the land seeped into his peripheral vision no matter how isolated he thought he was. This was different. It was easy for Ben to imagine that he was the first inhabitant of a new land, waiting to greet a high-riding outrigger that had come from the other side of the Equator, guided only by the stars.

Ben's reverie was broken as Nohea nudged his arm.

Nohea said, "It's five-thirty. The first workers show up at seven-thirty." He added that they still had more than a half hour walk— five minutes to the clearing, fifteen to twenty underground, and ten more on the asphalt road that had been carved through the Wao Kele O Puna.

"They don't work 'round the clock?"

"Usually … but there's an emissions problem. The County shut them down until they fix it. For the last two weeks they've been working on the venting … but first shift only. C'mon."

Shortly, they came to the clearing where the only ground cover was new *hāpu'u* no more than a foot high. The baby ferns were bright green and appeared eager to grow. Nohea told Ben that there were three varieties and he explained their medicinal value. Then, after telling Ben to watch his step, Nohea carefully continued to the center of the clearing. There were many fissures in this area, some wide and very deep. Falling into one could mean serious injury, if not death.

"There's a fissure just ahead with stone steps leading down to a huge lava tube. The tube runs to within a few feet of the roadway that leads to the well. That's how we'll enter the forest."

"I've been to the Thurston Lava Tube. Is it like that?"

Nohea snorted. "The footing is not quite as comfortable, but this tube is much wider and longer. You see, the entire Island is like a maze underneath. Most of the ancient lava flows were underground. In fact, as we speak, Kīlauea's main flow travels underground for much of its journey to the sea. Long ago, when the Hawaiian chiefs were at war, their armies used these tubes to move from one location to another undetected. But you have to know your way. Their are numerous offshoots. Some are dead ends. Some lead downward and disappear into the earth. And once you reach a certain point, the tubes are much too steep to climb. This one twists and turns, but it is reasonably easy to follow. Careful! We are close."

Up until now Ben hadn't broken the law. But he knew that as soon as they emerged from the underground subway, he would be committing a misdemeanor.

"Here it is," Nohea exclaimed. "Be careful, the steps are smooth and steep. The first few will be slick with rain. He disappeared before Ben could ask him not to go too fast.

The chatter and chirping of the early morning birds disappeared and the sound of running water took their place. It was cool and damp, at least ten degrees cooler than above ground. Ben looked ahead and saw the beam of Nohea's flashlight bobbing in the darkness. He unclipped his from his belt and flicked it on. He pointed it downward and then brought it around in a complete circle. The tube floor was smooth, except every few feet there were moguls—subtle rises and dips in the terrain like on a ski slope. He started after Nohea, who was imploring him to be careful but to hurry. Soon he was a few feet behind his friend, comfortable with the pace, and more at ease overall. Fissures above let in small portions of sunlight. Ben imagined that when the sun was directly overhead there'd be enough light to make it without a flashlight. Just as he was thinking that, they entered a larger chamber that was completely black.

"This is amazing! How many people know about this?"

Nohea answered, "Many know, but few know the way."

"You say these things go on for miles?"

"The longest stretch I've used goes about six miles. But I've heard about others much longer."

"Not much grows down here."

"Not true. Stop and look up."

Ben shone the beam of his light toward the roof of the tube. Where there were fissures there were roots and ferns and all sorts of mosses. Some of the roots that hung overhead were more than ten feet long. "What's it like above?"

"Dense rain forest. Right now we're under a large, old *'ōhi'a* and the forest floor is covered with ferns, and taro patches that our *'ohana* planted long ago."

"I guess it's not only safer down here … it's probably easier than finding your way up there."

"Up there moss grows on every side of the trees and the canopy blocks out most of the sun. So determining direction is next to impossible. When I've come with friends who are botanists at the University, guys who have been in the Wao Kele hundreds of times, hell … even they get lost sometimes. Now we mark our way with *ti* leaves

... well, I use *ti* leaves ... they use yellow plastic ribbons. You tie a leaf or a ribbon around a tree every fifty feet or so."

"So you've come in here undercover with some botanists," Ben surmised.

"A few times. I bring my cameras. Make believe I'm the group's photographer."

"Why do you come in?"

"Because I have a right to," Nohea answered, his voice strong and clear. Then softer, "... and to report back how far along they are."

They continued on. A few minutes later, Nohea commanded, "Keep low."

Ben hunched and bent his knees. Without seeing it, he could sense the walls of the lava tube and the roof closing in. As they waddled along, he thought about *his* right of access. Maybe they weren't trespassing. Maybe that would be his excuse if he needed one. *This is ceded land ... in perpetuity. This is my homeland.*

He shook his head.

The path narrowed to the point where Ben could brush against the sides of the tube with his hands. The lava walls were slick and wet. He shone his flashlight upward. The ceiling was still more than thirty feet high and had a sleek, silvery look. He could hear running water, but it seemed farther away now. He asked Nohea about that.

"The water is below in another tube. We've passed several other tubes ... they mostly lead downward toward the water."

Ben asked, "So it's this water, heated deep inside the earth, that they want to get at."

"Right."

"Putting Pele aside, that part seems pretty harmless."

"I don't put that aside."

"I know, I know ... don't get me wrong, I'm on your side. Maybe not for exactly the same reasons. I respect the environment. I don't want any animals or birds endangered. I don't want the air polluted, but the argument that makes most sense, the one you probably have the best chance of promoting, is the towers and cables." Ben laughed. "Hey, maybe your best bet is to make a compromise. Tell them they can resume the geothermal project just as soon as they complete Wailoa Bridge." Ben laughed again.

Nohea turned, held his flashlight under his chin and showed Ben a wide grin. Then he slapped Ben on the shoulder. "Don't worry, bruddah ... I won't let them catch you."

A minute later. "Quiet! We're close. Our voices travel."

Then there was the proverbial light at the end of the tunnel.

"Be careful just ahead. Near the end ... there's an *'ōhi'a* root that reaches the floor. It's over twenty-five feet long. You have to walk around it. A year ago it was only halfway down. You could push it back and forth. Now it's a good hiding place."

Fifty feet farther, Nohea beamed his light on the twisted column of roots. The tangled mass was more than eight feet wide. Some of the roots were as thick as telephone poles. Ben remarked that they looked like giant blood vessels.

"They are," said Nohea. "The arteries of the forest."

Ben sat poised on the steps. Nohea's feet were a few inches above his head.

Nohea whispered, "I think I hear a car. Remember, there's a guard at the front gate. It's a couple of miles away, but he leaves his post every two hours to check on the rig until the workers show up. We've got a ten-minute walk each way, so we can only stay up by the site for a half hour or so. Hold on. Here he comes."

The guard's car passed, headed back toward the entrance. Ben checked his watch. It was six. And then, as his eyes adjusted completely to the semilighted surroundings, he spotted a broad yellow ribbon about eight inches wide and three feet long. It had been tucked into a small crevice near the stone steps. Knotted to each end was a two-foot length of surgical tubing, thinner, but not unlike the kind he used for resistance exercising. He reached and pulled it out.

"What do you make of this, Nohea?"

Nohea turned and took the ribbon. " I guess someone who wasn't sure which *'ōhi'a* covered these steps wanted to mark it."

"One of your botanist friends?"

"No, they come in the main gate ... with permission."

"So a lot of your PDF people use this tube."

"No, not really. Only a few of us. Maybe this was a first-timer. Maybe some kids from the high school. They've been getting pretty brazen about all this. They've played a number of pranks on the security guard. Maybe they finally found out about this way in."

"I'm impressed if you've gotten the attention of the teenagers ... if they're serious about this, that is. That was one of the most impor-tant things to my grandmother. That the younger kids start taking an interest in their culture, so it didn't fade away and become forgotten. She used to say it would only take three generations ... seventy-five years or so," he paused, "... and ... it would be gone forever."

Nohea's teeth gleamed with his smile. "We've made everyone more aware. Some of the kids just run up to the rig and tie ferns and flowers to it. Sort of like handing a flower to a soldier. But I think they have also become more respectful of the land and of their el-ders. I think that is true in many places. Our grandparents were fine. The problem started with our parents. They saw a measure of pros-perity after the war. They never thought about the effect that build-ing fancy resorts and luring millions of tourists would have on the natural resources of the earth. Now we're paying." Nohea held up the yellow ribbon and surgical tubing. "Want this?"

"I think I'll put it back." Ben took the marker and stuffed it back into its hiding place. There wasn't quite enough room and some of the tubing hung out.

"Let's go."

The walk up the roadway was uneventful. They stayed close to the edge so they could dash into the forest if they heard anyone coming. Nohea warned Ben to be careful going back in. He explained that some very dangerous fissures lined the road. He added that this was probably the reason for the yellow marker. "You don't want to make a mistake, especially if you are in a hurry, like if someone's chasing you."

The sun was much higher now. It had rained on and off most of the night. In fact, Ben had had trouble sleeping through the frequent downpours beating on Nohea's metal roof. Yet, he liked the sound. It made him feel alive. It reminded him of how his ancestors lived. Houses with thatched roofs where the rain sounded like thousands of tiny hula dancers. Nohea had said it was Kāne creating a new waterfall to feed a stream so that farther down in the valleys taro fields would flourish.

Then, up ahead, Ben saw for the first time the ugly metal structure that loomed out of the forest, as alien-looking as a rain forest would seem on the moon. The closer they got, the more Ben understood Nohea's viewpoint and his anger.

As they walked around the rig platform, Nohea explained all the technical aspects of the project. Where the other pipes would run. How the generators worked, fueled by the steam created from the geothermal fluids. Why they had to vent to relieve the pressure. The toxic by-products that were channeled into the silica holding ponds. How messy it all was. He stopped talking for a few moments when he spied some burlap bags strewn on the ground near a shed. Nohea shrugged, but it was easy to see that the bags puzzled him.

"What?" asked Ben.

"Nothing."

After talking about the slant wells, which really seemed to upset him, Nohea jerked his head to the right. "Let me show you the real mess."

They walked up a small ridge. Loose sand and pebbles tumbled down the sides of the incline.

Ben marveled at the dense foliage in the distance. It was obvious that the bulldozers had destroyed many acres of land. On the perimeter of the clearing, weeds and tall grasses abounded. A few yards away, at the beginning of the dense forest, creeping vines and ugly weeds were wrapped around the *'ōhi'a*, the start of an unrelenting choke-hold that would eventually suck the life out of the native trees. Even at his feet there were patches of alien grass and common weeds. Ben bent and ripped out several of the offenders. His weeding was interrupted by Nohea's startled shout.

"Ben! Jesus! Ben!"

Ben ran up the rest of the incline and found Nohea, who stood frozen at the top of the ridge that overlooked the brine ponds. He was pointing. Pointing at a body, half in the silica pool, half out. A pole stuck out of the chest. A large dark shadow covered the upper body. A shadow of brown blood.

Ben's first thought was—*another murder!* He quickly envisioned the corpses from his last homicide case.

His second thought, knowing he was trapped, knowing that he had to report this, was—*How do I explain being here? I don't think they'll chalk this up to good detecting.*

The body was half submerged in the brine pond so they couldn't see the victim's face. Ben could tell it was a big man. There was a Hilo High School ring on the middle finger of the left hand, a black rubberized underwater watch around the left wrist. The ring appeared much too small. Ben knelt. The watch showed the correct time. There was a burlap bag clasped in the man's right hand. The bag had obviously absorbed some of the pond water. Salt residue ringed the bottom. The burlap bag bulged. Something was inside. Next to the bag, sitting in the middle of the pool of dried blood, was an angry-faced idol.

Remembering Tobi's number one rule upon discovering a homicide—study the victim's expression—Ben was tempted to drag the corpse out of the water. A significant number of murder victims died with their eyes open. And although the facial lines would be subtle, often times you could distinguish between terror and shock and surprise. Shock—the victim knew his killer. Terror—he did not. Those maxims only held true for murders where the killer had confronted the victim. When the victim was unaware, you saw surprise. Unfortunately, checking this man's expression would have to wait. They could not move the body. Dragging him out of the brine pond could destroy some valuable evidence. Ben would have to wait until Forensic gave him the okay.

Ben turned to Nohea. "You have to hang around."

"I know." His face was filled with concern. "I'm sorry. This really puts you in an awkward spot."

"Don't I know it," sighed Ben. "Shit! Stay right here, don't walk around. There may be other footprints. Is there a telephone?"

Nohea pointed. "I'm sure there's one inside the shack."

"I'll be right back. Don't touch him."

Nohea raised his hands and gave Ben an 'are you crazy' look?"

Ben ran back, careful not to kick up too much dust.

He found a phone and dialed Hilo HQ, a number he'd called many times. He asked for Detective Rodriguez and was told he wasn't in yet. So Ben quickly explained the situation to the desk officer, who said he would send a Pāhoa patrolman right out. After glancing at his watch, Ben decided Tobi would be on his way to work. He called Kona HQ and asked for a patch. Tobi, sounding disappointed when he heard that Ben had been trespassing with a repeat offender, told him to keep him posted, but to let Hilo handle everything. Tobi's unspoken criticism left him dry-mouthed with anxiety. The only comfort came from his mentor's last comment. 'Take a good look at his facial expression.'

After walking outside, Ben decided to have a quick look around. A minute later he spotted a late-model Toyota pickup, in view, but wedged next to the trees that surrounded the drilling site. He hurried over to it and opened the door carefully, using his handkerchief on the handle. The keys were in the ignition. Yesterday's copy of the *Hawai'i Tribune-Herald* was folded in half on the passenger's bucket seat. On the floor of the passenger's side was a wooden container resembling a carpenter's toolbox but smaller. Fitted into three-quarter-inch holes were a row of test tubes. Two were empty. Six others contained liquid—three shades of pink and three more of light blue. Using his handkerchief once more, Ben held the corners of the glove compartment latch and squeezed. He eased it open. Inside were maps. One of the Big Island, dirty and worn. Two others of the drilling site. He unfolded them. One contained a detailed diagram of the current rig; the other a layout of the future piping system—the connection grid from the new wells to the planned power plants. Tucked into the corner of the glove compartment was what he was looking for. The registration and insurance certificate. Both gave the name of Curtis Lyman. He didn't recognize the name; he hadn't expected to. But Lyman *was* an old Island family name. There were missionaries named Lyman, and a museum in Hilo named after a Lyman, and Hilo Airport was also known as General Lyman Field. Ben wondered if there was a relationship.

Then, wedged behind the seats, Ben spied another map. He reached and picked it up. The map was of the Big Island and had been pasted to a piece of cardboard. He was about to put it back when he noticed a series of small red crosses running from the drilling site, to the slopes west of Hilo, along the Saddle Road, cutting across just west of Waimea near Kawaihae, and then turning north to 'Upolu Point. The string of crosses ended there. He looked closer. A few of the red marks seemed darker. They were the ones between Waimea and Kawaihae. He read a few of the landmarks to himself. Pu'u Pā. *Pu'u* meant hill. Pu'u Huluhulu. He smiled at that one—

he'd gone hunting there once with a friend. And Wai'ula'ula gully.

He sat staring out the windshield for a few seconds, creased his brow, licked his lips, still deep in thought, then suddenly remembered they had a homicide victim half submerged in a silica pond. Quickly, he replaced everything, squirmed out, and shut the pickup's door.

As he was about to leave, he noticed that the bed of the pickup was surprisingly clean. The only thing inside was a large aluminum box near the cab wall. It appeared to be bolted to the frame of the trunk. The top was secured with a serious padlock. He guessed the key would be in the victim's pocket.

When he returned to the brine pond, Nohea was seated on the ground, arms wrapped around his knees. He remained silent. Ben looked at the body. The burlap sack had been moved.

He spun around and glared at Nohea.

"I opened it," declared Nohea in a loud voice. Then he ducked his head into his lap.

"Why?"

A shrug.

"Touch anything else?"

"No!"

Ben stared at Nohea until he raised his head. They held each other's gaze for a while. "Okay, what's inside?"

"'Io."

"A hawk?"

Nohea nodded.

Softly, "A hawk." Ben looked skyward for a second, almost expecting to see a soaring mate. "Nohea, do you know a guy named Curtis Lyman?"

Nohea's head snapped up and he scrambled to his feet, looking at the corpse with wide eyes. "Yeah! Is … is that him?"

"Could be."

"Holy shit!"

"Who is he?"

Nohea answered, "He works here. He's an inspector. Tests the air and the ground water and stuff like that."

"I take it you've had run-ins with him before."

"Many times. Many times. He was falsifying results."

"You know that for a fact, or would you like to believe it?"

Nohea looked at his feet. "Maybe they made him do it. Maybe that's why they had him killed. What do we do now?"

"Who had him kill ... ?"

The end of his question was effectively drowned out by the approaching roar of an engine. They both turned and saw a billowing cloud of dust and a flashing blue light.

Ben got his gold shield ready. Then he turned and faced Nohea. "Who had him killed?"

Nohea faced him. "The people he worked for! ... who else?"

Chapter Eight

"GODDDDDAMN!"

Patrolman Jimmy Oliveira had never seen a corpse before. He was six months out of the Honolulu Police Academy, one year out of a criminology major from UH, and his eyes were nearly out of their sockets. He turned and looked at Ben. "What do you think happened?"

I think someone killed him with a spear. "I believe his name is Curtis Lyman. The address on the registration is Kapoho. His pickup is parked behind one of the generators ... if it's *his*," pointing at the corpse, "pickup. If not, then Curtis Lyman is a suspect."

Suddenly, Oliveira spun around and faced Nohea. "Say, I recognize you. Last week we brought you in for demonstrating. Right?"

Nohea just stared at the police officer.

Oliveira eyed the body, then Nohea. "What are you doing here?"

Ben interrupted. "Oliveira, you're part Hawaiian, aren't you?"

"Yeah, so?"

"We came together ... " gesturing to Nohea, "... he just wanted to show me what was happening here in the rain forest. I'm off duty. We're old friends. We were trespassing. But that's it."

"You've been with him all the time, Detective McMillen?"

"From yesterday afternoon."

Warily, Oliveira said, "I see." He paused for a few seconds, as if he was deciding whether he should leave them alone with the corpse. "I'm gonna see what's keeping everybody."

"We won't touch a thing," Ben assured him.

Oliveira headed back to his car.

"He suspects me, doesn't he?"

"I don't think so. I think he's just as confused as we are. If this is Curtis Lyman though, it sure points a finger at someone who opposed the drilling. Why'd you say the drilling people killed him?"

"Because we wouldn't … no matter how bad things got. Even if they killed one of us."

Ben had a little trouble with that explanation, but accepted it for the time being. "You and the other activists are going to be questioned extensively. The drilling people are going to make a big deal out of this."

"When do you think it happened?" Nohea asked.

"Can't tell without touching him, but the blood's dry. I'd say at least six hours."

"What would he be doing here at night?"

"You know more about this place than me. You tell me."

"Maybe they take some readings at night."

"Can you tell from his build if it's Lyman?"

Nohea shrugged and ran the fingers of both hands through his hair. "Not really. I've only seen him a few times."

"That's Curtis."

Ben and Nohea both spun around toward the voice. The security guard was behind them. His eyes were frozen on the body.

"You sure?" asked Ben.

The guard simply nodded. After a few moments he added, "I let him in at eleven-thirty and he never came out. That's what he was wearing. I recognize his belt buckle."

"Anyone else with him?"

"Nope. Just him."

"Didn't you think it was strange that he stayed so long?"

"Curtis worked all hours. Sometimes two shifts back to back."

In the distance the sound of throbbing helicopter rotors grew louder. Minutes later, a police chopper landed at the end of the roadway. One man rushed out, carrying a medical bag. Ben was surprised to discover that it was Ken Asumura, a good friend and Kona's pathologist. What was he doing in Puna?

Ken was just as surprised to see Ben. He explained that Hilo's medical examiner was ill. He'd been hospitalized in Honolulu for tests, so Hilo asked him to help out. He'd been in Hilo for the last few days.

Engine noise and more flashing blue strobes caught their attention. Two patrolmen and Hilo's Forensic team hustled out of their cars.

The guard cleared his throat. "I gotta get back to the gate."

No one said anything, so he hurried off. As Ben watched him leave, he noticed the Hilo policemen, who were headed their way. The policemen intercepted the guard.

After introducing Nohea to Ken—Ken seemed to recognize Nohea's name right away and gave Ben an inquisitive look—Ben explained that he and Nohea were friends and that they had discovered the body. Ken didn't ask why they had been at the site. Ben guessed his own annoyed expression discouraged further questioning.

Thirty minutes later the Forensic team had finished with the area immediately surrounding the victim, including running a nylon drag net through the holding pond. Ken removed the spear after closely examining the chest wound. He confirmed that the lance had pierced the victim's heart. He indicated it was okay to remove the corpse from the silica pond.

Ben volunteered himself and Nohea. They lifted the victim's legs carefully, following Ken's instructions. The pathologist stopped them as soon as the victim's head was clear of the brine pond. Ken knelt and examined the victim's neck and scalp. In those six hours the silica bath had deposited a ghastly white crust over Curtis Lyman's features. Lyman's face looked so horrible that Nohea said he couldn't have identified him. Ken confirmed Ben's guess that the homicide had been committed around midnight.

"He's an inspector?" asked Ken, who seemed very ill at ease.

Nohea responded positively.

Ben bent over and studied Lyman's face. It looked as if it had been frozen in dry ice. Eyebrows raised and frosted. Mouth open, silica stuck to the lips. Eyes covered with white flakes, but open, wide open. No amount of brine could hide the fact that he had been surprised. If he knew his killer, he hadn't seen him.

Another speeding vehicle approached and skidded to a halt on the gravel at the end of the road. Out of a white Nissan 4x4, a pair of portable blue strobe lights permanently mounted onto a roof rack, scrambled two Hilo detectives. They approached the scene briskly, scanning the area to the left and right as they chugged up the incline that led to the holding ponds. Then, as the detectives trotted down the near side of the small hill, Ben recognized one of the men as Ernie Rodriguez, whom Ben had tried to reach. The other was a new man whom Ben did not know. Rodriguez's eyes widened when he saw Nohea. Grim-faced, he seemed anxious to question them both, but he approached Ken first.

When he was finished questioning Ken, Rodriguez turned and snarled, "Follow me."

Realizing the growl was for Nohea, Ben told Ernie, "Take it easy."

Rodriguez merely grunted and motioned them to move.

The two trespassers left Ken to his work and followed the Hilo detectives back to their 4x4, which was still running. The other detective reached in and switched off the engine. Both Ben and Nohea leaned against the front fender. The detectives stood a few feet away. Rodriguez's hands were on his hips. The other man, introduced as Detective Kala, was poised with a pen and note pad.

Rodriguez said, "Okay, Ben. Let's hear it ... from the beginning."

Ben explained how he knew Nohea. He wanted to get that out first. Then, after watching the Hilo detectives exchange glances, he went about explaining the entire episode. Rodriguez stopped him as soon as he referred to the lava tube.

"You mean you were sneaking in? Trespassing? ... with an activist ... with an activist who's been arrested at least a dozen times? You, a Kona detective ... ?"

Ben nodded slowly. He didn't like the sound of it either.

"Where's this lava tube?" asked Detective Kala.

Ben hesitated for a second. "Don't know."

Rodriguez's eyebrows arched.

"It was dark."

All eyes shifted to Nohea.

He didn't hesitate at all. "Ain't tellin'." Symbolically, he folded his arms across his chest and pressed his lips together.

"We can arrest both of you, you know."

Neither Ben nor Nohea reacted.

Rodriguez gritted his teeth, and Ben allowed himself a slight smile as he realized that his presence protected Nohea from arrest as a murder suspect and that the homicide made the trespassing charge seem ridiculous. Rodriguez wouldn't take them in. The newspapers would have a field day. It was the job of the Hilo Police Department to protect the drilling company from the demonstrators, so law enforcement personnel, which included Rodriguez, were considered by everyone to be proponents of geothermal. Page One would carry the trespassing story for several days, maybe longer than the homicide.

"Shit," Rodriguez snorted. He relaxed his stance. "Okay, tell me about how you found the body."

They did.

Another vehicle pulled up. It was another Nissan pickup, but metallic gray not white, and there were no blue strobe lights. Two men got out. One was a trim man with wire-rimmed glasses. He was an inch or two shorter than Ben and was wearing a fresh aloha shirt and pleated gray slacks. The other, the driver, tall and heavy at six-two and around two-twenty-five, was wearing a one-piece khaki field outfit. Jackson Hole's logo, a black drilling rig with a bright orange disk in the background, was embroidered above his left pocket. Both men wore shiny white hardhats.

"Who are they?" asked Ben.

Detective Rodriguez turned. "The big guy is Geddes. He's from the mainland. Jackson Hole's project manager. The other guy is Takehiro. He's their attorney."

The newcomers went straight to where Lyman's truck was parked.

"Can we talk with them?" asked Ben.

"That's where I'm headed," the detective answered.

Ben started walking. Rodriguez grabbed his arm. "Ben, let *me* ask the questions."

Ben's hands went up in mock surrender. "Fine."

Nohea said, "I'll wait here."

Rodriguez said, "Good idea, Konanui. Good idea. Tell you what … why don't you go for a swim." The Hilo detective gestured toward the silica pond.

"Up yours."

Rodriguez smiled and bowed.

Ben gave Rodriguez a friendly shove to get him moving.

"Mr. Geddes, got a minute?"

Geddes turned from Lyman's pickup. "What happened? Where's Lyman's body?"

"How'd you know?"

"Patrolman Oliveira called us."

Rodriguez frowned and pointed toward the holding ponds. Geddes and Takehiro started walking.

"Just a second, gentlemen. I've got a couple of questions."

Takehiro responded. "Sure, sorry."

"Lyman's been with you how long?"

"Eight years," answered Geddes, rubbing the back of his neck.

"Any idea why he'd be here at night?"

"It was his job. He took samples ... air quality, water table tests, checked the fittings for leaks ... that kind of thing. The environment's not a nine-to-five job. Curtis worked all hours."

Ben felt immediate contempt for the Jackson Hole project manager. *The environment's not a nine-to-five job.* Ben shook his head.

"Any problems with him?" asked Rodriguez.

"None," answered Geddes quickly.

The attorney said, "The problem with him is that someone murdered him, detective."

Rodriguez shifted his eyes toward Takehiro. "He have any enemies at work?"

It was Geddes who answered. "His enemy is right over there. Glad to see you caught him already." Geddes pointed to Nohea, who was observing them from the path that led to the ponds. Takehiro spun around, a surprised look filling his face. Geddes added, "He used to work for us. When he resigned he made threats. You can guess the rest."

The attorney stepped forward. "Excuse me, please. He's not handcuffed?"

"He's not under arrest," stated Ben.

"May I ask why not, and also, may I ask who *you* are?"

"I'm Detective McMillen ... from Kona ... Nohea was with me. I'm his alibi."

Geddes, now rubbing his left shoulder and squinting, looked

puzzled, "With you?"

Ben looked at Rodriguez. It was hard to tell if the Hilo detective was actually gnashing his teeth behind his tightly pursed lips. Ben exhaled. "Nohea and I found the body."

Takehiro furrowed his brow. "On what business were you here? It's customary for the police to let us know when they wish to visit the site. And why was he with you? We would *never* have let Konanui in."

"We were trespassing," Ben stated flatly. He gave Takehiro a dumb smile.

Takehiro produced a genuine smile that said—'big mistake, McMillen, big mistake.' "This will … "

Detective Rodriguez interrupted, waving his hand. "We have a homicide investigation here, gentlemen. No one, and I mean no one, goes public with this." He stared at Takehiro. "I better not see this in the paper."

"Far be it from us to meddle in your investigation. But I'll tell you this … Konanui's alibi isn't worth anything if they were both trespassing. Both he and Detective McMillen should be treated as suspects."

Takehiro appeared very angry, but Ben guessed he was anything but. The attorney seemed to be enjoying the irony of how it came to be that Konanui and a Kona cop had been caught trespassing.

Geddes stepped forward and pointed a finger at Detective Rodriguez. "This had better be wrapped up quickly. We won't tolerate the safety and well-being of our employees threatened by a bunch of activists who have never listened to reason. You keep an eye on Konanui, remember … he said he'd stop us when he was let go."

"I thought you said he quit," said Ben, trying not to smile.

"C'mon, Andrew."

They left, walking like they had won round one.

When they were out of earshot, Ben kicked the dirt and cursed. "Assholes!"

"Hey, Ben, don't 'asshole' them. You've got me right in the middle of a political nightmare. What a time for a hike in the forest! Shit!"

"What was I supposed to do? Leave the body for someone else to discover?"

"You should have known better than to come in here in the first place, let alone with Konanui. Damn!"

Shortly afterward, when Ken Asumura was finished with the corpse and had given his preliminary report to the Hilo detectives, he sought out Ben and Nohea.

"They've loaned me a vehicle. I'm headed over to Hilo Hospital. Need a lift?"

Nohea quickly said okay. Ben reminded him that they were dealing with a homicide investigation. "No talking until you see it in the paper first."

Nohea agreed. "I live a short distance from the entrance," he said to Ken. "Drop us off at my place and I can take Ben to get his Jeep."

Ben interjected. "Nohea, even though I'm not officially on this, I'll have to file a report. We'll drop you off and I'll go with Ken." Immediately, Ben realized that Nohea was thinking about the lava tube. "You can trust Ken. He won't tell anyone where I've parked."

"No offense, Asumura. It's important that that place remains a secret."

Ken said, "I understand. I'm on your side. I'm against what they're doing here."

"You are?" Nohea seemed skeptical.

Ken's jaw was firm. He nodded once.

After they had delivered Nohea home and followed the muddy dirt road out of the cane field, they proceeded on 130, headed for the Hawaiian Acres subdivision and Ben's Jeep.

"Does Tobi know about this?" asked Ken.

"Uh huh."

"And?"

"I think he's pissed."

"Why'd you do it, Ben?"

"Nohea and I were fraternity brothers."

"Yeah?"

Ben nodded. "Yeah. But I had no idea he even lived on the Island. The last time I heard from him was six years ago. I got a post card from some drilling site in South America. Last week, when he got arrested, I saw his name in the paper. I called … thought I might be able to help, but he had already been released. I got a hold of him right before the Ironman … "

"By the way, congratulations."

"Thanks." Ben cleared his throat. "Nohea was a little put off when I told him I was a detective, but we got together yesterday, and he said if I really believed in what PDF was fighting for, then I should see exactly what he was talking about. He said every Hawaiian should."

"He's right," Ken offered.

Ben turned and faced the pathologist. "You a supporter? I thought you were just trying to make Nohea comfortable."

"You bet I am. Have been for a long time. My family's from Puna."

"Yeah … right. I remember."

"The land swap is wrong."

Ben had never seen Ken this upset. His friend's teeth were grinding.

"Maybe you should have come with us."

"Maybe I should have," said Ken, staring ahead. A minute of silence passed before Ken asked Ben if he had any ideas about suspects.

"Well, on the surface, since this Lyman guy worked for Jackson Hole Geo, I'd have to guess it's someone who opposes the drilling. From what I've read and from what Nohea told me, I don't think it's any of the organizers. But like any activist group, there are always some followers who believe in being more proactive. Sometimes it results in violence. The murderer may be a survivalist or a marijuana grower living in the Puna forests. Those guys hate the system. They sided with the activists. It's easy to picture one of them taking matters into his own hands. Send a message. Scare the workers. Get them all to quit. That'd stop the drilling. At least for awhile. Let them collect munitions or grow weed in relative obscurity again."

"And you think Nohea's completely clean?"

"He certainly didn't kill Lyman. But, I'll tell you. He's changed. He's angry and he's committed. He knows a lot more than he's told me. And I believe he could name a few violent PDF members in a second. But he won't." Ben sighed. "On one hand, I'm glad I won't be investigating this. They're gonna be tough on PDF and the others. On the other hand, maybe I'd be able to handle it differently, since I believe in their cause. Maybe they would sense my concern and understand that if they helped me capture the killer it would help them in the long run."

"When you started out, you said 'on the surface.' You think there might be another angle?"

Ben grinned at his pathologist friend. "Could be a setup. Make the activists look bad. So I guess it could be someone connected with the geothermal project."

"You'd like to believe that, wouldn't you?"

Ben stared out the window, observing the lush vegetation. He didn't answer.

Ken concentrated on driving. Ben tapped on the window frame, glancing every so often into the rear-view mirror near his rhythmic right hand. He read the mile markers as they passed, making sure one hadn't been skipped. Watched the thick foliage in between. Thought to himself—*Yeah, I'd like it to be someone from the drilling company.*

As they neared Orchard Land Drive, just before Ken signaled left, Ben reached toward the steering wheel and covered Ken's hand.

"Go straight."

"Huh?"

"Go straight. Someone's following us."

———————

Nohea drove directly to PDF's offices outside of Hilo, a house off the Saddle Road just past Kaūmana Caves. No one was there. He got on the phone and finally reached one of the Defense Fund's officers who was attending a meeting at the University. He told her what had happened and warned that the police would be by. He got the sense that she was concerned but not worried. In turn, Nohea was advised not to talk any further to the police without PDF's lawyer present. Nohea agreed and hung up. Then he called a friend who taught at the University but also worked with BIRAG, the Big Island Rain Forest Action Group. She, too, expressed concern that someone had been murdered, but did not seem apprehensive. Finally, Nohea left a phone message for the local chapter head of the Sierra Club.

He got up and walked outside and sat in a frayed lawn chair that faced the hills beyond. Past the tree line, a gray mist swirled about the lava formations. Huge rain clouds hovered *mauka* and Nohea could see dark streaks in the distance. It was raining hard on the upper slopes. He could smell it. The trade winds were picking up. Soon the entire windward side of the Island would be covered in a downpour and the gullies and culverts would overflow with muddy water. North, in Hāmākua, flash flood warnings would be posted. A small-craft warning would be issued, and traffic would snarl at the Wailoa construction site. He shook his head. Four years on a two-hundred-foot bridge. It seemed ludicrous to think that the developers of geo-thermal energy thought they could span the Big Island and Maui with towers and connect them with undersea cables. Cables that would be laid many times deeper than any in the world. In seismically active waters, through channels that had been declared a natural preserve for the humpback whale.

He wished Pele would appear at a Jackson Hole board meeting and burn the entire crew. Something made him shiver. He knew he didn't mean that. Pele would find some other way to punish them.

His thoughts turned to Curtis Lyman.

Five hours later the preliminary results of the autopsy showed that Curtis Lyman had died of a spear wound to the chest. The tip had severed his aorta right where it connected to the heart. Death had come instantaneously. No surprise there. Ken Asumura had checked for traces of poison in the wound. He found none. Poison had been Ben's concern. After seeing the wooden idol by the body, he had conjured up visions of witchcraft.

Ken placed Lyman's death at around midnight, and he had died where they found him. Nothing else seemed out of the ordinary. But to Ben much was out of the ordinary. First of all, if he was he working at midnight, why weren't his instruments and vials of chemicals found by his side? They had been found in his truck. So if he wasn't working, why had he been there? What was the inspector doing with a dead hawk in a burlap bag? Ben couldn't remember any of his grandmother's stories that dealt with that. Except that many Hawaiians brought dead animals to the sea. Had he brought the hawk, or had he found it? His thoughts turned to the murder weapon. Why a spear? It took considerable skill to throw a spear so it would stick into anything, let alone accurately pierce a man's heart. The spear was five feet long and weighed two and a half pounds, and Ken had said that the depth of the wound suggested that the spear had traveled at least twenty feet. When Ben asked how Ken knew Lyman hadn't been stabbed, Ken explained that a stab wound would more closely match the size of the tip of the spearhead. This wound was much larger, longer, suggesting that there had been nothing to steady it during the impact. Like a hand. The weight of the shaft had enlarged the wound as it fell until it finally lodged against a rib. Ben thought— *Quite a throw.*

Ben had asked Ken to test the hawk. The results were simple as well. Paralysis of the respiratory system. They both knew what that meant. The unfortunate hawk had flown too close to the rig during a venting.

Wait until Nohea hears that!

The idol. Ben knew most of them resembled gods. This one he didn't know. But Ken told him it was one of Pele's brothers. Was it authentic? Ken said it was old.

"How can I trace it?"

Ken puffed out his cheeks and let out the air slowly. "Next to impossible, I think. I doubt there were prints. You'll have to ask Rodriguez or Forensic about them."

"What do *you* think about all this?"

"It's obvious that whoever did this wanted it to look like one of the activists is responsible."

Ben countered, "Maybe an activist *did* do it."

"I doubt it."

Ben stared at his friend for a few seconds. He had never seen Ken so serious. The flashing smile was gone. He asked, "Are you assigned to this?"

"Until Fitts gets back. He has kidney stones. Should be back in a week."

"What about Kona?"

"Drake's covering for me. It's much busier here. Much busier." There was obvious distaste in his voice.

"What's wrong?" asked Ben.

"Too much drugs. Too many kids involved."

Ben nodded. "I've got to write up my report. I'm going back tomorrow. Keep me posted, okay?"

"Sure. Where you staying, tonight?"

"Hadn't thought about that. With Nohea, I guess. What about you?"

"With my mother."

They shook hands. Ken gave Ben a small smile.

Ben patted him on the back.

Detectives Rodriguez and Kala were seated in the Captain's office although the Captain was not there. Rodriguez spotted Ben, called out, and pointed to the coffee pot. Ben poured himself a cup, then raised the pot toward the two detectives, who shook their heads simultaneously. Ben sat in one of the side chairs.

Rodriguez was behind the Captain's desk, twisting the end of his mustache. He was slightly shorter than Ben, had a deep complexion and wide brown eyes. The whites seemed whiter against his dark skin. He was wearing an aloha shirt and khaki-colored jeans. Same jeans as in the morning, different shirt. His shoulder harness was visible when his shirt rode up. His Smith & Wesson was on the desk, barrel pointed toward the side wall.

Kala had just been promoted. It was obvious that this was his first homicide—he was sitting up straight, attentive, all ears. He was shorter than Ben and Rodriguez, but he looked as if he weighed the same. His aloha shirt was too tight and his gun bulged just under his left armpit. It appeared that he was trying to grow a mustache.

Ben looked at the wall clock. It was a quarter to five. Some day off.

"Who was following us?"

"One of the patrolmen," Rodriguez answered in a flat tone.

Ben, sarcastically, "Great."

Rodriguez threw up his hands. "Can't blame a guy for trying. We'd like to seal off that tube."

Ben didn't comment. He stared out the window and watched the rain.

"You see Asumura's report?"

"Not the written copy, but we talked about it," answered Ben.

"Any ideas?"

Kala leaned forward.

"None."

Kala leaned back.

Rodriguez flicked at something on his gun handle. "It looks like one of the protesters did it."

Ben wet his lips. Mentally, he coin-tossed the two alternatives in his head. His Hawaiian heritage influenced how the coin landed. "I think it's too pat. I think someone made it look that way."

"Interesting. There's those who say Lyman falsified the readings. Made them look much better than they were."

"You believe it?" asked Ben.

"Don't know. Look, I work ... *we* work for the County." Rodriguez swept his arm across his body to emphasize that 'we' included Ben. He continued. "The activists have been a pain in the ass. Each week they get more brazen. If you can scare the workers ... it puts the entire operation on hold. Gives PDF more time. Time to gain supporters ... raise more money. They're losing all their law suits. They're running out of cash."

Ben didn't bother to comment. It wasn't worth it.

"Konanui's a *good* friend of yours?"

"Yeah."

"I gotta tell you, if it wasn't for the fact that he was with you, that you are his alibi, he'd be in jail right now. And it wouldn't be an overnight deal. I mean no bail. To me he seems to be the most committed, the most violent."

Ben shook his head. "He's not violent."

"Oh, yeah? He took a swing at one of the uniforms a month ago. Got three days in jail. The other protesters are serious, but they're always restraining him at demonstrations. Before, you said you were at his house last night. You know for a fact that he didn't sneak out while you were sleeping? Say around midnight."

"I'm a light sleeper. I'd have heard him. Besides, the rain kept me up half the night."

"Would you buy that ... if our roles were reversed ... and I told you I was a light sleeper? We got a homicide here. I want you to be sure your friendship with Konanui hasn't influenced your feelings."

"He didn't leave." Ben's tone was gruff.

"Okay. Okay. Pete, here," nodding to Detective Kala, "tells me that this is the second time this week that idols have been found out by the drilling rig. He said they're the type of carvings that are used to scare people."

Ben looked at Pete Kala. "The first time, was anything else found?"

"A tapa place mat. Some roots ... and there were two idols."

"Fingerprints?"

"Wiped clean."

"What about this time?"

"Clean," Kala answered.

"Same on the spear?"

The detective nodded. "Except one smear that was probably from Lyman's hand as he fell."

"Has Forensic compared the idol to the other ones?"

"Yeah. They're basically the same. Different images, but the wood's the same and old."

Ben stared at the floor for a few seconds. He was starting to feel the pieces of the puzzle shift. "What else did you find in Lyman's truck?"

The Hilo detectives exchanged glances. Rodriguez gestured for Kala to answer.

"Besides the test equipment ... the vials of chemicals and litmus paper you saw ... there was a pad of graph paper and a lap-top computer under the driver's seat. But ... ," he looked back at Detective Rodriguez, who nodded curtly, "in the back, in that aluminum case ... "

"Yeah?"

"Twenty-four sticks of dynamite."

Rodriguez stood and walked over to the window where he stared outside at the rain and the traffic. "He's not supposed to have it. The drilling company is checking their supplies to see if any's missing."

"What do they use it for?"

"Tree stumps. Some of the *'ōhi'a* they had to take down for the roadway were as round as that table." The coffee table he pointed to was at least two feet in diameter. "But they haven't used any in years ... so they say."

"Two dozen sticks would take out the rig," Ben postulated.

"Half dozen would," said Rodriguez.

"Think they were planted?"

"The lock hadn't been picked."

"What did the Jackson Hole people tell you about him?" asked Ben.

"Good worker. Nothing out of the ordinary. Been with them since eighty-three."

"What about before that?"

"Owned his own construction company."

Ben knew what that meant. Lyman knew how to use dynamite and, most likely, where to get it. "Was he scheduled to be there last night?"

"He made the schedule. Like Geddes said, they take readings day and night. Said they were concerned with the environment and no expense was spared."

My ass ... ... Ben thought. *Dynamite. Why did Lyman have it? No reason other than sabotaging the well.* Ben wondered if Lyman was being *made* to falsify records. *Maybe he was fed up. Shit! There are a lot of possibilities. Maybe Lyman was a disgruntled employee who finally decided to get even and someone killed him to shut him up and made it look like someone like Nohea did it. Or, maybe he was taking nighttime measurements and an overzealous activist killed him as a warning. Or ...* "Did you find the key to the aluminum container on Lyman?"

"In a small pocket in his coveralls." Then Rodriguez asked, "You still think it was made to *look* like an activist?"

Did the murderer take the key, plant the dynamite, and then return the key to Lyman's pocket? Why go to so much trouble? "Huh?"

"You still think someone's trying to set up the activists?"

"Ernie," said Ben shaking his head, looking down, "you're not Hawaiian. You don't understand what's really at stake."

"And you do?"

Ben raised his head. "I do now."

Chapter Nine

WHEN BEN FOUND OUT that Rodriguez and Kala planned to stake out the drilling site that night, he asked if he could go along. Rodriguez consented, but only after Ben added that he would be heading back home in the morning; it was their case. They agreed to meet in the Pāhoa High School parking lot at eight-thirty.

At five-thirty Ken Asumura drove Ben back to his Jeep parked in Hawaiian Acres. No one followed them this time. They parted with weary smiles.

Ben set out to look for Nohea. He was somewhat surprised that he didn't get lost in the sugarcane fields and arrived at the path to Nohea's farmhouse in twenty minutes. Nohea's relic Karmann Ghia was gone. There were no tire marks, probably meaning he had left before the rains came and hadn't returned. Most likely there was a lot for the Pele Defense Fund members to talk about. Ben hustled down the trail, hopped onto the squat front porch, went inside, found a pad of paper and a pencil, and left a note for his friend.

He drove back through the cane fields and turned left when he reached Pāhoa proper. As he headed up the sleepy town's main street, Ben realized he hadn't had anything to eat since a pre-dawn breakfast of a cinnamon roll and a funny-looking, overripe banana. Two cups of bitter coffee at Hilo HQ didn't count.

A short distance ahead he spotted a freshly painted building wedged into the row of storefronts. It housed the Paradise West restaurant. He made a sharp U-turn and parked in front.

Next to the entrance to Paradise West was a hand-painted sign that promised friendly service and fresh local fare. He ducked around one of the potted areca palms that guarded the front door of the restaurant. Inside, Ben was not disappointed. Light paint and simple furniture. It was friendly and airy. Ben ordered local gray snapper, *uku*, and a salad, then sipped a Beck's while he waited for his dinner. He began to think of Nohea. He wondered what his old friend was really like now. It had been eight years. People changed. He wondered about the threats that had been made when Nohea left Jackson Hole Geo.

Ben looked around. The restaurant was nearly empty. One couple was also eating dinner, and two locals sat on bar stools drinking beer. It was quiet. Gave him time to think about the Lyman homicide.

First, he admitted to himself, he wished it were his case. He realized it was a sensitive case, closely tied to the drilling project, embroiled in the controversies surrounding Native Hawaiian rights and the environment. Certainly a challenging set of circumstances. Rodriguez and Kala were going to start with the assumption that someone sympathetic to the activists was responsible. But Ben was convinced that they should start with exactly the opposite premise. That someone wanted to make the activists look bad. Why else would someone use a spear and plant idols? It was too obvious. Rodriguez thought the murderer had felt compelled to make an irresistible statement.

Rodriguez is wrong.

As he thought about that, his salad arrived, as did a large basket of steaming French bread. He postponed his mental investigation. He was starved. Five minutes later, empty salad plate and bread basket pushed to one side and a second Beck's in hand, he resumed thinking about the murder of Curtis Lyman.

Finding out about the victim was important. He wondered if Lyman *was* falsifying data. If so, was he doing it on his own or had he been coerced? Had *he* put the dynamite in his truck or was it planted? If the dynamite was his, had he planned to blow up the rig? Could there be another reason he'd have twenty-four sticks of explosives?

The waiter placed the broiled *uku* before him. It was nicely garnished with tiny carrots, zucchini, and slices of papaya. A small bowl of brown rice sprinkled with parsley flakes accompanied his entree.

"Thanks."

"Anything else?"

"Coffee."

The waiter nodded and left.

For the next hour Ben sat, finished his fish, ordered a slice of key lime pie, and drank several cups of coffee. And thought about the murder.

At eight he decided to see if Nohea had returned home. He hadn't, so Ben retraced his route and made it back to the high school parking lot by eight-thirty. Rodriguez was already there. They talked about Ben's return to the Kona police force instead of Curtis Lyman's murder. It helped clear Ben's mind. Ten minutes later, Detective Kala showed up in a Ford Explorer. Ben and Rodriguez got in and they left for the Wao Kele O Puna.

The main gate to the Jackson Hole well was close to Nohea's farmhouse. Maybe three-quarters of a mile away at most. From the high school Detective Kala drove straight back, bearing right at each fork until they were deep into the cane fields.

It was the night of the ascending half moon, an *'Ole Pau* night, the tenth night of the lunar month. The moon appeared twice the normal size and much brighter. Ben remembered a story—he wasn't sure if it was Hawaiian or not—about the phases of the moon. When the moon was a small ascending crescent, it was empty. As the month went on, it filled with lost souls, becoming 'full,' and when it descended, it emptied, dropping the lonely spirits of the dead into the sea to join their ancestors. Ben smiled; he liked it. He hoped the tale was part of Hawaiian mythology. He'd ask Millie Kalehua, the Major's administrative assistant, about it when he returned to Kona. Millie knew almost as much as Ben's grandmother had. Like his grandmother, Millie was a pure Hawaiian.

A few stars faded in and out of the clouds. The ivory-colored moon seemed to be watching them. Behind them was the yellow glow of Pāhoa. Ahead, lay the Wao Kele O Puna. After a ninety-degree turn, the road deteriorated into loose gravel and puddles. A quarter-mile ahead was the entrance gate. The only real light from that direction came from the red lights of the rig itself. As they approached, another beacon caught their attention—the interior light of the security guard's car as he opened the door and stepped out, prepared as usual to tell visitors that they were on private property.

The second-shift guard recognized Detective Kala, then peered inside and smiled at Detective Rodriguez. He gave Ben an blank look. The guard looked sleepy, his expression as empty as a wind sock. Detective Kala said they were going to stake out the well for a few hours. The guard frowned like he felt his authority was being undermined. He opened the gate for them, walking it slowly, his shoulders slumped. He reminded Ben of his sixth-grade teacher who had had the enthusiasm of a blackboard eraser.

As they made their way to the rig, Rodriguez turned around and faced Ben.

"I know I shouldn't have had you followed. Before, when you

declined to talk about the lava tube, I hoped it was because Konanui was there. So now, you wouldn't mind pointing out the spot you and Konanui used, would you?"

Ben snorted to himself. "I haven't the slightest idea where it is. It was dark. I followed Nohea." *Nice try.*

"But even if you did ... "

"Even if I did ... ?"

"You wouldn't tell us."

"But I don't."

Rodriguez's turn to snort. He turned around.

In the moonlight Ben could see the bristled hair on the detective's neck.

The ghostly well came into view. They drove around it and parked in a depression near the forest edge. Branches scraped against the Explorer's doors and panels. Ben and Rodriguez had to shimmy out. Ben glanced at his watch. The luminescent dial read a few minutes before nine.

"You think anyone will really come the night after the murder?" Ben asked.

"Who knows? Maybe he forgot something that we missed. He's more likely to come for it right away than risk leaving it for a few days. Besides, he's already come at least two times that we know about. Maybe it's a nightly ritual." Rodriguez pointed toward the rig. "Pete, position yourself behind that mound of dirt. You'll have a good view of the road and the well. Ben and I will be near the salt pond. It may be a while."

Both Hilo detectives carried lightweight backpacks. Inside each were a flashlight, a two-way radio, and a rain slicker with POLICE in shiny silver emblazoned across the back—Rodriguez carried two slickers. Also, each had a thermos of coffee, a few sandwiches, and a spare 9 mm clip. Rodriguez motioned Ben to follow. Moments later they were positioned in the forest behind a large *'ōhi'a*. Rodriguez raised Detective Kala on the radio, testing. Although they whispered, their voices were clear. They agreed to check with each other every fifteen minutes. Rodriguez was to initiate contact.

It started to rain again. Rodriguez pulled out the rain gear. He handed one navy blue slicker to Ben and they donned them. It was relatively dry under the forest canopy, so Ben pushed the hood back behind his neck so he could hear better. Rodriguez did the same.

The Hilo detective let out a big yawn. "Sorry, if I've seemed unfriendly. I need to toughen up Kala. Have to set a good example."

"You didn't seem tough to me."

"You know what I mean. Look, I know this is major conflict for you. And between you and me, I think this drilling project stinks. Maybe not for the same reasons. I'm not Hawaiian and I'm hardly a devoted environmentalist. Pele is a nice legend, but I don't believe in her. It has nothing to do with that."

"What's it got to do with then?"

"Year after year we get turned down for raises and better benefits. We risk our lives. The drug problem gets worse and worse, and the pushers get younger and younger ... *and* rougher and rougher ... and now they have other weapons besides their fists. Maybe I haven't been shot at like you, but who knows, someday ... any way, the point is we have to live with the fact that we carry a gun and sometimes the bad guys do, too. The state and the county want this project to go through. They want the royalties. And where will the money go? Not to a raise or dental coverage or more life insurance, I can tell you that. It seems every year the politicos buy new pants with deeper pockets."

"I hear you."

"And as far as the well goes, it smells like hell when it vents ... and it makes a racket. For days." He sighed. "I feel sorry for the people who live near here."

After a few moments of silence, Ben said, "You know, Ernie, this *is* a frame-up."

"I know. I want the drilling people to think we think it's an activist."

Ben smiled. "Good."

Rodriguez shrugged his shoulders. Ben patted him on the back.

They talked about the geothermal plan for the next half hour, both laughing at the Wailoa Bridge project, trying to guess which century the towers and cables to O'ahu would be operational. Rodriguez had to slap his hand over Ben's mouth. They were laughing too loudly.

The rain continued until about ten o'clock, then fizzled to a drizzle, and finally stopped about ten-thirty.

At five to eleven, Kala came on. Five minutes early.

"Ernie."

"Yeah."

"Someone's coming," he said hoarsely.

"The guard?"

"On foot. Up the road." His voice had an anxious edge to it this time.

"Hold your position. Let's see what he's up to."

Ben leaned forward and peered into the dark. He could see nothing, hear nothing.

"Damn!" whispered Kala.

"What?"

"The guy's got on a cape. He looks like Batman!"

"C'mon."

"Honest. A fucking cape. He's carrying a bundle of leaves or flowers, or something."

"Where's he headed?"

"Toward you. Toward the ponds."

"Stay where you are," Rodriguez ordered. "Keep your gun in your holster."

Ben edged forward a bit more. He still couldn't see anything, but now he heard soft footsteps. Not like shoes crunching gravel, but bare feet, barely audible. He could hear Ernie's breathing. Their shoulders touched.

Ernie said, "This is unbelievable, look." He pointed back toward the path. Coming up over the rise was a man. A cape floated and settled on his shoulders. He was carrying several large palm fronds. It was too dark to make out his features. But he walked like he was old. There was something tucked under his arm.

"What's he doing?" asked Rodriguez.

Ben answered, "Beats me."

The *kahuna* passed them and headed directly for the silica pond where Curtis Lyman had met his death. He stopped and knelt at the very spot where Lyman had been found. The area had been staked—a yellow crime band had been stretched around six wooden posts. Carefully, the *kahuna* stepped over the plastic barrier. He laid out the palms, then knelt on them. He took something from underneath his arm and placed it before him. The object looked like an idol. The *kahuna* started chanting.

"Let's get him."

"Let him finish," ordered Ben, eyes unblinking, staring at the old man—a man who hardly seemed capable of hurling a spear with any force. Ben felt strange, like he was witnessing something from the past.

The chant went on for ten minutes. Once, Kala called on the radio. But the *kahuna* hadn't heard. He seemed too engrossed in his prayer. Rodriguez hushed Kala immediately and told him not to use the radio unless something life-threatening was about to happen.

The Hawaiian priest stood, stepped back over the plastic yellow band, and retreated. When he passed them, Rodriguez sprang to his feet, and running as quietly as possible on the balls of his feet, soon overtook the *kahuna* and wrestled him to the ground. The *kahuna* showed surprising strength and overturned his attacker, but did not assault him or attempt to escape. He just sat there, staring into Rodriguez's eyes.

"Police!" shouted Ben. "Get off slowly. Hands up. You're under arrest."

The *kahuna* obeyed instantly. The word 'arrest' changed his expression from surprise to fear.

Rodriguez got up and brushed himself off. He shone his flashlight in the old man's face. The man had gray hair and wore a halo of ti leaves around his head. A white tapa cape covered his upper body. A simple *malo* covered his loins. He kept his head lowered even after Rodriguez ordered him to raise it. Rodriguez wouldn't touch him, however. Ben guessed he didn't want to hassle the old priest. Superstition or respect—it didn't matter. Ben guessed that Rodriguez was wondering if this old man could hurl a spear. Ben had already decided he couldn't.

They decided to take him to the Pāhoa station for questioning. After that, assuming there was some reason to suspect the old man of Lyman's murder, they would transfer him to Hilo. They left after Detective Kala returned with the wooden idol in an evidence bag.

The Pāhoa substation was small, a new two-man prefab office that served as a complaint center, a home for the radio equipment, and a place to change from civilian clothes into uniform. There were two officers stationed there. One was fresh out of school, Jimmy Oliveira. He had been the first patrolman on the scene earlier that morning. The other was an old veteran, Elias Whitney, who grew vegetables during the day, then worked a six-to-midnight shift. After midnight, and on weekends, Oliveira and Whitney were on call.

So from six to nine, Whitney patrolled the streets of Pāhoa, mainly looking for stray dogs and making sure anyone who looked like a marijuana grower was in and out of town quickly. At nine he went back to the substation and was rarely bothered unless one of the bars called with a disturbance.

When the detectives and prisoner reached the main street of Pāhoa, it was completely dark. No street lights. No house lights. All the shops seemed deserted.

Kala said simply, "Power failure."

With clouds covering their only source of light, Detective Kala drove cautiously. A minute later they pulled into the small lot in front of the substation. Kala had a key, but the door was unlocked. Patrolman Whitney was seated at the front desk, using a candle to read the newspaper. Kala flicked the light switch out of habit.

Rodriguez asked Whitney if he recognized the old man they'd captured. Whitney got up, carrying his candle. Ben thought it was amusing. Patrolman Whitney squinted into the old man's face. Finally, he stepped back, shook his head, then suggested Patrolman Oliveira might know him.

Kala radioed Oliveira, who lived close by and arrived in a few minutes wearing a fresh set of blues.

Ben smiled, thinking rookies treated their blues like new cars, but after six months ...

"Never saw him before," Oliveira stated.

Whitney yawned.

Oliveira told him to go home.

Ben guessed half of Whitney's hours were really Oliveira's.

The *kahuna* sat surrounded by three detectives, one rookie patrolman, and a half dozen flickering candles. Ben studied the old man's dress as best he could. The wavering light made it difficult. He hadn't seen a tapa cape before. He'd seen ones made from bird feathers. He remembered his grandmother explaining to him how the feathers were collected. *'I'iwi* and *'ō'ō* feathers were used. The *'ō'ō* was naturally attracted to the white flowers of the *pāpala kēpau*. When the flowers began to drop off, a gummy fruit developed and some of the yellow *'ō'ō* feathers would stick. The Hawaiians would shake the trees and keep only the feathers that fell off. To gather the red feathers of the *'i'iwi*, a special *kahuna*, who was said to be able to paralyze the spirit of the bird so it couldn't fly, was called upon. His magic was simple. He spread the sticky sap of a breadfruit tree on the branches of a tree whose flowers attracted the fragile *'i'iwi*. When the tiny bird got stuck, the *kahuna* carefully plucked a few of its feathers, then dabbed its feet with *kukui* oil before setting it free.

The old man had not spoken a word. Not when he was captured. Not during the drive to the Pāhoa substation. The only thing he'd done was shaken his head no when asked if he wanted an attorney. At least he understood English.

Ben studied him for a long time. His hair was gray but thick. He was about five-eight and couldn't have weighed more than a hundred and forty pounds. His fingernails were dirty. His skin didn't seem too weathered and the hair on his arms was black. Ben stepped closer to push back the cape. The *kahuna* raised his head and made a throaty noise, looking him in the eye. It was then that something about the *kahuna* seemed familiar to Ben. Suddenly, the old man let out a horrible scream. Ben took a step back. The *kahuna* leaned forward and blew out the candle that was closest to him. Ben didn't know what to do. The other three policemen were looking at him. Ben said, "I don't think he's going to tell us anything."

Oliveira sat mystified. The Hilo detectives moved to a corner and started talking in low voices. Ben reached for a chair, turned it around, straddled it, and sat, staring at the man in the tapa cape. *Kāhuna* had been his grandmother's favorite subject. She said it was a shame how Westerners associated the word 'kahuna' with a cigar-smoking—or, as she'd said, 'a smoke-stacking'—overweight Moose Lodge member wearing a tasseled hat. Ben had a different memory from growing up in southern California. Kahuna, to him, meant beach bum, surfer. But, his grandmother's teachings had made him understand that *kāhuna* were the wise men and women. Specially trained. Advisors, healers,

planners. The ones who knew which tree would make the best canoe, who knew that mind healing was more important than physical
cures. There were stories that seemed to include witchcraft as well.
Wishing a person to death, or creating fireballs that flew across the
sky.

Kāhuna —the priests of old.

Still there was something about this old man that seemed familiar. Ben looked into the old man's face once again.

The *kahuna* closed his eyes.

There was no real holding cell in the Pāhoa substation, just a room
with a solid-core door, fireproof, double locked from the outside, with
a heavy, insulated glass sidelight and nothing on the exterior wall.
That's where they put the *kahuna*. There was only one way out and
it led into the hallway. From there, to the right, was the front door
guarded by the patrolmen's desks. The rear exit, to the left, set off an
alarm when opened.

Ten minutes passed, and the *kahuna* just sat there with his head
bowed. He didn't utter a word in response to Rodriguez's questions.
First, Kala left, frustrated. He said he was going across the street to
see if he could find some coffee that was still warm. The rookie patrolman, Oliveira, followed, saying he thought Paradise West was open
until midnight. Ben and Rodriguez remained behind.

Rodriguez repeated several of his previous questions.

"Why were you there?"

No answer, not even a shrug.

"Where were you last night at midnight? Do you know about the
man who was murdered?" No answers. Rodriguez asked a half dozen
more questions with no success. Finally, he too, threw up his hands,
saying he was going out front to call Hilo. At least the phones still
worked.

Ben tried another approach. He explained he was sympathetic to
the cause, said he didn't believe the *kahuna* was the murderer. He

asked for help. Was it his first time in the forest? If not, had he observed anything strange during other visits? The *kahuna* raised his eyes at that. Ben peered into them but all he saw this time was a miniature reflection of lighted candles.

"Can you talk?"

The *kahuna* focused on Ben. He pulled his lips tightly together.

"Are you afraid to talk?"

No response. Just a hard stare.

Ben stood up straight, walked over to the rear wall, and turned, eyeing the suspect at length. The *kahuna* watched carefully.

"Why aren't you talking? Just tell me why?"

The *kahuna* bowed his head.

Ben shook his head and left to talk to Rodriguez. When he closed the door he realized he didn't have a key to lock it with. He looked down the hallway to the left, the light from the candles in the front shone over his shoulder. He could see the red warning sign—the security door was armed with an alarm.

How far can he get?

He joined Rodriguez out front.

Two minutes later when Ben and Rodriguez returned to the holding room, the *kahuna* was gone. All that remained was the ti leaf headpiece on the cold white tile floor. Rodriguez ran to the rear door. Ben groaned, realizing his mistake. Rodriguez pushed it open, shrinking instinctively, expecting to be crushed by the blare of the alarm.

No power ... no alarm.

Chapter Ten

A DEEP SIGH preceded, "Mornin', Tobi."

Tobi looked up from his desk. "*You* look well rested."

Ben raised his eyebrows. "I think the race was easier than my days off."

Tobi nodded and smiled. "Commander Diaz brought me up to date. Including last night. Your *kahuna* just vanished?"

Ben hesitated a bit, thinking how unbelievable it was, that the old *kahuna* had gotten away, disappearing into the night in just a couple of minutes. "Uh huh."

"I have never been in the Pāhoa station."

"There are no cells. There was a power failure when we arrived. We had him in the interview room. Rodriguez and I were discussing strategy out front. Without thinking, we figured if he tried to sneak out the back the alarm would go off."

"Even an old *kahuna* understands the principles of electricity." Tobi snorted softly. "You do not think he is the killer, do you?"

Ben raised his head and grinned a little. "Nope."

"Why not?" asked Tobi.

"I think someone is trying to make it appear that an activist is the murderer. Maybe someone's even trying to frame *this* guy. That would account for the idols and the spear. I think he goes there often to pray and leave things. Someone found out and copied it, figuring it was a perfect setup. The old guy's silence just makes it more convincing."

"He did not speak?"

Ben shook his head. "Not a word. I think he's just scared, or … maybe … "

"Maybe?"

Ben shrugged his shoulders.

Tobi inhaled sharply. "Well … now the case belongs to Hilo."

Ben didn't respond. There was *something*. Something when they had stared at each other, when Ben's frustration began to show …

… or maybe he's got something else to hide.

"Ben?"

"Sorry … I … nothing. Nothing, I guess."

"Whatever it is, it will come to you."

"I suppose so."

Tobi stood and walked to the window. His office reflected his heritage. The metallic gray police-issue furniture was gone, replaced by some of his own things—a *koa* desk and credenza, a glass-top coffee table supported by a two-foot-high bronze elephant, and old silk prints on three of the walls. In the corner, near the window, there was a tall Cook pine, its upper branches curving across the ceiling. Soon he would have to trim it or plant it outside.

Ben, looking over Tobi's shoulder, saw that the sky was overcast and the sun had disappeared. Boiling charcoal-colored clouds hovered over Mount Hualālai, threatening to tumble over the mountainside and bring a long rain to the entire Kailua area. The mountains behind HQ took on a purple tint and the newly planted palms just beyond Tobi's window bent *makai* in the wind.

Tobi turned and leaned against the credenza. "How is your load?"

"Besides the stolen boat, not really too heavy. I volunteered for an Eradication Team raid, but no one's called yet." Ben was pleased that Hilo had finally gotten serious about the marijuana problem. Now, two or three times a week, after a surveillance team spotted a crop, a specially trained team of police officers flew out to the site in helicopters. They rappelled like mountain climbers right into the field of marijuana and seized the plants. The weed was cut and stored for evidence. And the property owner faced jail and loss of his personal property. That meant his land, house, car, and anything else he owned. As far as Ben was concerned, no penalty was too severe. Marijuana led to stronger drugs. There was already an *ice* problem in the schools.

Framed by the dark sky outside, Tobi's aloha shirt made him look like he was part of a stained glass window. "I want you to check out a burglary."

"Where?"

"Construction company in the industrial park. Last night, someone broke in and took a case of dynamite."

"Dynamite!" His mind raced back to Lyman's pickup. He wondered if there was a connection.

"You know something?" Tobi asked, returning to his desk. He crossed his arms, resting his forearms on the back of his chair.

"The victim at the drilling site had twenty-four sticks in his pickup. I haven't run across dynamite in any case since I've been here. Now twice in two days?"

Tobi said, "This is a long way from Puna. I think many construction companies use explosives."

"I'll check it out. What's the address?"

"Jack has it. He went out there last night. He has to testify twice this week, so I would like for you to take the case." Tobi looked at his watch. "Better move it. He has to be in court at nine."

Ben found Detective Cooper hunched over his desk, a powdered-sugar doughnut held high in one hand, a stubby pencil in the other. On his desk was a long white form. Jack was a fanatic about forms.

While other detectives and uniformed officers sat down and entered their reports directly into the computer, composing on the fly, Jack prepared a handwritten draft, proofed it, made changes, and then entered it. Sometimes he even used *Roget's*.

The doughnut found his mouth. Ben wondered if the doughnut was trained or if Jack had consciously taken a bite.

"Hey, Jack."

The bulky detective looked up and gave Ben a white-powder grin. He chewed a few more times before he spoke. "I know ... I know ... what about my weight?"

"I didn't say anything."

"Besides, I'd rather be caught with a doughnut than caught trespassing." He laughed heartily.

"You know, I should have bought you a T-shirt I saw the other day. It only comes in extra-extra large and says 'CALORIES ARE OUR FRIENDS.' "

Jack's laughter tailed off into a series of snorts. He wiped his eyes. Then, earnestly, he said, "I can understand why you did it, but of all the luck to stumble on a homicide ... You know, it reminds me of when I was about fourteen. My parents had a rule. None of us were allowed in their bedroom when they were gone. And of course, my dad was all over us boys about stealing his beer. Well, one day, while they were shopping, I spilled beer on their bedspread." Jack burst out laughing again. "Pretty good, huh?"

Ben shook his head, smiling. "I need what you have on the dynamite theft before you leave."

"I'll be with you in a minute. Putting the final touches on this draft."

"I'll get some coffee."

In the coffee room Ben ran into Joyce Ah Sing, the detectives' secretary. For some time Ben had known that Joyce was interested in him, and she knew that he knew, but whenever they were alone, neither made mention of it. Usually, when they were by themselves, Ben would see her face redden and notice that she seemed a bit nervous. And he was sure that she observed the same things in him. But as he thought about it now, she hadn't acted that way for some time. Maybe he'd been so preoccupied with cases and the Ironman that he hadn't noticed. Typically, the month before the Ironman he was oblivious to almost everything.

Joyce was attractive, maybe a little too thin, but pretty. He wondered if he should encourage her to talk about her feelings. Maybe he should tell her about Lisa's move to the Island.

"Morning, Ben. Look!"

She held out her hand and flashed a small engagement ring.

Ben swallowed. "When did this happen? I didn't even know you had a boyfriend."

"Oh, it's a guy I dated in high school. He came back about two months ago. We started seeing each other again, and, well … " She beamed like an underdog who'd just pulled off an upset.

Stuttering, "Hey … congratulations!" Ben stepped up and gave her a small hug and planted a kiss on her cheek.

"Thanks, Ben. Wedding's in January." She grabbed her coffee cup and disappeared.

Well, old boy, you certainly had that one figured out!

Sitting backward in his chair with his arms resting on the curve of the support, Ben listened to Jack's description of the burglary. In the back of his mind, he was thinking about Lisa. He wondered if she could make it over for the weekend.

Jack's hands were free. Both the report and the doughnut were gone, which was for the best, since Jack was an animated talker. "The silent alarm went off at 2:10. The construction company, Classic Structures, is at 44-7786 Pāwai Place." He pointed over his shoulder toward town.

"That's just past the old Triathlon Headquarters."

"Right. Two uniforms arrived at 2:17. The side door had been jimmied." Jack made a crowbar motion. "They didn't find anyone, didn't pass any cars on the way in, didn't find anything overturned or vandalized. The owner showed up about ten minutes later. The safe was undisturbed, but he found a case of dynamite missing from a supply shed that's tucked into a corner not far from the door that was jimmied." "How many sticks in a case?"

"Sixty-four."

"What about blasting caps, detonators, wire … ?"

Jack waved. "Nothing else was missing."

"Meaning, maybe the thief has that stuff already."

"That, or he expected the accessories to be in the box."

"Interesting." Ben told Jack about the dynamite found in Lyman's truck.

"Long way from here … don't see the connection. Your guy had his at least a day before my guy."

Ben nodded. He was thinking how two of anything seems connected on an island that was eighty miles by ninety. "Go on."

"We dusted the door and the shed … must be a million prints. I asked the owner to prepare a list of employees and another list of people who had worked there in the past two years. He said he'd have them ready around nine."

"And you didn't find anything left behind?"

"Nothing. The place had just been cleaned. A maintenance guy comes in every other day at ten. He's gone by midnight or one. He was there last night. I have his name. Haven't talked to him yet." Jack spread his arms, palms up. He got up and went back to his desk and picked up his note pad. "Here, copy this down. Len Mahuna is the owner. He's probably there now. Said he'd be back in at eight. Jesse Perkins is the cleaning guy. He lives in an apartment on Ali'i … 76-6231, just across from the Bali Kai. Works six to two. According to Mahuna he's a one-man operation. Been cleaning up there for five years. Mahuna says he has four or five other places he does."

Ben closed his notepad, pushed back his chair, and stood. "Have fun in court."

"Yeah, right … Hey, you hear about Joyce?"

———————

While waiting for a lumbering semi to climb the hill on Kaiwi Street so he could turn left onto Pāwai Place, Ben thought some more about the *kahuna*. He and Rodriguez had split up and searched both ends of the main street. There hadn't been many people out. But the few he and Rodriguez had questioned—after giving the detectives strange looks—told them they hadn't seen anyone dressed in a *malo* and a cape. If the old man had a vehicle, it certainly wouldn't been parked in town. It would have been out by the drilling site. But Ben didn't really believe the *kahuna* owned a car. He joked to himself— A dirt bike maybe, but not a car. So where could he have gone? How could he have disappeared so easily?

They really don't practice magic, do they?

Then he thought about the maze of lava tubes. Were there lava tubes in town?

The semi finally passed and a soft horn bleated Ben back to the present. He waved into his rear-view mirror and turned left onto Pāwai. Classic Structures was near the end on the left. There was one unoccupied parking space.

As he got out, he noticed a man repairing the side door. Ben headed that way.

"Mind if I look at the old frame for a second?" The man gave Ben a careful look.

"McMillen, Kona detective."

"Oh, sure. Name's Marty Rosario." He straightened up and shook Ben's hand. "Follow me." Then he walked to the rear of the building and pointed. "Metal door, but pine trim. Real soft. I'd say someone just used a screwdriver. The new one," he gestured back toward the doorway, "door and frame are solid steel."

Ben examined the trim for a few seconds. He knew Forensic had taken the actual piece that had been jimmied. "Not too tough."

"Cake."

"Thanks, Marty."

Marty tipped his Dodger cap.

Inside, the building was divided into a showroom—a room with cabinet samples and bathroom fixtures—and four offices, two on each side of a narrow corridor. The hallway led to a larger area in the rear. The receptionist pointed down the hallway when Ben asked for the owner. He found Len Mahuna sitting by a long wooden table in the back near the tool shed. It was apparent that he had emptied the aluminum structure and was taking inventory.

"Mr. Mahuna?"

Mahuna interrupted his counting. "Yeah."

"Ben McMillen, Kona detective. Don't get up." Ben pulled up a chair.

Mahuna sank back down. "Someone called before. Said Detective Cooper had to be in court. You got the case now?"

Ben nodded. "You find anything else missing?"

"As a matter of fact, I did. A box of silver duct tape."

"Like you might use to secure some dynamite?"

"Exactly," agreed Mahuna.

"What will sixty-four sticks do?"

"Are you kidding? You mean altogether?" He half gasped, half laughed. "Blow up a mountain." His right arm swept across his body. "Level the entire industrial park."

Ben's eyebrows arched. "What do *you* do with it?"

"Most jobs ... we have to blast away some lava for the foundation."

"How much do you use?"

"Four sticks maybe. A steel mat keeps the debris contained."

"If they show up, how do I identify them?"

"If they've blown, you'll need experts."

"And if I recover them before they're used?"

"Red wrapping paper ... 'bout a foot long and three inches around. Brand's printed lengthwise in black ... *Texas Blasters*."

"Okay. You have those lists Detective Cooper asked for?"

"Yeah ... in my office. Follow me."

When Mahuna stood Ben realized how big he was. Six-four and heavy. Barrel chested with hands that looked like they could hold a half-dozen sticks each. He didn't walk; he lumbered like a longshoreman who didn't carry his beer well.

The office work table was covered with blueprints and paperweights. Mahuna fumbled with a few drawings before he handed two sheets of paper to Ben. One contained the names and addresses of about twenty employees. On the other list were six names with addresses and termination dates. Ben concentrated on that list first. He was looking for someone who lived in Puna, or Ka'ū, or Hilo. One address was Kea'au, a town just south of Hilo, where Highway 130 split off to Pāhoa.

"What about James Harrison?"

"What about him?" asked Mahuna.

"Says here he left three months ago. Why'd he leave?"

"We fired him when he showed up drunk just a few weeks after his second DUI."

"Two and you're in jail," informed Ben.

"They were easy on him. You probably remember the second one. He came up on an accident and pulled a lady out of a burning car. But when the police talked with him, they realized he was drunk. The judge went easy on him since he saved the lady's life. Probably too drunk to realize the danger he placed himself in. He was supposed to go for treatment. He did for a couple of weeks, but it didn't last. He started showing up late, and it was obvious he had been out all night."

"He worked here and lived in Kea'au?"

"No, that's a new address. We owe him pension money at the end of the year. He's got a job down there now."

Ben asked, "Construction?"

"He guards the road to Kalapana, makes sure no one walks over the lava flow. Works for the County."

Ben nodded. "They put him on for saving the lady?"

"Lady was a sister-in-law of one of the County parks guys."

"He make any threats when you let him go?"

"To the contrary … he apologized. Said he hoped we did well. He was ashamed, embarrassed. I take it you're short on suspects?"

Ben pursed his lips.

"You wanna talk to my employees?" asked Mahuna.

"How many are around?"

" 'Bout six. The rest are at job sites."

"None of them was here last night, right?"

Mahuna nodded in agreement. "You gonna go see Harrison?"

"I'll have someone in Hilo talk with him. I've got a few questions for the people here. Have the rest come by HQ either today or tomorrow and ask for Detective Cooper or me. Tell them it won't take long."

"Sure."

"In the meantime, if you think of anything, or find something else missing, call me right away." Ben handed him his card.

"You got it."

"Thanks."

Ben interviewed the receptionist, two ordering clerks, and three men who made up a site crew. They all said they had been home all night. He asked if they had any ideas about the burglary. None did. He asked if any of them had ever talked about the dynamite. The responses ranged from 'no' to 'just the family' to 'my girlfriend.' Except for one man who admitted he'd been in a Kailua bar one night, explaining how they blasted foundations.

"Telling who? ... friends?"

He shrugged like he couldn't remember.

"Anyone seem more than casually interested?"

"Don't think so. Don't really remember. It was awhile ago. A year or so."

Too long ago.

Ben told them to keep their eyes and ears open. None of them appeared to be nervous, but he'd have someone check out their alibis.

Len Mahuna escorted him to the front door.

As Ben stepped outside, Mahuna asked, "You think we're in for a big bang soon?"

Ben looked up at the threatening sky. Dark clouds blocked the sun. He returned his gaze to Mahuna. "Unfortunately, dynamite's one thing you don't steal to keep."

Len Mahuna grinned, agreeing.

"Just for the record ... where were you last night?"

Mahuna's grin widened. "It was my anniversary, McMillen. I'm as covered as I've ever been."

The Queen Kaʻahumanu Highway had been named after the favorite wife of Kamehameha the Great. The tourist maps referred to it as Highway 19, triathletes Ben knew called it the 'Queen K.' Locals called it Kaʻahumanu Highway. As Ben headed north on the Kaʻahumanu Highway, he realized that with so little to go on—he expected the other Classic employees would be unable to provide any leads—he probably wouldn't be able to follow up on the dynamite theft until something happened. Unfortunately, that something might be catastrophic, especially if someone set off all sixty-four sticks at once.

It started to pour. It became so dark that Ben assumed this would be no passing shower. He pulled over and unfolded the Wrangler's canvas covering. He cursed. Six inches from closure the zipper on the Jeep's roof flap stuck and it wouldn't budge. He gave up and started driving again. Soon he was trapped in a Chinese water torture, as dripping water brushed his nose. He shifted as far as he could, but there were several leaks and the water still got him on the cheek.

Surprisingly, the rain only lasted ten minutes. The clouds magically dispersed as if Kāne had sucked all the moisture out of them and a mural of steam created a haze over the landscape. The foothills behind Kailua seemed to be wavering. The sun peeked out from behind the last remaining cloud and almost immediately a pair of perfect rainbows spanned Mount Hualālai. Tourists pulled over and got out their cameras. Locals smiled, appreciating the temporary reduction of traffic. Ben brushed the water off of his face and lap, then turned right, and drove up the hill to HQ.

First thing, Ben checked with Hilo. Curtis Lyman's dynamite was a different brand. Different from Classic's. Different from Jackson Hole's, which was all accounted for.

The rest of the morning and early afternoon were spent trying to track down the boat that had been stolen from Honokōhau Harbor the previous week. No one he talked with along the rows of boat slips provided any help. By two, Ben was hungry. He could smell the fish and chips at the Harbor House restaurant. So he radioed in for messages—no messages—and let them know he was going to eat. That done, he headed for the harborside restaurant.

He hadn't gone but a few steps when a familiar voice hailed him. Danny Mitchell, perched on the bow of his charter, was waving for Ben to come aboard. Ben waved back and headed for slip #48 and Danny's new boat, *Dances With Fish*.

Leave it to Danny to name her that.

Danny had become Ben's best friend. He was the former owner of Mitchell's, a casual restaurant that turned into a dance bar at night, which had closed a few months before. Danny told Ben the long hours cooped up inside had been too much. And, he added, he had always wanted to skipper. Ben thought about long hours, something to which a detective was no stranger. At least they didn't have many stakeouts on the Big Island. Those, he imagined, would be torture, especially with the distracting scenery.

Danny had explained that although charter captains were up early, usually just before daybreak, they were done by six on full days, two on half days. Typically, there were more half days. But the important question was—is it really work? Cruising the Kona waters, trying to land record billfish, meeting interesting people from all over the world was entertainment, not work. Even keeping the boat in shape wasn't bad, as long as you didn't skip a day. 'A boat is like a workshop. If you put each tool back in its place, clean up the wood shavings and sawdust, you feel good about the place. But let everything accumulate so you're knee-deep in debris and you can't find your tools, it becomes a chore, not a hobby.' Danny never disembarked until *Dances With Fish* looked like it still belonged in a showroom.

He had told Ben—'All I want is to break even and eat fresh fish every night and never have to go inside.' Hearing that, Ben wondered how Mitchell's had ever opened.

Ben stepped over the gunwale and onto the deck. He shook hands with Danny, noticing right away that Danny's stomach was flatter. The athletic build that for so long had been hidden under the accumulation of malt and hops was starting to show through. Danny's brown hair was several shades lighter than when he'd rummaged around the bar, and his eyebrows appeared almost blonde. But, most important, his smile was full and genuine.

"How you been, mate?"

"Fine."

"Saw in the paper that you beat ten hours. Congratulations."

"Thanks."

"You eat lunch yet?"

"Nope."

"Pull up a chair, I just finished hosing her down."

Ben sat on a royal blue canvas deck chair. Danny handed him a beer. Ben held up his hand. "Can't now."

"You need a day off."

"I just had three, but I ended up working most of the time." He told Danny about the killing at the geothermal well.

Danny rubbed his hand over his stubbled chin. "The thing I don't like about *that* whole business is that no one knows what a cable carrying that much juice is gonna do to the fish. Especially the whales. I hear they plan to cross the 'Alenuihāhā Channel by 'Upolu Point and come up on Maui's south coast. Shit! That's a whale sanctuary. All that electricity must give off something. It could really screw up their sonar."

"I know." Ben sighed. "There's a million more reasons, but I think the politicians and the power barons are going to win this one. I wish I knew of a way to stop it."

"Blow up the fuckin' well."

Ben eyed Danny. "Why'd you say that?"

"Say what ... you mean blow it up? Hey, what else would work that quickly ... certainly not a law suit?"

"No, it's just that the guy who was murdered had twenty-four sticks of dynamite in his truck ... "

Danny's raised his hands in mock surrender. "I was just kidding."

Ben jokingly gave him an 'evil eye.' "I just came from the industrial park. A place called Classic Structures was burglarized last night. Someone took a case of dynamite and some duct tape."

"Enough of that." Danny threw a fish sandwich at him, which Ben one-handed.

Soon they were both eating and planning a fishing trip for the following Sunday.

Fifteen minutes later, Ben got up to leave.

"What's your hurry?"

"Don't know, really. I'm trying to get a handle on Simpson's boat. Thought I might go see him." He grinned to himself, thinking of old Buster Simpson, who would rather breathe sea water than air and had more fishing stories than the other Kona captains combined.

"I heard about that," Danny interjected. "No clues?"

"Nothing. No one's spotted it."

"You know, if no one's seen it at sea, then my guess is it's hidden or abandoned along the coast." He scratched his head. "Or sunk. But maybe not. The Coast Guard doesn't check every nook and cranny. They can't get close in, especially where the lava rocks come all the way to the reef. If you want to look, we can probably get closer, poke into some coves to the south. I've got nothing to do the rest of the day. Whaddaya say?"

"Might as well. I'm supposed to be working on it. Let me go back to the Jeep, radio in, and get my hat and binocs. Be right back."

Soon they were underway. The rain clouds had formed again but seemed stuck for awhile, wedged into the high valleys of the volcanoes. The sky over the ocean was clear except for a few cirrus wisps. Even Maui, floating far to the northwest like a raw emerald in the sea, was visible. The wind was comfortable at ten knots, making the eighty-degree temperature seem relatively cool.

Dances With Fish hummed through the harbor just under the speed limit, Danny at the helm. Ben was preparing two lines with squid lures. Might as well troll as they headed toward South Kona.

They chose that direction because there was considerably more foliage along the Kona shoreline than Kohala, which was composed of stark lava fields and was populated by several major resorts. A stolen boat would soon be discovered up there. South was interesting country. In the hills were coffee and macadamia nut farms, but much of the land was vacant except for small fishing villages that dotted the coast. Keʻei. Hoʻokena. Hoʻōpūloa. And Miloliʻi. In between, the jagged coastline looked the same as it had for centuries with scores of bays and points, and rugged cliffs that had taken the brunt of the sea for eons. Each small cove could shelter a boat, and without a close inspection, a craft could remain anchored, undetected and protected, for a long time.

Danny opened it up a little once they cleared Honokōhau Harbor. He kept it just under eight knots, good for trolling. Good for spotting the white hull with blue striping that was, or had been, Buster Simpson's pride and joy.

Dances With Fish was a forty-foot Hattaras fully equipped with a tuna tower, outriggers, and two Cummins engines. Inside the cabin there was sonar, an electronic fish finder, and even a microwave for cooking. The boat slept two below and any number on deck who wanted to sleep under the stars.

An hour passed. No luck trolling. No luck spotting Simpson's boat.

Ben and Danny discussed the geothermal drilling project for a time, but soon the conversation turned to the murder.

"Don't you feel like you should be part of the investigation?" asked Danny.

"Yeah, but it's out of our jurisdiction. They can ask for help. Maybe they will after awhile."

"So you think it's a setup."

"Yeah, someone's trying too hard."

"Who'd do that?"

"It used to surprise me when people in high places went to great lengths to make things work out the way they wanted. No more. It could be the Chairman of the Board of Jackson Hole for all I know. Money and power motivate more than all the half-time pep talks put together."

Danny took that in. "Ever get fed up with all the politics of the police force? Ever just want to be by yourself, work for yourself, live by yourself?"

"I get fed up, but I'd like to think I can help the people. From exploitation of the natural resources ... from the corruption of drugs."

"You're dreamin.' "

"Someone's got to do it ... and soon."

By Miloli'i Bay, only five miles from the end of the South Kona District, Danny spotted a small, protected cove that seemed filled with sea birds.

"That's unusual," he commented. "I think they're *noio*. Usually they hang out around the FADs." FADs were Fish Aggregation Devices, big buoys spread out along the coasts of the six major Hawaiian Islands. They attracted plankton, which enticed shrimp and baby squid. They, in turn, lured small fish and so on up the food chain to man and his big boats and rubbery squid lures. "There must be a huge school of fish trapped in the cove. Let's go have a look. We can pick up some live bait. I've got a full-day charter tomorrow."

Ben glanced at his watch. It was almost four-thirty, nearly time to call it a day. "Suits me." He picked up his binoculars and scanned the coastline. He could make out the birds clearly, but couldn't see the water below. The rugged land mass of Hanamalo Point blocked his view.

After reeling in both lines, Ben secured them in their fittings. Danny, peering from the bridge, slowed the craft to a couple of knots, then Ben scampered to the bow and squatted, holding on to one of the outriggers. He stared ahead, looking for the coral reef, but it appeared as if this part of the bay was clear. Why were the fish trapped? The tide was low, but not *that* low.

As they came closer and the entire cove came into view, Ben heard Danny shout.

"Buster Simpson ahead, mate!"

Ben looked up. He raised his binoculars. Anchored just off shore was Buster Simpson's boat. On the tailgate was a blue marlin. Or at least what was left of it. Black and brown noddies pecked at its flesh. Other birds cried out and soared above the fishing vessel. The high-pitched guttural call of the noddy filled the air. It was hard to hear. Suddenly, Ben felt as if a shadow had descended over him, mirroring his soul. He envisioned the bodies of two people sprawled on the ship's deck. Half-eaten corpses with crabs trapped in their rib cages. Bloated eyes staring into space, not believing the ceremony of death at sea.

Danny slipped the gears into neutral and gunned the engine. The noise scared the *noio* and most took flight. A dozen or so remained for a few last nips, but as *Dances With Fish* dropped anchor alongside *The Kona Wind*, the stragglers flapped off, crying like hungry wolf pups. Ben slowly raised his head, expecting to meet death in the eye, but the boat was abandoned and the only blood on the deck was that of the blue marlin.

Ben stepped aboard. The smell was awful. The marlin's stomach was completely torn open. It was then that Ben noticed a huge circular bite near the marlin's head. A shark had come out of the water and taken what it could reach. Ben's eyes scanned the small lagoon for fins. There were none.

Danny came aboard. "What a mess!"

"Solve one case, open up another."

"Huh?"

"What happened to the people who stole the boat?"

Instinctively, they both peered into the shallow water, shading their eyes. They saw no bodies. No clothes.

Then Danny pointed toward the rocky shore. "Let's hope they just left after realizing they weren't going to drag a two-hundred-pound marlin a thousand feet up to the main road."

Ben looked up and whistled at the sight of the imposing cliffs. Then he stared at the great fish, lying there, stripped of its dignity. Its exposed eye caught his attention. He leaned forward and studied the smoky orb. There was blood in one corner. Actually, it looked more bloodshot than like blood from a wound. Like a broken capillary. As he straightened up, the hairs on his neck and arms and legs bristled with a mixture of excitement and shock. It was there. It was close. His mind, like a slot machine, rolled through the combinations. Finally, the wheels rolled into place. Jackpot.

Now he knew. At least he thought he knew. The *kahuna*. The disappearing *kahuna*.

He straightened and took in a deep breath, oblivious to the stench in the air and the increased shrieking as the noddies glided closer, thinking only of the *kahuna*'s identity and what he would do about it.

Chapter Eleven

T HE MAN WAS BACK, but this time no cape covered his shoulders. It might get in the way when he had to run. And *he* would *have* to *run.*

He peered out from the rough stone steps of the lava tube, scanning the asphalt road for the security guard's car. As before, he was barefoot and wore a white *malo*. His chest was bare except for a whale's tooth that hung from his neck. The only thing in his dress that differentiated him from an ancient *kahuna* was the Chronosport watch he wore on his left wrist. He glanced at it now. The stainless steel dive model with a luminescent dial read a few minutes before 4 AM. Soon the guard would drive up, scout around the well, then go back to his post. The two patrolmen who had been assigned to watch the well had left two hours earlier. Dawn was ninety minutes away. He had plenty of time as long as the security guard left when he was supposed to.

He waited. Five minutes. Ten. He yawned. He looked at the lighted dial once more. Fifteen minutes and the second hand seemed frozen. He tapped the bezel. Finally, to his right, the mixture of shadow and light began dancing through the trees that lined the road. Closer, first creeping, then faster until two headlights clearly appeared, illuminating the smooth black surface. Instinctively, the man in the tapa loincloth ducked as the wash of light extended into the forest and found the base of the large *'ōhi'a* that disguised the entrance to the underground passageway. He saw the car pass quickly. The guard was speeding.

"Good," he whispered to himself, "he's in a hurry."

Ten minutes later, the guard had gone by again. It was clear. The figure in tapa popped out of the lava tube, slipped his heavy backpack over his shoulders, and began jogging up the road toward the rig. To the east, the moon was a swollen crescent wavering in the sky. Stars abounded; in fact, the sky had never seemed so full of light. Venus hovered to the west, a frozen flare of light. Jupiter, its companion this October, hung a few degrees to the south.

The going was slow, the backpack was full. Thirty-two sticks of dynamite, an Army surplus trench shovel, two flashlights, a thermos of water, a rubber mallet, thirty-two wooden stakes, some silver duct tape, and a Bic lighter.

The infrastructure of the drilling rig was directly ahead, outlined in red lights, its steel gleaming in the moonlight and casting a distinct dark shadow across the gray gravel clearing.

The man dressed as a *kahuna* stood before the well for a long time, weighing the repercussions of blowing up the rig. He wondered what it would be like to drop lighted sticks of dynamite into the well hole. He imagined that they would free-fall until that magic moment when the spark in the fuse met the compressed gunpowder and triggered the explosion. He guessed a single stick would be enough for the well hole. He shook his head and moved on.

As he trudged up the path to the silica ponds, he felt a cold shiver pass over his body and he stopped. His mind played back the sound of the spear he had hurled—to him it had almost sizzled as it flew through the air. Then there was the deep thud and the guttural gasp as the air was forced out of the inspector's lungs. Then the sound of the body hitting the ground, and finally, almost simultaneously, the splash in the pool of brine water.

Bile rose in his stomach, the muscles in his neck constricted. He had trouble breathing, and perspiration beaded on his forehead and ran down his neck. But it soon passed, and he took a deep but careful breath, then continued walking, now down the incline to the main pond.

He had hoped the rubber mallet would silence the pounding, but that was hardly the case. The ground reverberated. After the first noisy blow, there was an echo. He stopped and listened for other sounds in the forest. Like footsteps or an approaching vehicle. But there was only the hum of insects and the occasional cry of a bird. He smiled to himself. The guard was almost three miles away. The police had left hours before. And if there was anyone else in the forest, they'd probably come forward and help him, without so much as a word or a question. For the only other intruders in the forest would be those who would applaud his work.

Still, as he pounded the next two stakes into the hard earth, he stopped between each blow and listened for a second or two. After the third stake was securely in place, he became confident that he was the only one present. But he had to hurry.

It took a half hour to hammer all the stakes into the ground. Four broke so he only ended up with twenty-eight good ones. He decided to attach two sticks of dynamite to the stakes at the four corners of the holding pond. That would use up all thirty-two. He wasn't going to carry any explosives back in case someone stopped him at the other end of the lava tube. There would be no explaining the dynamite. Not for him.

He dropped to his knees by the first stake and extracted two sticks of dynamite from his backpack. He leaned them against the stake, then took out one of the rolls of duct tape, wedged the roll between his legs, pulled off two feet of tape, and ripped it off. Then he pressed the tape against the red cylinders, placed the cylinders against the stake, and wound the tape around. It was secure, six inches above the salt water. He scrambled over to the next stake. Twenty minutes later he was done.

Next, the fuses. It had taken him a long time to find the materials he now extracted from his backpack. Coils of specially treated, slow-burning magnesium wire each a hundred and fifty feet long. He had started out with six of them. The first, a full two hundred and fifty feet, would burn for six minutes, giving him exactly enough time to get back to the lava tube after he lighted the end. The other fuses had been cut into varying lengths, each calculated to reach one of the thirty-two stakes. When four had broken, he was careful to just skip them and not reposition anything. If he had figured the lengths accurately, then all the sticks should blow at once. He knew, most likely, that the fuse segments would burn at slightly different rates, but he hoped that most of the sticks would explode simultaneously. He knew if a stick didn't blow, it might be recovered and traced. That was a risk he had to take, although he was pretty sure no one would be able to connect him to the theft in Kona. And they'd never figure out how he knew the dynamite would be there in the first place.

For the next half hour, he set the fuses—it was relatively easy since each length had been marked and labeled, and his flashlight provided plenty of light. When he was done, he wrapped the twenty-eight separate fuses around the main fuse, keeping them as close together as possible, making sure they touched their neighbor. Next, he unrolled the main fuse, back up the incline and then down the other side. The end of the fuse fell out of his hands and caught in some dead *pili* grass. Leaving it there, he ran back to the top of the hill and then raced down the other side. Quickly, he checked each stick of dynamite, then the connection points, making sure nothing had loosened or moved as he was unrolling the main fuse. Everything had held. He ran back up the hill.

When he reached the end of the long fuse, he took the lighter from his backpack, knelt again, stared intensely at the magnesium coil, breathed deeply a few times, checked his watch, then lighted the fuse.

The man in the tapa loincloth fled, running like never before. His heart pounded. His bare feet scraped over the crushed lava, but he didn't feel a thing except exhilaration. Finally, the struggle would be over. All the years of work.

He made the lava tube entrance in just over five minutes and hugged the top step. Eyes focused on his watch. Then a smile, though his chest heaved as he tried to suck in some air. He had been running seven days a week, three miles at six minutes each, for many months, but still it surprised him that he had run a mile in almost five minutes.

Another thirty seconds passed. *Now.*

There was no explosion.

But just as he started to wonder what had gone wrong, he saw the sky light up with fire and white crystals. Then he heard it. A tremendous boom and he felt the shaking of the earth. He scrambled down the stone steps to safety, reached into his backpack, extracted one of the flashlights, and turned on its powerful beam. At first he was scared. The cavern seemed to be shaking. Small pieces of debris fell from the ceiling. Dust swirled in the beam of his light. There was much more loose gravel and stone on the cave floor than before. He wished he had brought shoes. He heard underground noises but they seemed far away. After filling his nostrils, he ran, passing the huge column of 'ōhi'a roots and disappeared into the black tube.

What he didn't see or hear after he was underground was the red lights leaning to one side, and then, as if in slow motion, the drilling rig crashing to the forest floor, crushing the tool shed. Fuel tanks, bottles of propane, and pipelines exploded, adding to the devastation.

The insects and birds had vaporized. They were no longer en-dangered.

*   *   *

The phone and the alarm rang almost simultaneously. Normally that combination would have been jarring, but Ben was so tired that he reacted slowly. First he slapped at the ALARM button on top of the clock radio. He nailed it on the third try. Then he reached for the phone. No matter how much he stretched, he couldn't reach it without getting up. He gave in and got up, annoyed. His eyes opened only a crack. "Yeah."

"Ben, I just received a call from Hilo. There has been an explosion at the geothermal drilling site."

His head cleared immediately. Tobi had his attention. "I knew it! Why didn't they stake it out?"

"They did, but the patrolmen left at two ... orders."

"Anyone hurt?"

"Do not think so," answered Tobi.

"Are you going?"

"No, but they asked for you. I am sending a helicopter to pick you up. Where is a good spot?"

"Geez. How about on the lava behind the house? There's a patch of *pāhoehoe*."

"How big?"

"About fifty feet across."

"Okay. You be outside in twenty minutes. You have any crime scene ribbon in your Jeep?"

"Yeah, I do."

"Good. Pick the smoothest spot. Make an X."

"Gotcha."

"Report in after you have looked around."

"Right."

Ben showered and dressed in five minutes. With wet hair he rushed outside, proceeded to his Jeep, retrieved twenty feet of yellow ribbon—which was all he had—and marched out onto the flow behind his house. About fifty yards away was a smooth spot where long ago the lava had moved quickly with no impediment. He made a yellow cross, anchoring the four corners with flat rocks he found nearby, then went inside for breakfast.

He poured the usual mixture of *Just Right*, *Mini-Wheats*, and *Corn Flakes* into a large bowl and added skim milk. Then a sip of reheated black coffee before he added raw sugar and skim milk to the remainder of the cup. There was no fresh fruit, but he found about two inches of pineapple juice in the refrigerator. He chugged it, finishing it before he realized it was a bit fizzy. He wrinkled his nose. The first few spoonfuls of cereal tasted sour, but soon he was wolfing it down, his mind far away, trying to picture what the explosion had done to the drilling site. He wondered if they'd find that the explosives had come from the construction company.

I'd bet on it.

He wondered if someone had used the entire case.

Rotors whumped outside in the distance.

By the time he'd put together a small overnight bag containing a change of clothes and toiletries, the police helicopter was a few feet from landing. He raced outside and watched as it swayed slightly in the wind, steadied, and gently touched down. The pilot motioned him to keep down, then extended his right arm, moving it in a counter-clockwise circle, outlining how he wanted Ben to approach the aircraft.

Ben bent his knees and his back and duck-walked around to the passenger's side of the helicopter. The bubble door was open and he clambered inside, pulling the door closed behind him.

"Camp Randall," said the pilot as he offered his handshake.

"Ben McMillen."

"Glad to meet you, Ben. Stow your bag under your seat and buckle up. I'll have you there in thirty minutes."

"Great."

"Suppose you've been in one of these before."

"Many times, Camp. Many times."

"Okay, here we go." As Randall eased the stick forward, the chopper lifted slightly, turned, then banked to the right. They skimmed the ground for a few seconds, crossed over the lava, and soon were above the water, gaining altitude and heading for Ka'ū, following the coastline. "After Kealakekua, we'll head *mauka* and cut across."

Ben leaned toward the pilot. Randall gestured to a headset looped around a handle attached to the glass bubble. Ben put on the head-gear. He heard Randall radio their position and time of arrival. At the end of the transmission, he heard something about an Eradication Team Raid. When Randall signed off, Ben asked him about the raid.

"I'm the backup chopper. There's one scheduled in Puna," he glanced at the stainless steel, four-dial watch that dominated his left wrist, "in about forty minutes ... not too far from the explosion site."

"Mind if we swing by the raid site?"

Randall turned and faced Ben, giving him a questioning look with a partially closed right eye. "I thought this explosion was high priority."

"It is. But it can wait fifteen minutes. I've trained for the eradication team. Haven't been called yet. I'd like to see one up close."

Randall smiled. "Okay, but we have to make sure we go in last. Don't want to ruin the surprise. We can hover in the distance if we're early. Can't stay long, though."

"That's fine. Thanks."

Camp Randall gave Ben a 'thumbs up.'

Ben watched ahead as they banked left and soared over the highway, passing south of Kealakekua, heading inland. Below, they flew over the lush vegetation that ringed the fruit and coffee farms. Upland, Mauna Loa's 1851 lava flow was a combination of grayish rock and *'ōhi'a*. From the vantage of the helicopter it was easy to spot the *kīpuka*, pockets of concentrated foliage, seeding grounds for new *'ōhi'a* that would eventually replenish the forest. And ahead and left was the volcano—Mauna Loa. Still active, but quiet since 1984 when the Pacific hot spot centered under the smaller volcano to the southeast, Kīlauea. Mauna Loa reached more than 13,000 feet into the sky, above more than ninety percent of the earth's atmosphere. It formed the western boundary of Hawai'i Volcanoes National Park and stood like a proud mother as little Kīlauea spewed rivers of molten magma.

They flew along the southern edge of the volcano passing over the Southwest Rift Zone at an altitude of 500 feet above the ground. Ben held onto the edging of the bubble window. Here, over the Ka'ū Forest Preserve, Mauna Loa's slopes were covered with *'ōhi'a*, but also there were groves of *koa* at the upper fringes of the woodlands, as well as mountain streams choking with rain water from recent showers. As the landscape flattened, they dipped lower, re-crossed Highway 11 near Kīlauea's East Rift Zone, flew over the Ka'ū Desert, then over the Chain of Craters Road, where Ben had driven just days before.

Randall brought them down to two-hundred feet and leveled out.

Peering to his left, Ben waited patiently, hoping for a glimpse of the drilling platform. When they finally came to the clearing in the Wao Kele O Puna rain forest, Ben shouted, "Holy shit! Do you see what I see?"

Randall let out a long Texas-style whistle. "There's nothing left. Shit, look there!" He pointed.

Ben saw it, too. The drilling rig was a crumpled, twisted heap on the ground. Charred propane tanks. A smoking generator. The smaller brine ponds looked as if they had been tilted and their silica poured out to one side. And just a little *mauka*, many trees were down. All that remained intact was the black roadway that led into the forest. The main pond was gone. In its place was a large jagged hole. It looked as if a huge meteorite had completely leveled the site.

"Still wanna see the Eradication Team?"

"I guess I'll have to pass. Bring her down."

Randall nodded and relayed their imminent landing on the radio.

As they got closer, Ben could see about a dozen cars, all bunched together at the end of the road. The tool shed was flattened and smoking. White crystals, sparkling in the sunlight, were scattered everywhere. There were men in orange coveralls walking around, like a cleanup crew after an oil spill. The crew looked up as the helicopter neared the ground, their orange suits reflecting the bright sun.

Camp Randall brought the bird down fifty feet from another police chopper.

Ben was greeted by Detective Rodriguez.

"Captain Otaki said there was some dynamite stolen over in Kona."

"My case."

The Hilo detective handed him a plastic evidence bag. Inside was a red piece of wrapper. "This match?"

Ben took the curl of paper and examined it. There was a piece torn away where the 'as' in *Texas* should have been and the 'Bl' in *Blaster* was partly charred. "I think so."

Rodriguez took back the bag. "No one was hurt. It happened near dawn. The only injury is the security guard. Jumped so high he cut his head on his sun visor." Rodriguez couldn't help but smile.

Ben ran his fingers through his hair. "Three miles away?"

Ignoring the question, Rodriguez looked at Ben. Stared him right in the eyes. "When Oliveira got here, Konanui was at the gate. We arrested him."

It didn't sink in at first. Ben was too busy surveying the scene.

There were new fissures crisscrossing the clearing. They were wide, more than a few feet, and they appeared to be deep. The smell of sulfur hung heavy in the air. Trails of steam and smoke slowly corkscrewed into the air. "Huh?"

"I said we arrested your friend, Konanui."

"What? What for?"

"Maybe it was the way he was smiling."

"Where is he?"

"Safe in a Hilo cell for the time being. We're holding him for questioning."

"He was probably here first because he lives so close."

"I know, but I had no choice. I came with Geddes and Takehiro. Maybe Konanui should have kept his comments to himself."

"What did he say?" asked Ben, warily, not really wanting to hear it.

Rodriguez snorted, "He bowed, extended his arms, and said 'Good morning from Madame Pele!' I thought Geddes was going to slug him."

Thirty minutes later Ben had examined the site as best he could. There was debris everywhere. The sheet metal had sharp twisted edges. Foot-long plywood splinters from the tool shed were embedded in PVC pipe. Some cast-iron pipe was cracked. The rig look like a giant Slinky that a gorilla had played with. A small column of sulfur steam was visible near the base of the rig wreckage. It came from the well hole.

Harry Puou, the lead member of the Forensic team, approached them. He removed his black rubber gloves and stuffed them into the pockets of his orange suit.

"Ernie."

"Harry, this is Detective McMillen from Kona."

"McMillen ... yeah ... I remember you from the other day."

"Call me Ben. What can you tell us?"

"In simple terms, some nut planted at least two dozen sticks of dynamite around the main pond."

Ben was surprised. "Around the pond? Not the well?"

"The pond," Harry confirmed. "Everything else went with the impact. That much dynamite makes one helluva explosion. Chances are the guy who did this didn't know much about dynamite. He didn't use blasting caps." Harry held up a short piece of wire. "Magnesium fuse. My guess is that he wired each of them to a main one and lit that. If he had a long enough lead he might have escaped. If not, he's become part of the landscape … what's left of it."

Ben wet his lips. He was thinking. Why the pond? Why not the well? But his thoughts were interrupted when he heard a familiar shout. The three of them turned. Ben saw Ken Asumura running toward them. He appeared excited and he was breathing hard. His face was covered in perspiration.

"What? What?"

"Ben," he panted, "Ben," still out of breath, "up there. There's … there's bones and artifacts. The explosion opened … it opened a deep fissure." He took two deep breaths, the second was much slower. "There's human bones and sennit wrapping … fishhooks, spears … all sorts of stuff. The explosion opened up an ancient burial cave!"

"Where?" asked Rodriguez.

"Follow me … "

They hustled to an area just two hundred feet from the fallen rig. Climbing over a large 'ōhi'a that had snapped at its base, they came upon a wide crack in the ground. Strewn about were bones, unmistakably human. Ben saw the tip of a spear, and one of Ken's assistants was holding a half dozen fishhooks, carved from shark's teeth long ago. Many of the bones were still partially wrapped in sennit.

Ben had a sinking feeling. He thought about his grandmother wrapped in her woven coffin, buried in a small fissure on the western slope of Haleakalā on Maui. Her bones were there to rest in peace forever. He wasn't sure what he'd do if someone unearthed them.

Then Ben felt someone's eyes upon him. It was Ken. He held Ken's stare for a long time. Ben wondered what he was thinking. Ken seemed to be doing the same. Finally, Ken turned and started walking back to his car.

Ben watched the retreating pathologist until his eyes came upon another large, fresh fissure. His eyes followed the fissure, which cut through the forest in a southwesterly direction. When it disappeared under a dense cover of *hāpu'u* ferns, he raised his eyes and stared in the direction of the lava tube he and Nohea had used to gain entrance into the forest. He was sure the two caverns met underground. Although he wondered what would be found down there, he hoped no one else saw it. Burial caves were supposed to remain untouched forever.

He looked about his feet. One skeleton seemed to be reaching out for him.

Chapter Twelve

AFTER A FEW DAYS RECUPERATION, Hilo's timeworn Medical Examiner, Dr. Fitzsimons, returned to work, his kidney stones smashed and passed. He was crankier than usual, however, for he had been ordered to confine his work to the lab for the next ten days. And his doctor, not trusting his venerable patient, had notified the staff— 'He comes to work, he stays in the hospital for a few hours, he goes home. Anything else, *you* call me.' So, for the time being, all field work on the windward side of the Island remained with Ken Asumura.

Ken had taken the Wao Kele O Puna remains back to Kona Hospital for testing. After working through the night, tearing the autopsy room apart, arranging and rearranging each bone many times, he had called Ben, waking him at six. The pathologist had startling news. There were six sets of bones.

Three were old. Three were not.

The autopsy room had been converted into what looked like an archaeologist's workshop. The two aluminum dissection tables held partially reassembled skeletons. Four other sets of bones were laid out on old wooden tables commandeered from the hospital's store-room. Lots of bones were missing, but what was there was conclusive. Many bones of the older dead were broken. Ken said this was caused by centuries of shifting earth and the weight of new lava flows. And, of course, some of the older remains were wrapped in shreds of sennit, tell-tale strands from woven caskets of long ago.

The new sets weren't broken. They were whiter and in much better shape. Even without radiography and ossification tests, it was obvious that they were considerably younger than their gravemates.

"Are you telling me we could have three homicide victims here?"

"That's my guess," answered Ken. "At first I thought maybe a few Puna families had been using an old burial site. People still do follow the old practices, you know."

"I know. I helped bury my grandmother six years ago."

Ken nodded. He started to say something, but stopped, and walked over to one of the wooden tables.

Ben noticed his hesitation, but decided to let it go. "You said, at first ... "

"Take a look at the skulls of the new ones."

Ben came over to the first wooden table and peered into the eye sockets. For a few moments he was mesmerized. Then he examined the hole where the nose had been—the nose is cartilage, not bone, and decays quickly—then the area around the jaw. "What?"

"Using ultraviolet light and a slice of the femur for osteon counting, I found the victims to be in their early twenties. According to the deterioration of the remains, death probably occurred somewhere between two and three years ago." Ken raised his hand, deferring Ben's question. "I was going to take impressions of the teeth and catalog the restorations for dental identification."

Ben nodded. "And ... "

"There are no teeth."

"What? ... Wait. My grandmother told me it was customary for the immediate family to keep teeth, fingernails ... even some hair."

"Maybe a long time ago, but people who follow the burial traditions these days just want their dead buried with their ancestors. They don't keep body parts. Not any more."

"All the teeth are gone?"

Ken was nodding. "All of them ... They don't all fall out that quickly. It takes many years. The blast may have dislodged some of them, but not all. And we found no teeth at the site. They'd be scattered but not *too* far away from the remains."

With his left hand Ben rubbed his cheeks and chin. "So someone didn't want them ID'ed.

"Exactly."

The entire investigation began whirling around in Ben's head like a tropical storm. It seemed pretty gristly—a killer extracting the teeth of his victims. "What else do you know about them?"

"They were all men. You can tell by the relationship of the pelvic bones to the chest plates. As you can see, I've reconstructed the humerus, radius, ulna, femur, and tibia. Two were about five-eight. The other around five-ten."

"Anything else? Can you tell nationality?"

"Nothing else. No jewelry. No calcification indicating bone breakage when they were alive. Honolulu should be able to determine some genetic traits. By using distance between the eye sockets, shape of the jaw bone, slant of the nose, stuff like that, they can usually come up with some generalities about race. But, without clothing, jewelry, and personal items, the only way you find out whose skeleton it is ... is by matching dental records."

"There's no other sign of foul play, except the missing teeth. No skull fractures? No bullet holes?"

"Nothing," stated Ken flatly.

"Then what's your guess as to how they might have died?"

Ken thought for a few seconds, rubbed his eyes, and leaned against the wall. "Strangulation would be one, but I don't have enough of the neck bones to see if any are broken. Poisoning, although I found no evidence of anything except traces of minerals that are found in lava flows. You know, sulfur, magnesium … the usual. Stabbing's a possibility. Even a gunshot wound, if the killer removed the bullet or if it exited cleanly. Hey, if he took the time to pull out the teeth, then digging out a bullet wouldn't be a big deal."

Ben looked for a place to sit. His only choice was an uncomfortable steel chair. But it was better than sharing a table with a skeleton. "If it was poison, what about residue?"

"Didn't find any … no organs, no residue." Ken shook his head. His teeth showed his anger.

"Ken, is there something else troubling you? Something you want to tell me?"

"What do you mean?"

"Something's bothering you."

"Besides this? Sure, there are things bothering me. Same as you. We have Curtis Lyman murdered and we don't have a killer. We have the whole geothermal thing. The rain forest. The possibility of three more murders, maybe others … what more do you want?"

Ben looked into his eyes. "No, I mean something else."

Ken opened his mouth. Nothing came right out. Then, "No … except this is upsetting my *'ohana*. My mother lives only a few miles from the rain forest. And remains … remains are sacred. You know that."

Ben exhaled deeply and stood. "I understand." He suddenly had no stomach for this, but he knew he had to continue. "You're sure the other three are authentic. Real old."

"Absolutely. At least a hundred years, probably more, but Honolulu will have to determine it exactly."

"The old ones aren't important. Put together profiles on the three new ones, everything you know, and add anything you think might help, even guesses. I'll start checking on Missing Ps."

"You'll have it by noon."

"Ken?"

"Yeah?"

"Get some sleep, buddy. You look tired. Your eyes are bloodshot ... more than usual." Ben patted the pathologist on the back. "Get some sleep."

Ken rubbed his forehead. "I will."

As he turned onto Highway 11, heading north, Ben decided he needed to talk with Ernie Rodriguez. The car radio was out, the volcanoes saw to that. But there was a Union 76 station ahead on the right, and he spotted a pay phone. Ben pulled in, got out, and called Hilo PD.

Surprisingly, he got Rodriguez right away.

"Rodriguez here."

"Ernie, Ben. I'm just leaving Kona Hospital. We got trouble."

"What trouble?"

"Ken tested the bones. There were six sets."

"There's gonna be some pretty pissed people. This'll put a hold on the drilling for a while. There was talk of clearing some more land and starting up another well as early as next week. But not with burial caves and artifacts in the area. At least I don't think so."

"Ernie, three of the skeletons weren't old. The victims were in their early twenties. Dead within the last three years."

"Well, I'm sure they were registered. I've come across this a few times. There are Ka'ū and Puna families who still observe the old burial customs."

Ben guessed Rodriguez wouldn't know much about old burial customs.

"What if I told you each of the new skulls had no teeth."

"Decayed."

"Not that fast."

"I don't follow you."

"Maybe they were extracted so the remains couldn't be ID'ed."

"Holy shit!"

138

"There *is* an old custom where the *'ohana* keeps certain body parts, like teeth, fingernails, hair ... but they don't keep teeth anymore ... certainly not all of them."

"What do you want me to do?" There was hesitation in Rodriguez's voice.

"Do your death records indicate if a body was buried privately?"

"The mortuary space is blank, or maybe it says 'private' or 'family.' But, if it's blank, it might also mean the family didn't know which mortuary they planned to use."

"Just in case we have a real burial, put someone on it, will you? Try for every burial in Puna within the last three years that you think was private."

"What am I looking for?"

"Males. Twenty to ... let's say thirty when they died."

"Okay."

"Ernie ... how about if you work on Lyman's murder and I take these?" Ben hoped Rodriguez felt so overwhelmed that he would forget about jurisdiction. "I'll treat these as Missing Ps until I get the burial reports from you."

"Sounds okay. I'll tell Commander Diaz. Say, Ben, who knows about this?"

"You, me, and Asumura. I'm headed in to tell Tobi ... you can tell Diaz."

"You oughta go public. That'll stop them from clearing new land."

Ben laughed.

"What's so funny?" asked Rodriguez.

"Pretty soon you and Nohea will be best friends."

Rodriguez snorted. "By the way, we released Konanui an hour ago."

"But you have someone tailing him."

Silence.

"Thought so."

Ben pulled into Kona HQ. The parking lot was nearly empty. He entered through the side door, took a left down the hallway, then cut through SUPPLY and marched into CIS—the Criminal Investigation Section. Home.

Feet on his desk, fresh coffee by his right hand, and a furrowed brow. And Joyce Ah Sing standing next to him, staring out the window. He could only see part of her face.

"What's up?" she asked with a faraway look.

Ben snapped his fingers.

Her eyes fluttered and she gave him a silly grin. "Sorry."

"I need Hilo, Puna, and Ka'ū Missing Ps from the last three years. Just the males who would have been between twenty and thirty when they were reported."

"Hilo, Puna, and Ka'ū?"

Ben told her about the three sets of bones and his assignment to a case out of their district. Noticing her detached expression when what he had just said should have caused alarm, he asked her what was wrong.

"Nothing."

"C'mon."

"We had a fight."

"Everybody fights."

"Not like this."

Ben straightened. "He didn't hit you, did he?"

"No."

"Then what?"

"The engagement's off." Joyce covered her face with her hands.

Ben felt bad for her, but also he felt a bit like an ex-husband paying alimony. He wanted a partner for her. "Joyce, it'll be okay. You still want to marry him, right?"

She dropped her hands. The corners of her mouth turned upward and her shoulders moved in a barely perceptible shrug. Lips pursed, thinking.

"I'm sure he's talking to someone right now, just like you, saying the same thing. Give it a day or two, I'm sure you'll be back together."

Joyce gave him a small smile. "Maybe you're right … " Then her eyes opened wide. "Jeez! Three skeletons! I'll get these as fast as I can."

"Thanks. And keep this to yourself. Tobi doesn't even know yet."

"Gottcha."

"Joyce."

She turned.

"Chin up."

She tilted her head and sucked in her lips. "He better call."

"He'll call."

For the next hour Ben worked on his report of the explosion. He called Len Mahuna at Classic Structures and said he'd be by later that morning to confirm that the dynamite used in Puna had been taken from his place. Hilo Forensic had found several partial wrappers and had given him one. Over the phone Ben's description of the red wrapper fit. He added that to his report and typed the words 'PRELIMINARY MATCH' next to his description of the tie-in to the Classic theft. Then he made a copy of his report and headed for Tobi's office. Several of the uniformed officers stopped him in the hallway and asked about the explosion. It was the talk of the Island's police stations. They all whistled when he described the discovery of the bones. He didn't tell them that three sets were new. He wanted to see how Tobi wished to handle it.

Jack Cooper was with Tobi. Tobi waved Ben inside.

"We heard about the burial cave," said Jack, fidgeting with the collar of his faded blue aloha shirt.

"There's more."

Tobi's eyebrows crested. Jack dropped his hands and shimmied forward in his chair.

"There are six sets of remains. Only three sets are old."

Jack's mouth opened but nothing came out. Tobi's face wrinkled. Both of them sat unblinking. Ben explained the rest of Ken's findings, emphasizing the implications of the missing teeth.

"What do you think?" Tobi asked.

Ben sat in one of the matching side chairs, arms on the arm rests. In his lap his fingertips touched and flexed, mimicking what Tobi did when he was engrossed. "It's hard to tie the Lyman homicide to the other three. Those bodies are two or three years old and Lyman's body wasn't buried … it was left for all to see. On the other hand, all four were discovered on Foldagger property … all near the well. I'm convinced there's a lot more to Jackson Hole and the Foldagger family than meets the eye." Ben thought about the people who owned the land on which Jackson Hole drilled.

The Foldaggers were one of the major landholders in the Islands. They began as sugarcane plantation owners in the 1850s. Back then their family businesses controlled all aspects of the sugar cane business, from the cane fields, to the transportation of raw sugar, to the refineries on the mainland. They factored into every transaction. The Foldaggers had extensive land holdings on Oʻahu, Kauaʻi, Maui, and the Big Island. But they were no longer involved in sugarcane, as that business had diminished greatly after World War II. Now they were in real estate—major office buildings, industrial parks, resort communities, and among their land holdings, the result of the land swap when their original drilling site was covered by Kīlauea, was the Wao Kele O Puna.

"Let us examine the facts," offered Tobi. "We have four bodies. One we know was the victim of a homicide. The other three probably were as well … unless, as you say, you find evidence of private burials. Since we agree that is highly unlikely, let us assume that there are four homicides. So first, what is the motive?"

"Two possibilities," suggested Ben. "First, what if the three guys whose remains we found were a threat to the success of the drilling project, and then Curtis Lyman finds out something three years later and is used by the killer to frame the activists? That would explain why the others were buried and why Lyman's body was left out in the open where he'd be discovered. That's the version I favor."

Tobi asked, "And the other, which I guess is obvious?"

Ben spread his arms apart, palms up. "Yes it is ... too obvious. Lyman was killed by an activist or someone sympathetic with their cause. But I don't believe that."

Jack shifted to the edge of his chair. "I don't understand the frame-up."

Ben leaned forward until they were only a few feet apart. "Most of the public has sided with the activists. However, if they thought the activists had turned violent, then the drilling company would face a lot less resistance. The activist movement would be tarnished, the drillers would gain more public support ... no ... I take that back ... they'd achieve their real goal... public indifference, and the State Attorney General would keep PDF, BIRAG, and the Sierra Club tied up in court for a long time. The movement would run out of money. Besides, as far as I'm concerned, the most likely suspect is Nohea Konanui ... and he was with me."

"So you think the homicides are connected," stated Tobi.

Ben confirmed that he did.

Tobi stretched and then rested his hands on top of head. "What if there is more than one person involved? Maybe Nohea has a partner and the partner murdered Lyman."

"There may be more than one person involved, but Nohea's not one of them."

"Why, Ben?"

"You have to trust my judgment. Nohea may be hot over this, but he's not a murderer."

"What about the *kahuna*?" asked Tobi.

"It's not the *kahuna*, either."

"How can you be sure?"

Ben shifted in his chair. "Trust me on that one, too. It's not the *kahuna*."

Jack asked, "Then why'd he run away?"

"We're talking about a genuine *kahuna* … no cell can hold him. If he had remained, it would reveal a weakness … his *mana*, his power would be questioned."

Jack made a prune face. Ben knew Cooper's belief in Hawaiian folklore and mythology was based more on his respect for his friends than on actual conviction.

Jack asked, "You think he was just in the forest to pray?"

"Yes … to get Pele to cover the well. Just like in '85."

Tobi stood and walked over to the tray of potted orchids that sat on his window shelf. Slowly he stroked the leaf of one of the dendrobiums. Facing outside, he said, "To me … that means you think that Nohea is the *kahuna*."

Ben narrowed his eyes. "Or someone like him. Lyman's murder was made to look like a *kahuna* or someone sympathetic to the cause did it. It's a frame-up."

Tobi turned and faced Ben. He looked hard and long. He seemed to be searching for another question about the *kahuna*. Instead, he queried, "The dynamite is the same?"

Ben said he was sure it was.

"What are you going to do? You have ruled out the two likely suspects, Nohea and the *kahuna*. If you had no penchant for solving homicides, I would push you toward the two of them. Do you have a hunch?"

Ben gave Tobi a serious look. "It's not my case."

"Your expression says you are convinced Hilo is wasting their time."

Ben shrugged. "I think I may be able to track down the killer through the MPs. I'll work it from that angle. We'll see who ends up solving this first." Then he turned toward Cooper. "Jack, are you available?"

"Court case ended this morning."

"If you can work with Hilo on the burial records, then I can start on the Missing P angle *and* take some time to talk with some of the Jackson Hole workers. Someone there must know something."

"You got it. Who do I call?"

"Try Ernie Rodriguez. If you can't get him, try a Detective Kala."

"He new?"

"Uh huh."

Smirking, Jack pushed himself out of the chair and left, saluting as he crossed the threshold and disappeared.

The sun ducked behind the clouds and Tobi's office took on a somber tone. Tobi opened the blinds more to let in more light. He asked, "You think Geddes is the man?"

"I think maybe there's someone behind the scenes that Geddes keeps on as an aid of some sort. Someone who's been with him a long time."

"Like a bodyguard?"

"Maybe a bit rougher than a bodyguard. But I haven't run across anyone like that."

"Who else?"

Ben got up. "What about a Foldagger? Those are the people with fortunes at stake. They have the most to lose if the drilling project doesn't pan out."

"Ben ... let me tell you something *my* Captain once told me." Tobi sat on the corner of his desk. "The man with much to lose *has* much to lose because he has achieved something worth losing." Tobi paused. "And since he has done it once, he knows he can achieve prosperity again. He is not desperate like the man who has never been prosperous. It is that man who is most desperate who usually resorts to crime." Tobi winked his eye. "Think about who has the most to gain, not who has the most to lose."

"It's hard for me to eliminate the wealthy. They have the resources to protect themselves ... to cover this up." Ben paused for a few seconds. Something flashed through his mind, but too quickly, and he lost it.

Tobi was watching him carefully.

Ben added, "It seems to me ... that the rich always want to get richer."

"Just a suggestion."

Chapter Thirteen

FIRST, THE MISSING Ps.

Joyce had brought seven folders. Inside were National Crime Information Center reports from the FBI's computer database of Missing Persons and another database of Unidentified Persons. The NCIC reports contained everything from personal descriptors such as age, sex, race, height, weight, hair color, eye color, tattoos, scars, needle marks, medical information, optic data, clothing and jewelry worn at the time of disappearance to a tooth-by-tooth dental record including restorations and their type, appliances, chipped teeth, and missing teeth.

The seven folders were for males who had been between the ages of twenty and thirty when they were reported missing from the Hilo and Puna districts. Joyce found none from Ka'ū. Of the seven, five were from Hilo, which was to be expected based on Hilo's larger population.

It had been too noisy in CIS—one of the vice detectives had just become a new father—so Ben took a cup of coffee into the squad room, which was usually empty during a shift. There he was alone.

The first folder was for Roy Oba. He was twenty-one when he

disappeared, a student at UH - Hilo, who had lived at home in Hilo with his parents. Missing since the previous June and last seen drinking coffee at the Student Activities Center just before six p.m. But he was listed as five-four. Too short. Ben went on to the next folder.

William Ferdette. Six-one. Too tall. Next folder.

Ben quickly discovered that only two of the seven were between five-eight and five-ten. One had lived in Puna, the other in Kaiwiki, a small town just *mauka* of Hilo. From the hallway came the sounds of scuffling feet. Soon one of the clerks came into the squad room with an armful of baby presents. There were more footsteps down the hall and Ben realized the celebration was headed his way. He went back to his desk. Now CIS was empty. He called Ken and was told the pathologist was in a staff meeting that should end in ten minutes. Ben left a message.

The man who lived in Kaiwiki worked construction. He was employed by the State as a maintenance worker at the Hilo airport. The report said he disappeared one Sunday. Supposedly, he went fishing, but his boat remained anchored in Hilo Bay all day. There was no record of his boarding an inter-Island flight. He had simply disappeared.

The second man, the Puna man, lived alone in Kaniahiku Village, *makai* of Pāhoa, just below a development called Nānāwale Estates and near the entrance to Lava Tree State Monument. He owned a small orchid farm. After a week of missed deliveries and no answer to their telephone calls, two of his customers had gone out to see what the problem was. The place was deserted. The farmer's truck was there, breakfast crumbs and a moldy crust of toast on the kitchen table, a pot of old coffee on the counter, reading glasses by the telephone. This Missing P had been reported in April, two years before. The man's name was Wadel Kitano. What interested Ben most was a note on the bottom of the second page of the MP report. Wadel's hobby was spelunking. Some cave exploring equipment was found in his bedroom, and it was obvious from his collection of rocks and books that he had been a serious spelunker. Someone who would have more than one set of equipment. So it was possible that that's where he had gone. Ben's mind flashed back to the Wao Kele O Puna lava tube and to its tributaries and deep fissures. He thought about the new fissure he had spotted. He wondered if Kitano had gone underground alone. He wondered if he had had any connection to the drilling project.

Maybe he stumbled onto something. Something Jackson Hole wanted kept secret. Something Kitano thought he should talk about.

Ken called back.

"Just wanted to know if you determined race yet?" asked Ben, tired, trying to hold in a yawn.

"I should have that in about an hour. Any leads?"

"One, maybe. I've got a Missing P who was a spelunker. The report says his friends think he went caving and never came back."

"Where was he from?"

"Near Pāhoa."

"Hmmm. He go alone?"

"That's what I'm going to find out. I'll call you back in an hour. I'll be out for awhile."

"Make it eleven. I'll have everything by then."

"Fine."

Ben called Detective Rodriguez and asked who had worked on the Kitano Missing P. Rodriguez put Ben on hold. A minute later Detective Howard Burrell came on the line.

"Burrell here, McMillen. What do you need to know?"

"The Kitano Missing P ... 'bout two and a half years ago ... "

"Yeah, I remember it."

"You think he disappeared caving?"

"Seems most likely."

"Go on."

"We interviewed both of his caving buddies. The three of them went every Sunday. The last time they saw him they dropped him off at his place after a day of exploring. One talked to him during the week, letting him know that they couldn't go the following Sunday. Funeral."

"Who couldn't go?"

"The other two. That's why we figure he went on his own, got lost or ran into some trouble down there."

"Experienced guys don't go alone."

"He didn't run away with the milkman."

Ben didn't laugh. "His friends look over the stuff you found in his house?"

"Yup," answered Burrell. "They said some was missing. Light stuff. Like he was going to go where he'd been before. Makes sense if he was going alone. Probably a place he'd been to before. Maybe an earthquake opened a new fissure. Maybe he was just careless. Caving's probably like driving … most accidents happen within … "

"I get the picture. Got their names?"

"Sure, hold on."

A few minutes later Ben had the names, thanked Burrell, and hung up.

On the way over to Classic Structures, Ben thought about the disappearance of Wadel Kitano. He wondered if the man had been a supporter of PDF. Something else to check out.

Len Mahuna was outside inspecting the new side door. He turned when he heard Ben's Jeep pull up.

"Howzit, Detective?" said Mahuna.

Ben turned off the engine. "Okay, howzit by you?"

Mahuna answered, "Not bad. Not bad."

Ben got out holding a plastic evidence bag containing part of the red wrapper found at the well site. It had been dusted for prints, but only smudges had been found. Ben separated the Ziploc-like top, extracted the wrapper, and handed it to Mahuna.

"Looks the same. Without the serial number, I can't be positive, but I did some checking on my own. We're the only firm on the Big Island that gets dynamite from these guys in Texas. I needed another case. Asked for an air shipment. It'll be here tomorrow or the next day. You can have a stick to compare wrappers."

"Looks like you're doing my work for me."

"Glad to help."

"Anything come to mind the last two days? Any suspects?"

Mahuna shook his head. "No. Nothing. You check out Harrison?"

"Hilo did. He had an alibi."

"I hope not in a bar."

Ben shook his head. For a few seconds the whitecaps in Kailua Bay caught his attention. The Ironman seemed like a month ago.

Classic's owner cast his eyes toward Puna. "You been out to the geothermal well?"

"What's left of it."

"Pretty big blast ... huh?"

"Never seen anything like it," said Ben. "The whole place was leveled."

"He use it all?"

"Half. What do you use to detonate this stuff."

"Us? We use electronic detonators. Why? What did this guy use?"

"Looks like a long old-fashioned fuse."

"Dangerous. Your suspect may be hard to find."

"Why's that?"

"He may have cremated himself."

Ken Asumura said all three victims were probably a mixture of Japanese and Hawaiian.

After packing enough things for a few days, Ben left his house and headed toward Ka'ū on Highway 11. This was no sightseeing trip. He did sixty on the straight-aways and screeched around curves at forty. The tach never dipped below 3000. He had his portable blue strobe attached to the roll bar so no one would stop him.

Just under two hours later he was near Kīlauea Crater. Traffic slowed. Since he had come around Mauna Loa, he could just barely raise Hilo on the radiophone. Rodriguez wasn't in but Detective Kala was. They had found a half dozen private burials, but one of the Hawaiian detectives whose family had lived in Puna for many years had told him not to bother checking them out. He said the private burials had occurred in family plots on family land, probably Christian style. Any bodies that had been taken to the caves wouldn't be registered. And no one was going to talk about it. Cave burials were to remain secret. Burials had been one of the most sacred ceremonies in Hawaiian culture. Kala said he didn't think anyone would keep the teeth, but he couldn't be sure.

Ben replaced the transceiver softly, resigned to the fact that the three people whose remains had been unearthed had been murdered.

In Kea'au, at the junction of 11 and 130, Ben turned right and continued south toward Pāhoa. Twenty-five minutes later he was standing on Nohea's *lānai*. The orange Karmann Ghia hadn't been out by the road, so Ben stepped inside the farmhouse without knocking. The note he had left previously was still there. It hadn't been moved. He had no idea if it had been read. He added to the bottom of the note that he'd been back and wanted to talk. 'Call me at Hilo HQ.'

Forty minutes later—it would have been thirty-five except there was a tie-up at the Wailoa Bridge construction site—he angle-parked in front of Hilo Pua Nani florist on Kamehameha Avenue.

Ben hopped out of the Jeep and flexed his legs. The fresh, ozone smell of recent rain was in the air. Shoppers, mainly townspeople, peered into store windows, each carrying a half dozen small parcels, as if they had to distribute their purchases evenly among the row of merchants that faced Hilo Bay. Small puddles receded right before his eyes. Wet footprints disappeared seconds after they imprinted the sidewalk. It was near eighty and the temperature would head higher as soon as the sun pried its way from behind the cloud bank that was slowly being sucked up the side of Mauna Loa to the southwest.

Ben liked Hilo. He'd rather have it rain rain than rain tourists.

Ronald Taketa, the second-generation owner of Pua Nani, was a member of Wadel Kitano's spelunking team. His floral shop specialized in Hawaiian flowers and, in a new market, exotic silks. Handcrafted silk flowers had recently become an art form, sold for small fortunes, and didn't seem to impinge on the regular flower trade. Pua Nani's collection was one of the finest on the Island.

As soon as Ben stepped inside, he was greeted with a display of gingers—whites, pinks, and reds—sassy, heliconia, and dozens of other exotic flowers. A young woman appeared from behind a tall silk palm and asked if she could help. Ben asked for Taketa. She pointed toward the back of the store. Ben thanked her and worked his way through a maze of hanging heliconia and the predictable beaded doorway to the workshop.

Ronald Taketa was trim, even skinny. He was about five-ten. His skin was dark. Ben pegged him as part Hawaiian, but mostly Japanese.

"Mr. Taketa."

The owner of Pua Nani turned, smiled, and took a few paces toward Ben, offering his hand. "Aloha. Call me Ron."

"Ron. Ben McMillen. I'm a Kona detective. I'm helping with an investigation in Puna. Can I talk with you a second?"

"Sure. Is something wrong?"

"Nothing for you to worry about, but I wanted to talk to you about Wadel Kitano."

"You found him!"

"Not sure. Let me explain. You know about the explosion at the geothermal site."

Taketa nodded. Ben thought he saw a hint of a smile.

"An ancient burial cave was unearthed in the blast."

Taketa's eyes widened, then he looked behind him and pulled up a tall stool, motioning to Ben to do the same. After they were both seated, Ben continued.

"Several sets of bones were discovered. Some of them were not ancient remains."

Taketa's face screwed up. He appeared lost.

"We think the old burial cave may have been used to hide three fairly recent homicides. It's possible that one of the bodies is Wadel. It's a long shot, but I need to know everything you can tell me about him."

"I see." Taketa took a deep breath and let it out slowly. "Wadel and I and another spelunker, Gene Au ... we used to go exploring every Sunday. We were in the Wao Kele O Puna hundreds of times, since, oh ... 1980 or so ... when we got together."

"You think he went out alone the day you and Gene Au couldn't make it?"

"Yes. Gene's clothing store is around the corner. One of the other merchant's father passed away that week. The funeral was that Sunday. We canceled caving. Wadel probably went alone, which he shouldn't have done, but maybe he went to an easy cave, one he'd been to many times before. He probably just needed it so badly. You see, Gene and I love spelunking, but Wadel, he was consumed. I imagine he kept track of how many consecutive Sundays he'd gone caving. I think he might have gone out, picking a familiar cave, just to keep his record intact."

"What do you think happened?"

"I doubt he got lost. My guess is that with all the seismic activity, a new fissure had opened up, maybe one just around a corner, maybe one just beyond an old one, one we used to jump over. Gene and I looked for him. So did the police. We picked the most likely spots, but we found nothing. There were a few new fissures, but none of them were very wide. We came back with dogs. They never found the scent. They don't like the lava tubes."

Ben wondered about a connection between these caving enthusiasts and the geothermal project. He thought of two possibilities. "You guys ever find artifacts, burial caves, anything like that?"

The owner of the flower shop nodded. "Artifacts all the time. Mostly *'opihi* shells and gourds, but we found a burial cave once."

"Where? In Puna?"

"In Puna. On the edge of the Wao Kele near Hawaiian Acres."

"Did you report it?"

"We told the Department of Land and Natural Resources. The location was kept secret so there wouldn't be looters."

"Was it close to the drilling site?"

"No. Miles away."

"What about the geothermal project? How did Wadel feel about it?"

"You kiddin'? The venting was killing his orchids. He was strongly opposed to it."

"He ever demonstrate?"

Taketa nodded vigorously. "At least once that I know of. He was jailed overnight."

Ben wondered if Nohea knew Kitano. "He belong to PDF?"

"Belong is probably not the right word, but he contributed. We all did. And we're all members of the Sierra Club."

As Ben was digesting this, he noticed there were tears in Taketa's eyes.

The florist wiped his eyes with his fingers. "Sorry," he said. "Talking about Wadel ... "

Ben stood and held the man's shoulder. "Hey, I understand."

"You think he was murdered? You think there's a connection?"

"I don't know. The people at Jackson Hole Geo know Wadel? ... like they know Nohea Konanui? You know Nohea?"

"I know who he is. Wadel went on a demonstration once, like I said, but it was for the old well."

"The ORMAT well?"

"Yeah."

"And he was arrested for trespassing?"

"Yeah."

Ben glanced at his watch. "Hmmm. Tell you what. It's almost one. What say we find Gene Au and grab something to eat."

"Sounds good to me," said Taketa. "Let me tell my sister." He walked through the beaded curtain, wiping away more tears as he entered the front part of the shop.

Gene Au had already eaten, but he turned over his shop to his mother and joined them. Taketa suggested they get some sandwiches and sit in the park across the street. He said it was a shame, when it wasn't raining, to waste a lunch time inside.

As Ben and Taketa ate, Gene Au, who was a more experienced spelunker than Taketa, admitted for the first time that every Sunday morning since Wadel had disappeared, before he and Taketa went exploring, he spent a few hours checking out sites in Puna that Wadel used to frequent. He'd start at six and be done and at Ron's house by ten.

Taketa said, "You shouldn't go alone. I should go with you. Why would you repeat Wadel's mistake?" He was extremely upset.

Gene Au put his hand on his friend's shoulder. "At first, I really expected to find him, and since you were closer to him than me, I wanted to spare you the pain. Later on ... I don't know ... I kept going alone because I thought you'd think I was foolish to keep looking."

Firmly, Taketa said, "From now on I go ... we'll do this together."

"Agreed, my friend." Gene turned to Ben. "I must have been in fifty caves by now. Not a trace. You know, in some of them, the ones with finely crushed lava floors, footprints remain for a long time. I've found plenty, but none belonging to Wadel."

"How do you know whose they were?" Ben asked.

"Wadel had tiny feet. Size seven. All of these were bigger. No children go caving and very few women."

"Gene, what do you think happened?"

"All along I've thought he fell into a new fissure, something an eruption or an earthquake caused. I never thought about murder. Not for a second. But now that you've found three skeletons, I don't know."

"I asked Ron if he knew anything about Wadel's past that might help us ID the remains. What about it?"

"You mean like broken bones?"

"Precisely," confirmed Ben.

Gene, a tall man of Chinese and Hawaiian ancestry, scratched his head. He wore his black hair extremely short, and his fingernail made a sound like he was scraping sandpaper.

"I can't think of anything."

"Does he have relatives in the area?"

"Ron told you Wadel's wife died five years ago?"

"On the way over to your place."

"They never had kids. He had a uncle that he used to visit, but I don't remember his name or where he lived."

"That's okay," said Ben. "I'm headed for the Hilo station later. They'll have something. I need to talk to the person who knew him the best when he was growing up."

Gene Au sighed. "Poor Wadel."

"Last question, then I have to go. Anyone ever threaten him, like after the demonstration?"

"We weren't there," answered Ron. "He just told us he went."

"Any neighbors I should talk to?" asked Ben.

"Yeah … try old Mrs. Pukui. I should have thought of her before. They call her Auntie Eleanor. She used to cook and clean for him after his wife died. But she moved to the other side of the Island a few years ago."

"Eleanor Pukui?"

Both men. "Yeah."

"Where's she live?"

"Kailua or Keauhou?" said Gene.

Taketa shrugged.

Ben stood. "Thank you both. I'll keep you posted. And please … keep this conversation to yourselves. If Wadel was murdered, we don't want the person responsible to know we're investigating his disappearance again."

"We understand," said Taketa, solemnly.

Gene Au nodded in sober agreement.

It started to rain and lunch in the park was over.

When Ben reached Hilo HQ, neither Rodriguez nor Kala was in. The duty officer showed him a desk he could use. Ben called Jack Cooper and asked him to find Eleanor Pukui and ask her about Wadel Kitano.

"Concentrate on anything that might enable Ken to determine if one of the skeletons is his. Be gentle with her."

"You got it."

Ben had Jack transfer him to Tobi. When Tobi picked up, Ben quickly brought him up to date. Tobi asked him if he'd checked out employees of the drilling company.

"They're next."

Chapter Fourteen

B EN THOUGHT ABOUT THE THREE MEN he was going to see. Jeffrey Geddes, the geothermal drilling company's project manager, who split his time between the mainland and the Big Island. Andrew Takehiro, the one-time State employee, now Jackson Hole's attorney. And Henry Helenihi. He had replaced Nohea as the on-site supervisor of the geothermal project.

By Hilo standards, the rain had stopped. It was only drizzling. Ben walked through the mist up Pauahi Street and turned left on Aupuni. Jackson Hole Geothermal had leased two thousand feet on the second floor of an office building directly across the street from the County Office Building adjacent to Kaiko'o Mall. Handy for filing permits. That's where Takehiro and Geddes had agreed to meet him.

Ben had done a little research on the man who acted as the spokesperson for the drilling company. Takehiro had been born in Hilo. His parents had both worked in the Suisan Fish Market, his mother as a bookkeeper, his father an auctioneer. The Market, just off Bayfront Highway where the Wailoa River meets the ocean, was a busy place where Hilo's early morning catch was auctioned amidst a frenzy of jabbering and bidding—some in English, some in Japanese, and the auctioneer in what amounts to the universal language, a mixture of everything, pidgin English. Restaurant owners bidding alongside the locals and a small number of tourists.

Always a good student, Takehiro graduated from the University of Hawaii with a B.A. in Political Science and earned a full ride to UH's Law School. He was third in his class, graduating with honors. Yet, his only job offer came from the State, and he had labored in various departments for fifteen years, but mainly handling legal matters for the Department of Land and Natural Resources. He had been involved in some of the issues concerning the first geothermal well on the Big Island—the UH HGPA project, which was later shut down because of hazardous conditions.

Takehiro had left the State's employ in November 1984, when Jackson Hole Geothermal, recognizing his value, hired him. He had contacts in government ... *and* ... he was part Hawaiian.

As Ben climbed the steps to the second floor, he wondered what Takehiro would say about the burial ground and the remains.

A receptionist greeted him and offered him fruit punch, which he declined. She then asked him to wait for a few minutes. She told him Mr. Takehiro was on a conference call that was nearly over. Ben wondered how she knew it was about to end. Instead of asking her that, he asked her how well she had known Curtis Lyman.

Her dark eyes blinked a few times. "Oh, very well. It's a shame. He was a nice man, although he didn't seem quite himself the last few months. I think he was working too hard."

"Like what ... was he nervous? Grumpy? Upset?"

"I'd say upset."

"Any good friends at work?"

The woman swung away from her typewriter and clasped her small hands on top of her desk. "You mean socially?"

"Yeah."

She gave Ben a puzzled look. "There are just two women here. We're both married."

Ben smiled. "I meant a friend. Someone he would confide in."

"Oh ... gee, I don't think so. His job was different from everyone else's so he typically worked alone. And he didn't have a fixed schedule."

"He work here?" Ben's head went left and right.

"No," she answered. "We have a small laboratory at the University. When he wasn't in the field, he was there. Oh, Mr. Takehiro's light just went off. I'll see if he's ready."

Andrew Takehiro stood in the doorway. The receptionist almost bumped into him. Quickly, she spun around, smiled at Ben, and clumsily regained her chair.

"Detective McMillen." Takehiro extended his hand.

Ben took it, felt the man's exceptional grip, nodded once, and then followed the attorney into his office.

"Something to drink? You're on duty ... maybe iced tea?"

"No, thanks. I'd like to get to the questions."

Takehiro pointed to a stiff chair, waited until Ben was seated, then lowered himself into a comfortable looking leather chair on the other side of the desk. Takehiro assumed what Ben called 'lawyer's pose.' Erect, leaning slightly forward. Elbows on the desk, hands together, thumbs supporting his chin, and the rest of his fingers against his lips and chin in prayer. "Go ahead, detective."

Ben watched him for a few seconds. The attorney was calculating something. "First of all, I want you to know that Detective Rodriguez is heading up the investigation of the Lyman homicide."

Takehiro nodded.

"I'm working on the remains that were unearthed during the explosion."

"Have you identified any of them?"

"No."

"And you're sure they're not old?"

"Positive."

"Hmmm."

"Any ideas?"

"About?"

"About why three people were killed and buried in a lava tube near your drilling site."

Takehiro licked his lips and let his tongue hang there for a few seconds before swallowing it like a lizard. "Since none of our people are missing, I'd guess we have three activists who were trespassing and who got lost in the labyrinth and starved to death."

"What if they were murdered?"

Smoothly, "Then the same person who killed Curtis probably killed them."

"Under those circumstances, you still think they were activists?"

Takehiro raised his eyebrows a bit. Then he grinned. Finally he answered, "I believe figuring that out is your job, not mine."

Ben gave Takehiro a firm look. "Let's get back to your employees … you sure there's no one who might have a motive for sabotaging the well?"

"There's one *ex*-employee," the attorney answered sarcastically.

"He was with me."

Takehiro remained silent, but his smile widened.

Ben breathed slowly, staring at the attorney, trying to look calm. Then he stood and walked to the window that was behind Takehiro. He heard the attorney's chair swivel. Ben put his hands by his thighs and clenched his fists. He turned and faced Takehiro and asked, "Why do you think Lyman was carrying dynamite in his pickup?"

Takehiro adjusted his glasses, pushing them higher on the bridge of his nose. "No idea. We have not had any dynamite in more than four years. The last was used to clear a few stumps that blocked construction of the roadway."

"You have none in supply?"

"None. We checked yesterday, knowing you'd ask."

"When you did … had any ever been stolen?" Ben asked. He crossed his arms.

"No. As I recall, we only purchased a small quantity to handle a few trees. That was it."

"Where'd you get it?"

"I don't recall … that's not something I'd get involved with. You can ask Henry Helenihi. He'll know."

"Tell me about Curtis Lyman."

"I thought you said Detective Rodriguez was working that case."

"Just a few questions … background for me."

"He'd been with us eight years. His title was Chief Inspector. He was responsible for taking readings … water table, hydrogen sulfide, weather conditions, temperature, wind … that sort of thing. All the measurements we are required to report to the State agencies and the EPA. It's critical to us that we comply with health, safety, and environmental regulations."

Give me a break. "Are you?"

A lawyer's smile. "Of course."

"He hang out with anyone?"

Takehiro's expression turned puzzled.

Ben played along. "Any friends at work?"

"I wouldn't know. Again, ask Helenihi."

Ben held in a cough and swallowed carefully. "Okay for now." He stood and headed for the door. As he reached for the doorknob, he turned and asked, "Is this the first time you've uncovered a burial site?"

"We didn't uncover it. Whoever blew up the well did."

"What about before?" Ben leaned against the door.

"Never. In fact, McMillen, think about this. What if one of the activists planted the bones after the explosion? Some old … some new."

Ben gave him a stern look.

"Remember … they're the ones who are desperate."

Geddes was in a conference room at the end of the hallway. He stood hunched over the table, staring intently at some plans. A gleaming white hard hat that hadn't seen much field work anchored one end of the drawing. A telephone covered the other end. Geddes broke off his examination of the drawing when Ben rapped lightly on the door. As soon as Ben saw the catlike smile wedged into Geddes's jaw, he realized this interview would be a waste of time as well. He decided to make it short and hoped that Henry Helenihi might be more cooperative. That is, if the field supervisor already hadn't been prompted how to answer.

"C'mon in, Detective. Have a seat." Geddes gestured toward a corner setting of two armchairs and a small couch. The furniture was rattan, natural bamboo. The cushions were a subdued light blue print of seashells and small starfish.

Ben indicated he'd stand. Geddes backed up and leaned against the wall, careful not to brush against a relief map of the Wao Kele O Puna.

"Just a couple of questions. How often do you come here?"

"To the Islands? Oh, every two or three months."

"You were here when Curtis Lyman was murdered, correct?"

"Yeah. So what?"

"Why?"

"Routine inspection."

"What do you inspect?"

"Unless I'm a suspect, let's keep these questions on the explosions and your unidentified remains."

Ben was thinking that Geddes came to the Islands only when there were problems. Like venting problems. Problems meeting the schedule. Maybe employee problems. He wondered what had prompted this visit. It was obvious he wasn't going to get the answer from Geddes. "What's your theory?"

"You're the detective, what's yours?" Geddes grinned.

"Let's say I think we've found three activists."

Geddes's grin melted.

"See … what I'm trying to figure out is whether the score is three to one or four to nothing?" Ben gave Geddes a long stare.

Finally, Geddes broke the silence. "What's that supposed to mean?"

"Whether someone murdered three activists or four."

"Curtis Lyman wasn't an activist."

"Oh? I've heard he might have been falsifying reports."

"Nonsense!"

"Under pressure."

"Look, McMillen … I don't have to sit here and take your accusations. I'm trying to cooperate. You probably have the bones of three activists who were sneaking into the forest … "

"Who got lost and starved to death, right?" Ben placed his arms across his chest and widened his stance.

"You'd be foolish to think Takehiro and I didn't talk over the possibilities. Look … you have three people who got lost in the caves. Maybe they were activists, maybe not. And … " he raised his hand to hold off Ben's response "… one valuable Jackson Hole employee murdered. That much, and only that much, we know for sure. In my book, the score's one to nothing."

Ben tried another track. "Let's talk about Curtis Lyman. Why do you think he was killed?"

Geddes gave him an annoyed frown. "I thought Hilo was investigating that."

Geddes and Takehiro … same response. I wonder what else they're sharing? "They are. I just want a few facts. You don't object to me helping with the investigation of a murdered Jackson Hole employee, do you?" Ben could see Geddes's face redden. A vein pulsed just above his left eyebrow.

Geddes cleared his throat roughly. "I expect he was out there at night, simply doing his job, when he ran into this witch doctor, or whatever he is, and got killed." Now Geddes folded his arms across his chest. "If it's not Konanui, then that old man you captured *is* your man. You know … the geezer who disappeared right before your eyes. Three detectives right there. Was there a poof of smoke and a flash of light? Hah!"

"I don't think it was the *kahuna*."

"*Kahuna*! I'd expect that shit from Konanui, but a Kona detective? You've been to college, haven't you?"

Ben felt the taste of bile in his throat. He knew Geddes was baiting him.

Geddes snorted. Then he seemed to change his demeanor. "Curtis Lyman was a valuable and trusted employee. We want his murder solved without delay. Our other employees are afraid to work. We've had to hire armed guards."

"Work at what? The well's gone. The whole area's devastated."

"We're moving farther into the forest. We have no choice. Right now we're clearing a new site. It'll be no more than a month before we start drilling again. That'll show those activists that blowing up our well won't work."

"You got a permit, even after the discovery of the remains?"

"We promised to keep clear of the burial area."

Shit. "You really believe the activists set off the dynamite?"

"Who else?"

Ben inhaled, held it for a few seconds, then slowly let his breath seep out between his gritted teeth. "What about the fact that dynamite was found in Lyman's pickup?"

"Planted."

"Like to hazard a guess who would do that?"

"Konanui."

"Not him."

Geddes glared for a few moments. Then a smile crossed his face and with raised eyebrows, like he'd had an illuminating idea, he said, "Maybe it was someone who was with him. Someone no one would suspect."

Fuck you. "I'd suggest ... "

Geddes raised his hands in mock surrender. His expression said there'd be no more low blows.

Ben ignored the gesture. His tone was cold when he said, "I want a list of all your employees starting from day one."

"I'll see that you get it," Geddes said in a placating voice.

"Now."

"Okay, now," he said pleasantly. "Follow me, *sir.*"

When Ben found him, Henry Helenihi was at the new location, another few hundred yards into the Wao Kele O Puna, supervising two bulldozers. The sight of it made Ben sick. There were chain saws biting into the bark of hundred-year-old *'ōhi'a*. What had been a forest floor covered with *hāpu'u* ferns was now a track of dark earth, scored with huge tread marks. Here and there, dying ferns popped through the volcanic soil. Worst of all, a giant pig hung from a hastily constructed tripod, its flesh bleeding from jagged wounds, gashes that could only have been made with a chain saw.

Before he had driven down from Hilo, Ben had checked to make sure new permits had been filed. He was told that Jackson Hole Geothermal had several sites already approved. The explosion had just forced them to move to the second location a little sooner than anticipated.

Ben trudged through the uneven, newly excavated earth, smelling the rich soil, feeling the humidity of the decomposed lava, and fuming at the sight of more destruction in the rain forest. He wondered what Nohea was doing. He had a strange feeling that his friend was in the area, watching. As he approached Helenihi, who was signaling to one of the crew, Ben's eyes skirted the forest edge, looking

167

for Nohea.

The noise of the bulldozers made it necessary to shout. Henry Helenihi didn't see Ben until one of his drivers pointed in Ben's direction. The supervisor took a few paces forward and shouted, pointing to Ben's head. "Where's your hat?"

Ben shook his head. "I don't work here … I'm Ben McMillen, Kona detective. I need to ask you a few questions."

The color drained from Helenihi's face. He swallowed. "This way … where we can talk." He pointed back in the direction from which Ben had come.

Helenihi lead the way. Past the Jeep, maybe fifty yards, in the direction Helenihi was headed, was a newly constructed shack. Every few paces the supervisor turned and looked at Ben. The man was nervous. Anxiety evident from the manner in which he licked his lips and tried to swallow. When they reached the temporary wooden structure, Helenihi held the door, Ben stepped inside, and the site supervisor followed. Ben heard a deep, pained sigh. This was a man who *had* been told what to say, who knew something worth knowing, and he hoped, a man who could be persuaded to reveal the truth.

"I've been with Geddes and Takehiro."

Henry Helenihi's jaw remained firm. "Coffee?" he asked, close-mouthed. He pointed to a smoky brown Pyrex pot sitting on a cooktop.

"No thanks."

There were two folding chairs and a table made from a half sheet of plywood and two saw horses. The plywood was finished on the top side. Several blueprints were tacked to the tabletop, overlapping one another, edges curled and dirty.

Ben took a seat. So did Henry. Henry still appeared nervous.

"A Hilo detective has the Lyman homicide. I'm working on the remains we found."

Henry's body jerked.

"This where you keep the dynamite?"

Henry appeared puzzled. "We have no dynamite."

"Never."

"Before ... for ... for stumps. But now we have better excavating machinery."

"You just dig deeper."

Henry looked as if he was ashamed.

Ben leaned forward. "You've been told that some of the remains were not our ancestors?"

"Yes." Henry worked his fingers through his thick, wavy hair.

"Any ideas?"

"Geddes thinks ... "

"I'm not interested in what Geddes thinks, I want to know what you think." Ben gave him a serious frown.

Henry exhaled. Ben could smell stale coffee on his breath.

"It could be cavers who became lost." A small smile trickled from Henry's lips.

Ben sat silent.

"Could be some of the protesters," his face suddenly brightened, "or maybe three high school kids. They've been playing pranks on the guards. Maybe they found a tube opening and got lost."

"That was recent. The remains are between two and three years old."

"Oh."

"How long have you worked for Jackson Hole?" Ben asked.

"Since '85."

"You became field supervisor after Nohea quit."

"Uh huh." At the mention of Nohea's name, Henry's expression became sullen.

"That bother you?" Ben asked.

Henry Helenihi took a deep breath. His expression still laden with worry, but the fear in his eyes had departed somewhat. "I know what you're thinking. Here I am, a native Hawaiian, a pure blood at that, working for a company that's trying to destroy our land and our heritage. It's not easy for me, but I believe Hawai'i has to become independent of foreign oil. I wish there were some other way. Maybe we don't need this now, maybe oil prices have stabilized for now … but how long will it last? This project is going to take a long time, much longer than Geddes or Takehiro say. What if ten years from now we are ready, and the Middle East erupts again and oil prices skyrocket? That's why I work here, that's when this will make sense. You can't judge it by what's happening now. This is a project for the future. Hawai'i's future." Henry had become a bit more at ease now. His eyes were wide open and he was using his hands to reinforce his words.

Ben shook his head. "Henry … when does it stop? When all the *'ōhi'a* are cut down? When all *'io* have crashed to the ground with toxins in their lungs? When the Happy Face spider has no smile? When all of Puna's people are disabled because they have been drinking toxic by-products for five years? How about the unborn children? Think about the Hawaiian babies who may be born deformed or carrying the curse of cancer?

"And what about energy conservation? Wouldn't the geothermal dollars be better spent making solar energy more cost effective? Especially here in Hawai'i. Why aren't we developing solar power? Why not apply some technology to that? We're a gold mine of solar potential." Ben gulped more air. His chest was heaving.

Softly, Henry said, "I have to go." The fear was back in his eyes.

Ben shook his head and stood. "No you don't. I'm not finished with you." Ben extracted a small wad of folded paper from his breast pocket. I made a copy of the employee list Geddes gave me. I'd like you to go over it carefully tonight and see if there is anyone on it who may have left unexpectedly."

Henry remained seated. "You mean missing?"

"Missing, quit after an argument or an altercation, anything you feel might shed some light on this mess. And let's keep it between you and me, okay? You owe the people of Hawai'i that much, don't you?"

Henry licked his lips. He bowed his head.

"Concentrate on the ones that would have been in their twenties. But chances are, what we're really looking for are names that are *not* on the list. People not on the list who should be. Understand?"

"I understand."

"And Henry?"

Henry Helenihi looked up and held Ben's stare.

"This afternoon ... when you bulldoze another *'ōhi'a*, think how valiantly it struggled to grow from a flower seed to become a tree. Think of how many fail to germinate in the middle of barren lava fields ... how so precious few survive the hot sun and the wind, trying to get a foothold on life. Think about that."

Chapter Fifteen

SATURDAY CAME JUST IN TIME. Ben needed a day off. Friday after noon had been spent talking with several Jackson Hole employees. No one had been willing to answer questions about Geddes and Takehiro. After, with Takehiro always nearby, Ben had spent two hours in the office going through personnel records. He hadn't come up with anything helpful. Ben wondered if any of the employment records had been altered.

Jack Cooper had found Auntie Eleanor, the woman who did housework for Wadel Kitano. She remembered that Wadel had broken his right wrist when he had just started caving. Ken Asumura had all three right wrists. There had been no evidence of a break. Kitano was still missing, probably somewhere in the maze of lava tubes, but he wasn't one of the three unidentified remains. Ben wondered how many other people had met their deaths in the underground cemetery.

But enough of that. Although he knew that thoughts of the murders would work their way into his head throughout the course of the day, Ben was determined to spend this Saturday relaxing.

He popped out of bed and headed for the bathroom and then for the *lānai*. The surgical tubing wrapped around a support post reminded him of the tubing tied to the yellow ribbon he had found on the steps of the lava tube. He smiled at that. Next, Ben focused on the water surging against the lava formations that rimmed the small bay behind his house. His thoughts remained with the *kahuna*, debating, re-testing his decision to keep the man's identity a secret, hoping he was right that there was no way the *kahuna* had murdered Curtis Lyman. And no way that he had caused the deaths of the other three victims.

He had slept later than usual, so the swarm of sea birds was missing. Only a few lazy ones remained behind. Maybe they were too full of mullet to fly. Ben sat on a heavy bench, bent and grasped the tubing that encircled one of the wooden posts. He wound the ends around his hands and began to alternately pull and stretch his arms and shoulders. He lost count of the number of repetitions as the face of the *kahuna* floated before his eyes.

Half an hour later, after sit-ups, hamstring stretches, and pull-overs, front and back, Ben was sweating profusely. He vaulted over the *lānai* railing, landing carefully on a worn patch of *pili*, walked over the *pāhoehoe* lava, and dived into the sea. Within minutes he was two hundred yards offshore, rising with the swells, disappearing from sight in the troughs. After another hundred yards, he turned and headed for shore. He felt much better.

Just as he stepped from the shower, he heard the phone ring. Walking briskly, leaving distinct footprints on the slate bathroom floor, he reached his bedroom door just as the phone ceased ringing. Ben frowned and turned back. Holding a towel about his waist, he detoured into the kitchen and began to rinse the coffee pot. The phone rang again. This time he grabbed it before the second ring.

"Hello."

"Ben, it's me."

"You just call before?"

"No."

"Where are you?"

"Kahului. At the airport."

Ben grinned to himself. "When's your flight?"

"The next one leaves in forty-five minutes."

"I'll pick you up." Then he had a second thought. "It's not work, is it?"

"No, kiddo, it's you."

Much bigger grin. "I'll be there waiting with a *lei* in hand."

A small gasp escaped from Lisa's mouth. "They'll arrest you for that. Keep it in your pants."

He called Danny Mitchell, who picked up after the first ring.

"Danny, Ben."

"Hey, partner. How's it going?"

"Okay," Ben said.

"Anything on the guys who stole Simpson's boat?"

"I gave that to Jack. I'm working on the remains that were discovered after the explosion."

"I read about that. Quite a deal, huh?"

"Sure is. Hey, you got a charter today?"

"Nope."

"Want to take Lisa and me out?"

Ben could hear Danny clicking his tongue against the roof of his mouth. "I've got a meeting with the bank at one and a doctor's appointment at two."

"You okay?"

"Insurance exam."

"Oh." Ben was disappointed. No boat ride.

"Doesn't mean you can't go by yourself."

"You sure?" When they'd gone fishing together, he'd taken the helm almost as often as Danny, but Danny had never offered the boat before.

"Yeah. In fact, I don't have a charter until tomorrow afternoon. You can anchor in some nice romantic cove for the night, if you like. The boat's on me. Bait, food, and gas are on you."

"We'll be there by eleven. Thanks."

"If I'm not here, you know where the key is. If you're gonna stay out, just make sure you get a weather report and let the harbormaster know where you're gonna be."

"Yes, mom."

"Yes, Mother, sir!"

Lisa came through the crowd of passengers carrying a single overnight bag. Ben spotted her, waved, and when he had her attention, he pointed to the *lei* in his other hand. She quickened her pace. They met at the gate and hugged and kissed.

"Your *lei*, madam." Ben bowed from the waist, then slipped the orchid necklace over her head. It rested regally on her shoulders.

She gave him another kiss.

"How long do you have?"

"I have to be back tomorrow night. But I can take the last flight."

"How's the transfer going?"

"They're looking for a replacement. I guess it'll be a couple of months. Depending on who it is, I may have some training to do before I can leave."

They started walking to Ben's Jeep, which was parked by the curb near Baggage Claim. "Danny's loaned me his boat. I thought you might like to go fishing or just for a ride. Danny suggested we anchor in a cove and spend the night in our own little hideaway. How's that sound?"

Lisa smiled. "Okay, I guess. Let's see how I feel after an afternoon at sea."

"How about if we splurge on a big gourmet picnic basket … wine, chicken, fruit, dessert … ? If the water's too rough, we can always dine on my *lānai* and watch the sunset."

"You're getting good at foreplay."

They both laughed.

Ben checked his watch. It was nine. "Let me check in for a few minutes, then we'll head into town, pick up our feast, and find Danny. I told him we'd be there around eleven."

"The station?"

"Just to check with Jack. No more than ten minutes. Promise."

Lisa gave him a doubtful face that said 'We know better, don't we?' "How about if I drop you off, go shopping, and pick you up in a half hour?"

"Ten minutes is all I'll be. Honest." 'Honest,' the one word he always waited to hear when interrogating a suspect. It was a sure sign of guilt. He gave Lisa a sheepish smile.

"I'll drop you off."

Ben didn't argue.

Forty-five minutes later, Ben emerged from HQ, chin on his chest, raised eyebrows, and his hands in his pockets, mimicking a child about to receive a scolding, but hoping for pity. Lisa patted him on the head. They left the parking lot in a cloud of bleached dust, made a right on the Kaʻahumanu Highway, and soon reached the entrance to Honokōhau Harbor. A few minutes later they were parked by berth #48. *Dances With Fish* was there, but Danny wasn't aboard. Ben spied a note fastened to the wheel.

"Guess he's gone already."

"You sound like you don't want to be alone."

"Oh, I do, do I? Wait 'till we're a few miles out."

Lisa smacked her lips.

"C'mon. Let's get the food stowed."

Lisa had bought enough for a small weekend party. There were four small white Styrofoam coolers. One for wine and beer and juice. Another with fruit and a large container of pasta salad. Turkey sandwiches and breaded chicken breasts in another. Dessert in the fourth, a kiwi torte.

Danny's note said there was live bait in the tank. Two lines were fitted with squid lures and two more were ready for the bait. Below, he'd left out a navigation chart of the Kona coast and another of the Ka Lae—South Point—area from Hāwea Point on the Kona side to Kamiʻo Point windward. His note had ended with the words— 'big blues and *ahi* at South Point,' and two warnings, 'sometimes rough water at Ka Lae,' and, 'remember ... practice safe sex at sea.'

Twenty-five minutes later they were under way. Ben had spotted the harbormaster, Jim Frans, when they were making ready and told the old sea captain that if they weren't back by six, they'd be in by eleven the next morning. Jim told Ben to anchor leeward of South Point. He said the cliff there provided protection from the trades, but he added that calm conditions never lasted long at South Point. Ben said they'd be careful. He assured him they'd come back up the coast near Miloliʻi if it was too treacherous at South Point.

"Good idea," said Jim, rubbing his chin.

It was a perfect day. Just enough billowy clouds to break up the sun's relenting rays. There was a slight breeze and the sea was calm. A flock of sooty terns, *ʻewaʻewa*, followed along. For a while the terns' incessant shrill screeching filled the air. Finally, they headed inland, skimming the water, occasionally diving for baby squid. When they were gone, it became strangely quiet, even with the engine going.

"How've you been?"

"I was wondering when you were going to ask me that," said Lisa, brushing her hair back with her fingers.

Ben cocked his head at an angle and gave her a wry look.

"I've been fine, but I've missed you." With that, Lisa pushed off the railing that enclosed the bridge and gave Ben a big hug, pinning his arms to his sides. The hug ended in a long kiss and then laughter. Lisa stepped back. "I've given a lot of thought to the prospect of living together and I'm comfortable with it. What about you?"

"I'm ready. When do you think it'll really happen?"

Lisa rolled her lips together, letting her tongue peek through. "They want me over here before Christmas."

"That's less than two months. Great!"

"You really mean that, Ben?"

"Of course I do. What about you? You don't mind driving all the way up there every day? Most of the hotel people live in Waikoloa Village. It's almost an hour to my place."

"*Our* place." There was a pleased, peaceful expression on her face. "That's fine. Gives me a chance to unwind."

"No more questions … I don't want you changing your mind." He gestured for her to take the helm, gave her a quick kiss, and then climbed down from the bridge. "Let's get the lines in the water."

Lisa gave him a 'thumbs-up.'

Ben pointed toward the horizon. "See the FAD out there?"

Lisa squinted for a few moments, her eyes scanning the horizon, until finally she spotted the buoy.

"Keep her headed for that, speed at eight."

"Aye, aye."

Ben spent the next ten minutes putting out the two lines fitted with squid lures. One, an orange Zinger, was Danny's favorite. It was the same lure that Ben had used to catch the big blue two weeks before. The lures skimmed along the surface about fifty yards out and a little more than a boat-width apart. Ben thought about putting out two more lines with live bait for 'ahi and mahimahi, but decided to wait.

Then, as he went below to look for sunblock for his nose, he wondered if Lisa would really like his small house and the long commute. Maybe they could add on to the house. An extra room would help. But there was nothing he could do about the commute. December. Did it seem far away, or was it too close?

An hour later they had circled the FAD several times without a bite. Ben reeled in the lines, secured the lures to the downriggers, and asked Lisa if she was ready to eat.

"Sure."

"Here, or would you like to find a cove?"

"Drifting is fine. We can save the cove for dinner. It'll be more romantic."

After turkey sandwiches, a couple of bottles of orange-mango Koala, and some sliced kiwi, Ben indicated it was time to head for 'the Point.' "That's where Danny said the marlin are. Besides, it's beautiful there. I envy the fishermen who live near there." He set the throttle ahead, and soon they were skimming across the ocean at twenty knots, too fast for trolling, but he put the lines out again anyway. He didn't tell Lisa that South Point might be a bit rough. He didn't want to make her anxious. He didn't believe the swells would be too bad.

Lisa came up to the bridge, locked her arm around his waist, and put her head against his shoulder. The sea air whizzed by their ears, making it hard to hear, but actually, there wasn't much to say. Lisa tightened her grip around Ben's waist. As they came closer to shore near Hōnaunau Bay, Ben eased up on the throttle, knowing there were a few reefs that extended pretty far out. He wanted to follow the coastline south, partly for safety, partly for the beauty of the land and seascapes, framed by Mauna Loa, which was haloed by white clouds around its highest slopes.

No sooner had they slowed to eight knots, than Ben heard the whine of the line. He turned and saw the rod on the port side bending and releasing. It wasn't a marlin, especially this close to shore. But maybe a *mahimahi*. Or more likely, since they were close to the reef, a barracuda.

Lisa, watching also, seemed mesmerized.

"You want to take it?" Ben asked her.

"No. You. I'll take the wheel."

"Just keep us away from the reef. You don't have to worry about staying with the fish, it's not a billfish."

"I'll head out a little."

Ben hurried down the ladder and jumped to the deck, skipping the last rung. He took the rod out of its aluminum holder, gave it a quick jerk to set the hook, then pulled back, testing the line. Based on the drag, he believed he had something that weighed ten to fifteen pounds. Either a skipjack or a small *mahimahi*, maybe a big barracuda. He reeled in some line, pulled back on the rod, and reeled in some more. Suddenly he felt the line jump. It played out at a frantic pace and then, just as quickly, the line went dead.

"Shit."

"What?" Lisa asked, twisting around to see what had happened.

"We lost him."

"What was it?"

"Not sure, maybe a skipjack."

Ben reeled in the line, hoping Danny's favorite lure was still there. The line didn't feel empty. It felt like there was bait on the end. As the leader surfaced, Ben could see a silvery shape trailing. When the barracuda's head broke the surface, he let out a yelp.

Lisa watched, eyes wide.

That was it—a barracuda head. The rest of its body was gone, torn just behind the gills. Something bigger had taken a meal. Maybe a bigger barracuda. Marlin were known to slash at a caught barracuda, but they were too close to shore, and the jagged cut ruled out a billfish. Marlin killed their prey by slicing them in two with their bills, then circling back to devour the meal. The back of the 'cuda's head had been bitten off. Shark? Probably.

Ben brought the barracuda head alongside the boat, leaned the rod against the gunwale, and grabbed the dead fish by the gills. The squid lure was punctured in several places, but otherwise it was fine, although rows of razor-sharp teeth were going to make the extraction process difficult. After struggling with it for a few minutes, Ben decided to sacrifice one of the hooks, reached for a wire cutter, and cut off the impaled barb. He threw what was left of the barracuda into the sea. It floated for a second and then disappeared. Chances were it would never reach the bottom.

At five they reached South Point. They had seen only two other charters on the way down. Neither flew flags. It hadn't been a good fishing day.

Ten minutes later, Ben said, "Let's anchor." He gave Lisa the wheel, pointed to a spot about a hundred yards offshore just leeward of Ka Lae, a spot protected on both sides by high lava cliffs. The water was fairly calm. He climbed forward and slowly fed the anchor overboard. At a hundred and fifty feet the anchor still hadn't reached bottom.

"We've got to get closer."

Lisa looked worried. "There's a lot of rocks."

"No choice. We'll be okay. Just go slow."

A few minutes later they were anchored. Ben climbed back into the cockpit, then arched his back, stretching his muscles.

"How 'bout a beer?"

"Sounds good," said Ben.

Lisa went below and returned with two Beck's. Ben took one and sat on the gunwale. Lisa settled into one of the fighting chairs.

Both were silent until, after grinning at each other for a few moments, Lisa said, "We're just like two married people who've run out of things to say."

"Well, we can always talk about work."

Lisa furrowed her brow. "You serious? Whenever I ask, you don't want to talk about it."

"It's just that some of the recent cases have been very personal."
He watched Lisa shudder as she remembered the Dagdag case.

"Okay ... what *are* you working on now?"

Ben sat on the railing and crossed his arms over his chest. He
explained about the geothermal project. Lisa said she had heard a
little about it but didn't realize there was such strong opposition. Then
Ben told her about Nohea.

"How come you never mentioned him before?"

"I lost track of him after college, except for one postcard. It wasn't
until two weeks ago, just before the triathlon, that I saw his name in
the paper. He was the friend I told you I was going to visit in Pāhoa
after the race."

"I remember."

Then he told her about Curtis Lyman. "Hilo's working on that
one, but here's the intriguing part." He described the *kahuna*. His
escape. And then the dynamite theft in Kailua. And then the explosion and the remains. He didn't tell her his suspicions about the
kahuna.

"Three ... more ... murders?"

Ben nodded. "Within the last three years."

"Right at the drilling site?"

"Close by."

"What do you think is going on?"

Ben felt good. Something had changed. Usually he liked to work
through his cases by himself. When he was biking, or running, or
just sitting on his *lānai*. Now he felt like he had a partner again.

"I think they're connected to the drilling project, but I'm not sure
if this is the work of a single murderer."

"Go on."

"I don't think the activists had anything to do with the Lyman
homicide. I think it was made to look that way. As far as the other
three are concerned, without some identification, it's hard to tell. It's
their missing teeth that makes me think they are connected to the

Lyman murder. But why did the killer leave Lyman's corpse in plain sight? It doesn't make sense."

"Do you think there might be other victims?"

"You know ... I hadn't really thought about that. Ken mentioned that possibility the other day. I hope not."

Just then, Ben looked up. The sun had disappeared behind a bank of clouds, and the sky had darkened considerably. He stood. He didn't like the look of the clouds to the south. They were starting to rise, forming large thunderheads, something the month of 'Ikuwa was noted for. Then he saw a flash of light in the distance. He waited but heard no thunder. He assumed the storm was at least ten miles away.

"Think we'll be okay out here?" asked Lisa, nervousness evident in her voice.

"We shouldn't be out on the water during an electrical storm." He turned and scanned the shoreline beyond South Point, then out to sea, and watched the approaching clouds.

"It seems to be heading up the Kona Coast. But I think we better haul anchor and head around toward the boat ramp at Kaulana. Maybe we can skirt it. If not, and it gets worse, we can pull the boat up." *If there's someone there to help.*

Ben went to the radio. Nothing but static.

Fifteen minutes later they were nearing the boat ramp. No one was around. They could see the lights marking the homes of the local fishermen who lived in the tiny village of Pōhakuloa.

"It's probably not a bad idea to anchor near the ramp and find some shelter on land. I think there's a park and a picnic area near here. We can spend the night there... unless the storm passes quickly. Then we can come back on board."

Another flash of lightening, and this time, there was loud thunder. The wind began to pick up. They turned for shore.

Five minutes later they had secured three lines to the sides of the ramp and covered the cockpit. They scampered off *Dances With Fish* and headed for a small picnic shelter. Ben carried a cooler in which Lisa had consolidated their food. She carried blankets tucked under her arms. It began to rain and the thunder reverberated like drum rolls in the shoreline caves. They started running. The sky took on a greenish color.

Up ahead a man carrying a lantern trotted toward them. When he was within fifty feet, he stopped and shouted, "Aloha."

Ben raised the cooler in greeting. He and Lisa slowed down. Lisa was breathing hard. They walked, though briskly.

"You guys better stay at my house tonight," the man offered. "This is gonna be a long storm. Your boat okay?"

Ben said that it was.

"Give me the cooler. My name's Skip. Follow me."

Thunder echoed up and down the coastline.

Skip said, "Bad time for a picnic, bruddah."

He led them to a small brown house with a roof covered with tar paper where the shingles had blown off. In front a badly sagging gutter gave life to a few small ferns. There were catchment barrels at two corners of the house and one where the gutter overflowed. The night's rain might fill them. Steam was escaping from the roof.

As they stepped onto the porch, Ben could see two tiny faces peering out of the front window. When he waved, the faces ducked out of sight.

"My kids," said Skip. "Good kids."

Just then, the sky opened up and the rain came in force. Darkness arrived an hour early.

The interior of the house was quite large. One central room served as the kitchen, dining room, and living room. The wood-burning stove was glowing hot. Off the back, facing the ocean were two bedrooms, one for the children, and one for Skip and his wife. He introduced her as Alekanekelina, which she shortened to Aleka for them. He told them his real name was Peleki Alu. His young son, four, whose eyes were bright and black, was named Pali, and the little girl, who hid bashfully behind her mother's wide skirt, was named Ke'elikōlani after Princess Ruth Ke'elikōlani, granddaughter of Kamehameha the Great. Although just two, her shiny black hair flowed to her waist.

Ben introduced himself and Lisa. The rain pounded away at the roof and thunder rumbled deeply, shaking the dishes on the shelves.

Skip looked skyward. *"Ka'a ka pōhaku* ... the stones roll."

"Please eat with us," said Aleka. "Skip made a good catch today."

"Thank you." Ben knew better than to refuse their hospitality. "We have some things in the cooler, too."

Aleka smiled. Ke'elikōlani came out from hiding and stood next to the cooler. Lisa patted her head and asked if she'd like to look inside. Shyly, she nodded.

"You wanna beer?" offered Skip.

"Sure," said Ben.

Lisa refused.

"Your boat?" asked the fisherman.

"A friend's. He has a charter service out of Honokōhau."

Skip frowned. Ben thought he probably didn't like the idea of Kona boats fishing his waters.

"No luck." Skip wasn't asking, he was stating a fact.

"Just a barracuda head."

Skip smiled. Fishing superiority had been established. "You from here?"

"My *kupuna wahine* was a *kahuna lapa 'au* on Maui, near Kula. That's where we were from."

Skip nodded solemnly, showing he respected the grandson of a *kahuna lapa 'au*.

Right then, with the walls of his home casting streaky shadows in the poor light, Skip looked like he belonged on South Point—a kind and confident man, a man who was self-sufficient and who respected the land and the sea. "How come you guys come over here?" His face was weathered from the sea, and the lines around his eyes and mouth made him look older when he talked.

"Just wanted to get away from the crowds," Ben said.

"This is a good place for that."

For dinner, they enjoyed fresh *pāpio* cooked in taro leaves, smothered in papaya, mango, and tomatoes. Lisa cut up the two large slices of kiwi torte into thirds and passed them around. The torte looked very much out of place in the fisherman's house. Ben was embarrassed about it. But it was a special treat for Keʻelikōlani and Pali. They devoured their slices in a few bites and went into their room to play, licking their lips all the way.

Aleka made coffee to which she added some cinnamon.

"This is delicious," Lisa said, "... best I've ever had."

It was then that Ben focused on Skip's T-shirt. It showed a volcano erupting in the background. A white flower from the *ʻōhiʻa lehua* was in the foreground. Across the top were the words 'Pele Defense Fund.' And the bottom said—*Ua mau ka ʻāina i ka pono*. ... the land is preserved in righteousness. In smaller print—Mā lana Wao Kele O Puna. Ben gestured to Skip's shirt. "You support PDF?"

"Sure, bruddah," answered the fisherman. "Everybody in Kaʻū does."

"Do you know Nohea Konanui?"

Skip nodded fervently.

"He's a friend of mine," said Ben.

"You know about the explosion?" asked Skip.

"Skip, I'm investigating it. I'm a Kona detective."

Their host jumped to his feet. "You said you were a friend of Nohea's."

"Please sit. I am. I'm on your side. Nohea *is* my friend. He took me into the forest. He trusted me enough to show me the underground way."

Skip's scowl departed, but his expression remained wary, quizzical. But he sat.

Ben ran his fingers through his hair. "The explosion unearthed artifacts and remains."

"I know," Skip said angrily.

"Three of the skeletons are recent. They are not ancient remains. Have you heard of anyone disappearing at the site?"

Skip's mouth opened, but nothing came out. He crossed his legs. Both Lisa and Aleka remained silent, but their eyes went left and right watching the two men closely.

Skip placed his hands on the table. "No. But a few years ago I saw a man walking from the rig, carrying a lantern and I think a shovel."

"Three years ago?"

"About."

"Can you describe him?"

"Too far away. When I got closer the lantern went out and he disappeared."

"Did you report it?"

Skip laughed. "Not supposed to be there. Anyway, I thought it was the inspector."

"Was it?"

"Maybe."

What if Lyman killed the other three and someone avenged their deaths? ... but why wait three years?

"Ben?"

Lisa got no response.

Maybe it took someone that long to figure out it was Lyman.

"Skip ... you know Lyman's dead?"

Skip nodded.

"How well did you know him?"

"Not well."

"Do you think ... did he ever ... was he someone a PDF member would have feared?"

Skip wrinkled his brow. "He was okay. I don't think he killed anyone."

"Why?"

Skip shrugged. "He seemed more Hawaiian than *haole*." He opened another beer and took a sip. "You know, geothermal is not the only thing. There's Hawaiian Homes and the boat ramp."

Ben leaned back in his chair.

"Tell us about them," said Lisa.

Skip appeared trancelike for a few seconds, as if he were plotting. He blinked a few times before he spoke. "There's plenty things the big *haole* landowners and politicians are doing to ruin our land. You know geothermal, but they also got plans to shoot rockets from here."

"Where?" asked Ben incredulously. "Here?"

Skip nodded, his face framed with concern. "I think that's under control for now. They want to build a boat ramp first. Then a big dock. Before you know it, bruddah, they come with big boats with stuff for the rockets. What's that gonna do to our fishing? How we make a living ... learn to be astronauts? I go barefoot. Don't wear moon boots." He snorted. "I don't think so, bruddah."

Lisa slowly shook her head. She seemed mesmerized and it was evident from her face that she was a bit uncomfortable being a *haole*.

Ben turned back to Skip. "Tell us about Hawaiian Homes."

"How come you don't know 'bout that? How much Hawaiian are you?"

"More than half. My mother is pure. My father's got some Hawaiian blood, but he's mainly *haole*."

"You more than half ... you can get yourself on the list."

Lisa asked, "What list?"

Skip explained how it worked. How you registered. How they checked your ancestry. Then you waited for land to become available. Foreclosures, lease expirations. Then you were offered a parcel.

"Halfway across the Island," he said. "Rocky land with no chance to grow crops. Far from your *'ohana*. Far from your friends." His eyes narrowed. "I was offered some land near Waimea. Was I supposed to leave my friends? I fish here. I was taught the old ways of fishing Ka Lae, where the cliffs are high and the water rough. I know the water here … and the weather. I will teach my son." He hung his head. "But like a fool," Skip mumbled, "I said no. A friend of mine was next on the list. He has family near there. He could get a job in Waimea. He could live closer. I thought I was helping him. Only later, the land was leased and he didn't get it. He was still next on the list."

"How can that be?" asked Ben.

Skip shook his head. He didn't know.

Someone took Skip's place?

There was a loud clap of thunder. It seemed to jog Ben's memory.

"Where near Waimea?"

Skip scratched his head. "Right in the middle of nowhere … between Waimea and Kawaihae, right next to a cinder cone—Pu'u Huluhulu. Not good for nuthin' … except for my friend."

Huluhulu! Ben remembered the name from the map he had found in Lyman's pickup. The transmission towers were supposed to go through there.

The towers and …

Chapter Sixteen

THEY MADE IT BACK the next morning. Danny was waiting for them. It was evident from his expression that he had spent an anxious night.

"What happened? ... You didn't answer the radio. You get trapped in the storm?"

Ben flashed him a big warm smile. "Sorry ... we had to leave the boat. When I tried the radio, all I got was static. But we found safe anchorage and a fisherman let us spend the night. We're fine and the boat's fine."

"I was worried. A half dozen boats were lost along the coast."

"Sorry."

"Well," said Danny, looking somewhat relieved, "catch any fish?"

"No fish."

"No fish?" Ohhh, I get it ... you guys follow the instructions in my note?"

"Not another word, Mr. Mitchell," Lisa warned.

"He let you down ... huh?"

Joking and laughing they spent the next hour cleaning up *Dances*

With Fish, getting her ready for Danny's afternoon charter.

When they finished Danny grinned and asked, "Did you at least put the lines in the water?"

Lunch was leftovers from the fishing trip. After, they sat on Ben's *lānai*, not talking much, just taking in the cool breeze and the glorious scenery and giving each other thoughtful looks. When he hadn't been thinking about Lisa, Ben had thought about Curtis Lyman. He'd dismissed the possibility of him having murdered the other victims. If it had been Lyman who Skip had seen, he had probably been working, not burying. If it had been someone else, then it might have been the killer, but without a description, it didn't matter.

Out of nowhere Lisa said, "Ben, explain *'aumakua* to me."

Ben cocked his head, a puzzled look on his face. "Since when did you become so interested in Hawaiiana?"

"I know it's important to you ... that your Hawaiian heritage is important to you. I'd like to know more about it. When we first met, you were ... " She seemed to be searching for the right words.

"More *haole?*"

"Well, not really *haole*, but you were more interested in yourself ... what was going on right then. You never mentioned the past. What's changed you is your interest in your ancestors. I like it. It's made you someone special. I'd like to share it with you ... unless a real *haole* isn't supposed to believe in those things."

"Oh, no. Being Hawaiian ... thinking Hawaiian ... should be shared by everyone. Not just Hawaiians ... all races. You trace most ancient cultures, you'll find the same things. Gods for fishing, gods for rain, gods for the land. People were thankful for what nature provided and people respected her."

"So explain *'aumakua* to me."

"'*Aumakua* is a family's guardian spirit. It can be almost anything,

191

but most *'ohana* chose animals or birds or fish. Some, like Nohea's family, chose gods and goddesses."

"How was one chosen?"

"Usually something happened that led to good fortune, like a bird showing you the way home if you had become lost, or if something saved your life. Sometimes an *'aumakua* was chosen just because it was indigenous to where you lived, so you saw it frequently.

"For example, if I were lost in the mountains and an owl appeared and flew from tree to tree, and I followed, and finally I came upon my village, the *pueo* would become my *'aumakua*."

"Yours is the dolphin, right?"

"The spinner dolphin."

"Do you know how it started?"

"I've heard two stories. My grandmother said that an uncle from many generations before was a fisherman. Once, when he was fishing in the stormy months, like yesterday, he was swept into the ocean by a huge wave that came across the rocks. When he fell he bumped his head and was only semiconscious. A spinner dolphin came up beside him and nudged him toward a small beach and pushed him onto the shore."

Lisa's expression showed that she was pleased with his story. Maybe a little incredulous, but pleased. "And the other one … "

"This one is very interesting. This same ancient uncle … "

"When you say ancient, how many generations are we talking about?"

"Geez, I have no idea. But before Kamehameha, like maybe the 1600s."

"How far back can you trace your family?"

"That's one thing I don't know. But someday I'm going to spend some time on it and find out. I'll have to go back to Maui for that. Anyhow, when this uncle was a little boy, he was fishing. He was with his father. They fished all day. His father caught many fish, but the boy caught none. Finally, near the end of the day, when it was time to go back to the village, the boy caught a small fish. Just then a baby dolphin swam close to shore ... they had been fishing from a cliff and the water below was very deep. The small dolphin was injured. It was bleeding from the right side of its torso. The father said that a shark had bitten it and that it would probably die, since now that it couldn't swim fast, it would not be able to catch fish to eat. The boy took his small fish and threw it near the dolphin's mouth. The dolphin ate it, rose a little out of the water, as if to say thanks, and disappeared. From that day on, any time the little boy came near the ocean, the dolphin would appear and follow the boy.

Lisa smiled warmly.

Ben held up a finger. "But the amazing part of the story is that when the boy was older, he went with his father to Maui by canoe. The dolphin lead them the entire voyage. And it waited near Hana where they had gone ashore until the boy and his father were ready to return. Then it led them back here."

"You know, it's probably true."

Ben had a thoughtful look on his face. "You think so?"

Lisa nodded. "I think we should describe humans as dolphinlike, not the other way around."

Ben gave her a kiss. "And so now you need an 'aumakua."

"In the worst way."

"Has anything happened to you like that?"

"No, except when you saved my life."

They hadn't talked about the burning boat in a long time.

"So I guess you'll just have to be my 'aumakua until I find a more traditional one."

"My pleasure." His expression was solemn.

They took a walk along the water, watching the sun rays create a field of shimmering diamonds on the surface.

"Pick one out," said Ben.

"Pick what out?"

"One of the sparkling diamonds on the water."

Lisa, shielding her eyes, gazed across the sparkling water. "Is it my engagement diamond?"

"For now."

"That's sweet."

"It's also cheaper."

Lisa sighed. "I think I'd rather have a make-believe diamond from the ocean than a real one."

They walked hand in hand back to the house.

Later, Ben dropped Lisa off at Keāhole. Her flight was boarding, so their good-bye was hurried. They promised to call each day. She told him she thought she'd be back in two weeks, and then wishing him well on his geothermal case, she rushed through the gate, across the darkened tarmac, and up the steps to the plane.

Ben waited until the plane's wing lights were tiny specks in the night sky before he left.

During the drive home, he thought about what he was going to do the next day. First, he'd check with Rodriguez and catch up on the status of the Lyman homicide. Then he'd go over the list of Jackson Hole employees and see if he had missed anything. He also wanted to talk with Nohea. And finally, he was interested in Hawaiian Homes. Skip's story about his land at Pu'u Huluhulu intrigued him. He wondered if there *was* a connection between the Department of Land and Natural Resources and the geothermal project. Something that was hidden, something that didn't meet the eye.

The phone was ringing when he pulled up in front of his house. He ran inside and jerked the receiver off the cradle.

"Hello?"

"Detective McMillen?"

"Yes, who is this?"

"Henry Helenihi."

Ben's heart started racing—detective's intuition. The hairs on his neck bristled. "Yes, Henry. What is it?"

"I've gone over the list. No problems with anyone on it."

"What about missing names?"

Henry cleared his throat. "Yes ... yes ... some college interns ... from O'ahu."

College age. "From UH?"

"Yes."

"Graduate students?"

"Yes."

"How many?"

"Just three."

Three was plenty.

"Let me have their names."

"No ... not over the phone."

Henry hung up.

Chapter Seventeen

BEN ANGLED THE FRONT WHEELS, pulled back hard on the emergency brake, and turned off the engine, all the time thinking about what would happen to his Jeep if it started rolling back down what Henry Helenihi called his driveway.

The incline was about ten degrees, rocky, and severely rutted from Henry's mammoth pickup. Ben had to hold onto the Jeep's roll bar to keep his balance as he stepped out. He started climbing the rest of the hill that led to Henry's house, which sat on a cliff near the Puna Trail in a place that wasn't really part of any village or town.

Henry was sitting on the front porch steps, smoking a pipe. He nervously puffed on his pipe like a locomotive trying to make a steep grade. The stiff wind carried the pipe smoke above his head, where it soon disappeared. Henry looked worried. Maybe he had a reason to be.

"I'm glad you called."

Henry looked off toward the ocean. "I'm not so sure *I* am." His eyes moved back to Ben. "Can you keep me out of this?"

"For now. You'd be smart to tell me everything you know. You'd be even smarter not to mention a word of this to anyone else. Not anyone. Understand?"

Henry swallowed and nodded once.

"Give me their names." Ben flipped back the cover of his notepad.

"Loy Ellis. Wayne Enoki. Ray Kamakani."

"Spell the first one."

"L - O - Y."

"Tell me about them. When they worked. What they did."

"Do you think they're the three remains?"

"Maybe. The more you can tell me about them, the better our chance is of finding out."

Henry took a deep breath, held it in his cheeks for a few seconds, and then slowly exhaled. He started rocking back and forth. "They were students. We used to have a work-study program. Brought graduate engineering students over to work for a semester."

"Used to?"

"The company stopped it two years ago."

After wiping his brow of perspiration, Ben jotted that down. "Go on."

"Loy ... he worked the rig. Tested samples."

"For what?"

"To see what they were composed of. You know ... whether the slant well would be productive."

"Do you know where he was from?"

"O'ahu."

"You know what part?" asked Ben, looking over his shoulder for a second, making sure his Jeep was okay. He assured himself that he had pulled the emergency brake all the way back.

"No, I don't. There should be records in Hilo."

"Since these names aren't on the list ... we won't find their records at Jackson Hole. Were they all from O'ahu?"

"I think Loy and Wayne were. Ray was from Moloka'i. I knew him the best. He was assigned to me. Field work. Clearing the roadway, building the platform. He was a civil engineering student."

Ben was angry with himself for not checking MPs on all the Islands, instead of just the three Districts he had Joyce look into. "He work with dynamite?"

"Clearing the roadway, sure."

Ben gave Henry a sharp look. "Let's get back to Ellis. When did he leave?"

Henry stopped rocking and rubbed his chin. "About three years ago."

"What about Enoki?"

"He worked in the lab with Curtis."

"With Curtis Lyman?"

Henry swallowed again and nodded. He breathed deeply before continuing. "Come to think of it, Ellis worked with Curtis for a time as well."

Ben's mind filled with a vision of a man carrying a lantern and a shovel. "What can you tell me about Lyman?"

"I liked him. He talked rough to others at times, but he was usually nice to me."

"How'd he get along with the three students?"

"I don't know. Okay, I suppose. Wayne and Loy never complained about him, if that's what you wanted to know."

"Lyman ever have a run-in with Geddes?"

"I saw them argue a few times."

"About what?"

Henry shrugged.

Ben referred to his notepad, "Let's get back to Wayne Enoki. When did he leave?"

"He went back about the same time as Loy."

"Went back where? ... UH?"

"I guess their work-study time was up. One day they were here ... the next they were gone."

"Wouldn't they have said goodbye or something?"

"Ray, maybe. Not the other two. I didn't see them much. I spent some time with Loy. We had a few beers now and then. But that was at the beginning of the summer. I don't think I saw him during the last month."

"So Wayne and Loy just left?"

Henry raised his eyebrows as he nodded.

Ben drew a line underneath their names. "And what about Ray?"

"Ray came around to say goodbye."

"You sure, Henry? This is important." Ben shifted his feet and leaned against the porch post with his left side.

"Yes. In fact, we went out for a beer."

"How'd you find out that the other two had left if you didn't see them much?"

"One day I just asked."

"Who?"

"Geddes."

Ben pushed off the post and straightened. "Can you remember the conversation?"

"I just asked if they had gone back to school."

"And?"

"Geddes said 'yes.' "

"What else did he say?"

Henry wrinkled his brow. "We were having a few beers and it came up. Geddes just said their time was up."

"Strange way to put it."

"Well, not like that. No double meaning or anything. Just the semester was up."

"What do you think now? ... no double meaning?"

Henry was silent. His expression was somber.

Ben blew out a deep breath. "I'll check it out, all right. Henry, you keep this to yourself. Remember, there's already at least one dead man ... and three others that may turn out to be your interns."

Nodding slowly, Henry said, "Geddes says he thinks Nohea did it to get even, for losing his job. Told me to be careful because I was the one who had the job now."

"When did Geddes say that?"

"Day before yesterday, right before you came."

Geddes. "You spend much time with him?"

Henry snorted softly and took the pipe out of his mouth. He tapped it gently against one of the porch posts. Then he stuffed it into his back pocket. "Hardly. I was kinda surprised he came by. Even patted me on the back when he left. Usually, he's not too buddy-buddy with anyone."

"You said you were drinking with him," Ben stated flatly.

"That was a few years ago. He's not very friendly anymore."

Ben looked around Henry's property, wondering if anyone was hiding behind the thick bushes, listening, waiting. He glanced at his Jeep once more.

"You don't believe Nohea has anything to do with this, do you?" Henry asked.

"No, I don't."

"That *kahuna*?"

Ben shrugged.

"What are you going to do next?"

"I'll check these names with the local police. Once I have the background they shouldn't be too hard to track down ... a relative, a friend ... someone should be able to help."

"Good luck."

"Thanks, Henry. You ... "

"I know, don't say it. I did the right thing ... except I don't feel so good about it."

Ben gave the frightened man a thin smile. It was the best he could do.

Where to now?

Under normal circumstances he should confront Geddes about

the three engineering students. Ben decided not to do that, at least not until he had more information. Maybe he'd find all three back in class. Alive. He decided to go to Hilo and make some calls.

He found his way back to Highway 130. A steady drizzle began to fall although the sun still shone. A fragmented rainbow arched across Hilo Bay. Ben counted five parts scattered across the sky. They resembled the footbridges that spanned the ponds and streams of the Japanese-style gardens near the west end of Banyan Drive. When the rain picked up in intensity, Ben pulled over and zipped up the side flaps on the Jeep. For some reason, this time the zipper didn't stick and the seam didn't leak. He headed for Hilo again. His wipers streaked two rainbows of brownish earth across his windshield.

He sat upright, leaning a bit forward in his seat. He was tense, both hands gripping the wheel. His neck was sore and he had a dull headache, the kind that would hang around all day. He thought about his prime suspect—Geddes. He didn't really think Geddes had committed the crimes himself. He'd have had someone do it for him. One of the workers. Someone big and strong—someone who could hurl a spear, someone who could carry three bodies down into the maze beneath the Wao Kele O Puna. Ben decided to run all the regular employees through the computer. Maybe one of them had a record. But, he asked himself, what was the motive? What was in it for Geddes? Why would anyone risk so much to frame the activists when they were low on funds, experiencing setback after setback in the courts. And the only hope the activists had of gaining an injunction was with the government, the same body who would share in the geothermal royalties. Maybe there was another motive. Ben's mind drew a blank.

The wind picked up, waves slapped the shoreline, and a bank of gray clouds covered the sun. The rainbows over Hilo Bay instantly disappeared.

He couldn't remember a time of so many consecutive days of hard rain.

Rodriguez was in, and after a brief discussion, he showed Ben to an empty desk. Rodriguez's update had been simple. No progress. The Hilo detective's eyes had widened when Ben told him about the engineering students. He asked if Ben needed help. Ben gave Rodriguez the students' names and asked if he could have someone check the MP lists.

"All Islands?"

"O'ahu and Moloka'i."

"Anything else?"

"What's the fax number here?"

"9-3-5 and all '3s.' "

"I can remember that one."

Ernie's hands, palms up, and raised eyebrows asked if there was more he needed.

"Nope," Ben said, "just a phone for a couple of hours."

They agreed to meet for lunch.

Ben called Information, identified himself as a Kona detective and gave his badge number. He waited patiently while the operator confirmed his ID. She was back on the line a minute later.

"How can I assist you, Detective McMillen?"

"I need the telephone numbers and addresses for three men." He gave her the names. "First check if they are in the student directory at UH."

"Manoa campus?"

"Start there, then do Hilo, and then the community colleges if you have to."

"Okay."

"Next, do the same thing for regular listings and for all families with the same last name ... just O'ahu and Moloka'i."

"They're will be quite a few Ellises and Enokis."

"I know. Fax me the stuff as soon as you can. I'm investigating several homicides. I need this by noon." He gave her the fax number.

"You'll have it in fifteen minutes. It's all computerized now, except, of course, for the student directories. I'll call the University."

"Thanks. What's your name?"

"Lehua Williams."

"Thanks, Lehua."

"My pleasure, detective. Next time you're in Honolulu, look me up. I'm in the book." She giggled and said goodbye.

Ten minutes later a clerk handed him the fax—a cover sheet and four pages—containing the names, addresses, and telephone numbers from the regular listings of eight Kamakanis, more than fifty Enokis, and about a hundred Ellises. There was also a note that explained there were no matches for the three students in the University directory. And on the bottom of the last page, a handwritten telephone number. Lehua's.

This was not the place to start—there really were too many names. Ben found a phone book and looked up the University of Hawaii. He placed a call to the Student Services office. After talking with three people, he finally found someone who knew where to look for past registration information.

"Three years ago?"

"Yes." Ben heard the clack of a keyboard. The keys clicked at a furious pace. That gave him confidence.

"Okay. Give me the names."

He did.

She found all three. Three years before they had been engineering graduate students. Ray Kamakani in mechanical engineering, the other two in energy-related fields.

"Are they registered now, maybe as post-grad students?"

"I'm checking."

There was silence except for the keyboard and the sound of the woman clucking the roof of her mouth with her tongue. Then, "Not here."

"When did each of them leave school?"

A minute later. "That's strange."

"What?" He was excited.

"They each took part in a work-study program and never registered for the next semester. What's up, detective?"

"Just looking for them. Do you have home addresses and telephone numbers?"

"Uh huh. Ready?"

Ben compared these addresses to the fax. They were all there. He went looking for Rodriguez.

Detective Kala had been working the MP lists. He handed Ben a fax copy from Honolulu. Only one of the students was on the missing person list—Wayne Enoki. Ben read the report. Enoki had been reported missing by his parents when they found out he was no longer enrolled at UH and couldn't find him. The last time they had seen him was when he left for the Big Island during the summer after his first year of graduate school. Someone at Jackson Hole had been interviewed but no name was given. The report stated that there was no implication of foul play. Honolulu Police had given it low priority.

With a dry mouth and that familiar churning in his stomach, Ben tapped out the number for the Enoki family on Iwi Way in Wilhelmina Rise just *mauka* of Diamond Head. He checked his watch. It was ten twenty-five.

It was Wayne Enoki's mother who answered.

"Mrs. Enoki, this is Detective McMillen of the Kona District. I'd like to ask you a few questions, if I may."

"Is it about Wayne?"

Ben could hear the tension in her voice. "I'm not sure, and I want to apologize for not being there in person to talk with you, but … "

"Kona, you said? I understand. Have you found a body?"

Ben was surprised at the directness of the question. He guessed that after three years you still have hope, but you also understand reality. "We've found some partial skeletons near the geothermal well where Wayne did his work-study. Now that doesn't mean anything, but I'd like to know if you can tell me anything about Wayne ... did he break any bones as a child, have any kind of surgery ... ? There's nothing on the missing person report, but I thought maybe there was something, even something small."

There was faint sobbing on the other end of the line. He waited.

"Sorry."

"That's okay. Take your time."

"We have a set of dental records. We were advised to keep them available."

"I'm sorry, Mrs. Enoki, but there were no teeth found with the remains."

"No teeth?"

Ben lied, "That's not unusual." He hoped she wouldn't pursue it.

"He had surgery ... " her voice trailed off.

"Mrs. Enoki?"

"He ... he broke his thumb. Actually, he chipped a bone. That's all I can remember right now."

"Which thumb?"

"His right one ... he couldn't write for a while. He was six ... in the first grade. When will you know? Should I come to ... "

"No, not now. Like I said ... "

"I want to come."

"Please, Mrs. Enoki, I realize how hard this is for you, but wait until we know more. It may not be your son. It could be anyone. I'll get this checked immediately."

"You call me right away, Detective McMillen. Right away."

She hung up crying before he could answer.

Next he called the Ellis family. There was no answer. He asked one of the claims clerks who didn't appear busy to track down the parents' workplaces. Then he called Moloka'i. Ray Kamakani's father answered. He lived alone. He hadn't talked with Ray in more than two years. He sounded gruff and angry. He asked if Ray had gotten into trouble.

"Did you report him missing?"

"Missing? What do you mean missing? Sure, he's missing. Missing his life here. Too many go to the college and never come back. What will happen to the people of Moloka'i if none of the children stay. What good is a *haole* education if you don't come home and help your people with what you have learned?"

"Mr. Kamakani, we found some bones after an explosion at the geothermal well site here on the Big Island. Your son worked here one school semester. Did you know that?"

"No."

"It's possible … "

"He's dead?"

"We have no idea. We're checking out everyone who used to work here. He's not registered in school. I was hoping you could tell me where he was."

"We fought."

"Mr. Kamakani?"

"He should have stayed here and helped with the farming."

"So you don't know where he is?"

Softly. "No."

"Mr. Kamakani, I know this is difficult, but you can help me by telling me anything that might help identify the remains. Did Ray break any bones when he was younger?"

"No."

"Did he ever have surgery?"

"The *kahuna lapa 'au* mended him when he needed healing."

"Yes, I understand. But is there anything you can think of that might help. Understand, maybe something you tell me will eliminate the possibility that the remains belong to Ray."

The man was sobbing now. "I want my boy back."

Both men were silent for a few moments. Then Ben said, "Mr. Kamakani, take down my number in case you think of anything."

"I need him back … I'll … I'll get a pencil."

Ben felt miserable. He hated talking to these people over the phone. But he didn't want to send someone else, and he couldn't justify the time to go Island-hopping without something solid to go on.

A small woman in a tight skirt came to him and handed him a piece of paper. She simply said, "From claims," and left.

Both Ellis parents worked at the Royal Hawaiian on Waikīkī Beach. Ben called the hotel. He asked for the father, thinking he might spare the mother the pain of talking to a stranger on the phone about her son. He was told the father was somewhere on the grounds. Ben gave his number and asked that they find Mr. Ellis and have him call back right away.

The phone rang ten minutes later. It was Ellis, and with the answer to Ben's first question the investigation took a turn in the wrong direction.

Ben was temporarily stunned. "You had dinner with him last night?"

Chapter Eighteen

LOY ELLIS LIVED WITH HIS GIRLFRIEND in a one-bedroom apartment a few streets from of the UH campus. The telephone was listed under her name.

Ben took a two o'clock plane from Hilo. He was met at the airport by an off-duty Honolulu officer who had volunteered to drive him around Honolulu. The policeman's name was Bertram Kahani. He told Ben that everyone called him Buzz.

They headed directly to the University, but instead of taking H1, which Buzz said was at a standstill because of an overturned truck, they followed Nimitz Highway to Nu'uanu Avenue, then turned onto South King Street, and took that to Kapi'olani. Soon they were wedged between the high rises of Honolulu's commercial center and the equally tall tourist barracks that blocked the view of Waikīkī Beach. Then north on University until they entered the maze of apartment buildings that flanked the *makai* edge of campus. Buzz knew the area well, and without slowing down he engineered a series of lefts and rights, then pulled to the curb in front of a two-story, stucco building that was nicely landscaped.

"Here we are."

Ben nodded and got out. Then he leaned over to the window. "I'll be about fifteen or twenty minutes. You can come in if you want."

"That's okay. I brought a book. Think I'll sit here and read."

Ben saluted and turned to face the apartment building. Behind, the lush Ko'olau Range framed the scene. Dark clouds sat about three-quarters of the way up its slopes. It was raining up there, providing Honolulu drinking water. Over Punchbowl, half a rainbow arched across the sky, abruptly disappearing into the heavy clouds that clustered farther up the mountain range. The *pali* and the sky took on a deep purplish color. It looked like nighttime in the mountains.

The walk to the main entrance was guarded by areca palms, none taller than four feet, each without a trace of spotting, dead leaves pruned away. The tradewinds caught the fronds. The lower leaves strained to stand at attention. The upper fronds waved and bobbed as if they had something to say.

Loy Ellis had told him apartment 206, in the back.

On the side of the stucco building was a garden and a hedge of plumeria. Twelve mailboxes were built into the stucco. The small brass nameplate next to 206's mail box said Kaulukukui. Ben looked up and eyed the wooden stairs. A heavy, dark man was waiting for him at the top.

Ellis was short and husky. He looked to be of Samoan descent. He shook Ben's hand and gestured to the kitchen table. The apartment was small. The kitchen reminded Ben of the one in Patrolman's Keli'i's apartment, the place where he had first stayed when he returned to the Kona force, while Keli'i had been on his honeymoon. This kitchen was the same, one-way—compact people only. Ben wondered if Ellis could turn around in there without inhaling.

Ellis's girlfriend was sitting on a stool at a counter that faced a pair of half-cut French doors that gave access to the kitchen sink from the eating area. She was Hawaiian, taller than Ellis, thin, dark, and had breasts that were much bigger than her frame was meant to carry. Her halter top was at the limit of its elasticity.

Ellis cleared his throat. Ben guessed he was used to men staring at his girlfriend. And he tolerated it up to a point. To the point when he cleared his throat.

"This is my girlfriend, Maile."

"Pleased to meet you," said Ben.

Her smile remained reserved.

Ellis said, "You're from Kona, you said."

Ben faced him. "Uh huh. I'm investigating an explosion at the geothermal drilling site in Puna. Human remains were unearthed." Ben hadn't told Ellis anything over the phone. He wanted his candid reaction to what had happened in Puna. "When were you there?"

Maile got up and walked over to the window. She leaned against the sill.

"For a semester three summers ago."

"Did you know Wayne Enoki and Ray Kamakani."

"Wayne and I took the same classes. Ray and I met a few times, but he was a year younger and worked in a different area. I haven't seen either of them since the project. Why? I don't understand what this is all about."

"They've been missing since the work-study program. Quite frankly, Enoki and Kamakani match the physical stature of the remains that were found."

"What! When you said remains before, I thought you meant old stuff. I was thinking ancient Hawaiians and artifacts. You mean, you think someone murdered them?"

"Or they had an accident," Ben offered quickly. He wondered why Ellis had said murdered. He hadn't mentioned anything about a homicide.

Ellis, who had been sitting, stood, stared at Ben for a few seconds, and then walked over to his girlfriend and squeezed her hand. He turned and faced Ben. "And until you found me, you thought that I might be one of them."

"Yes. Until I spoke with your father this morning. You see, the explosion uncovered six sets of remains. Three were old ... bones of our ancestors. But three were new. Remains no older than two or three years. Someone hid them in an old burial cave, thinking that if they were ever discovered, it would be many years from now, maybe the next century. It would be assumed that they were a natural part of the burial cave. No one would test the remains." Ben paused. "I talked with Henry Helenihi."

Ellis smiled. "How *is* Henry?"

"He's fine, but he's scared. He noticed that the list of company employees excluded the three of you. So far, I have no proof that Enoki and Kamakani are dead, but that's my guess. That's why I'm here ... I need your help. What can you tell me about them? Did anything suspicious happen while the three of you were there?"

Ellis took his time. "When I first was chosen for the program, I was excited about being part of the plan that would make Hawai'i independent of foreign oil. But when I learned about the land swap, and saw how the environment was being ruined, I wanted to quit."

Maile stood and walked over to her boyfriend and hugged his neck. "I'll make coffee." She went into the kitchen.

"But I didn't do anything about it. I was a month from completing the program. I needed my degree. I needed good references. I had to get out of ... I had to help my family. You see, I am the first in my family to go to college. My parents work two jobs each, demeaning jobs, not the jobs of Hawaiian royalty. I know I shouldn't talk about my lineage, but it is there. I'm ashamed. I kept quiet about what was going on. For a job, for a stupid job ... I disregarded the old ways."

Ben inhaled slowly. Watching the lost look in Loy Ellis's eyes caused him to reflect on the past. From the missionaries and their religion to the annexation and overthrow of the Queen. From the sugar plantations to the resort communities. From the idea of *ahupua'a* to

211

the rape of the rain forest. Where was Kamehameha when they needed him? "I thought you might be Samoan."

Loy shook his head. "My ancestors … I know I should not talk about this … but I am proud of my ancestors. They go back to the royal court here in Honolulu." He gnashed his teeth. "I have a question."

Ben gave Loy a sincere smile. "It's okay to talk about your ancestors."

"No. I shouldn't brag about my royal blood."

"You said you had a question."

"My question is about Curtis Lyman."

"I was going to ask you about him," Ben said.

"I read about his murder. I saw that he was killed with a spear. I called the paper and talked with the reporter who wrote the story. He couldn't tell me much more. Now Wayne and Ray. Is there a connection?"

"Hilo is investigating his murder. As far as … "

Loy's head snapped up. "You were the Kona detective they said found him … right?"

A nod.

Ellis stared without blinking at the floor. Ben let him think. Soon Ben realized that Maile was standing in the doorway, listening. She had a worried look on her face. Ben tried to make eye contact, but she avoided it.

"I think someone from the company killed him," Ellis stated flatly. "And for that matter, maybe Wayne and Ray, too." He shouted that.

Ben straightened. In a calm voice, he implored, "Tell me why."

Ellis turned and faced him. "Because Curtis was an honest guy. He was brought up Hawaiian. I wondered about it when I read about his murder, but I thought an activist was involved, like the article hinted." He swallowed hard and stared directly into Ben's eyes. "They were making him falsify his lab work."

"You're sure?" Ben angled his head.

Ellis held Ben's stare. "Ray told me. Simple things at first. Like lowering the parts per million, even though the real readings were within environmental guidelines. He told me it was to set a lower trendline. He said that with more wells, the level of pollutants would go up. By lowering the early numbers, the company could show increases but keep the totals within the government's accepted standards."

"He complained?"

"He said he did."

"Why didn't he expose them?"

"He needed the job. He was near retirement. He was counting on his pension."

"But *you* think he had finally had enough?"

Ellis's lips trembled. "Yes." He lowered his head. "They killed him."

"Who's they?"

"Someone who worked for the company."

"Who? Look at me!"

Ellis's head snapped up. His expression angry. "I don't know."

"Any one you suspect?"

"I have no idea."

"You must be thinking about someone."

Ellis emptied his lungs. He didn't seem to inhale until after he said, "Geddes."

Geddes. Ben's tongue circled his lips. "What about Enoki and Kamakani? Were they upset when they found out what was going on?"

Ellis seemed to be having trouble listening. His head was bowed again and his hands were clasped under his chin. Finally, he raised his head a bit. Slowly, he rubbed his beefy cheeks with his palms. "They were vocal with management. They called the University and complained. They joined PDF."

"They joined the Pele Defense Fund?"

"Yes."

"When? While they were working for Jackson Hole?"

"Yes."

"Did anyone at Jackson Hole know?"

"I don't think so. At least not until the demonstration."

"When was this?"

"Maybe two weeks before the end of the summer … right before the program ended."

Ben sat and thought.

Maile went back into the kitchen. She turned off the coffee maker. She came back into the dining area empty-handed. No one was interested in coffee.

Ellis was still bent over. Maile stood behind him and began rubbing his shoulders. After awhile he looked up.

"What are you thinking?" Ellis asked.

"I'm wondering why the University didn't press for an investigation when they didn't return here."

"They keep track of who's here, not who's not."

"And *you* didn't miss them?"

"I thought they went back home."

"You stayed there?"

"For another month. I took some vacation time. Maile came over and stayed with me. I wasn't that close to Ray and Wayne. Besides, Ray lived on Moloka'i, and he talked about working on the mainland. I don't think he got along with his father. Suddenly, Ellis leaped to his feet. "Fuck!"

Maile jumped back.

Ellis looked as if something had exploded inside his head.

"What?" asked Ben. "What?"

Ellis was staring out of the window.

"Loy?"

"I think I know who the third person is."

"You do?"

"There was this guy, a local. He was real good friends with Ray. In fact, he had a big influence on Ray. They always hung out together. He was the one who got Ray and Wayne to join PDF."

"What's his name?"

"Eddie something. He lived in Pāhoa, I think, or close by. I bet you'll find him missing."

"Describe him."

"I think he was eighteen or nineteen. Five-nine, five-ten. Dark hair." He pointed to Ben. Like yours. Same length." Then Ellis marched over to the window. He seemed to go into a trance again.

"Loy, what else?"

"Nothing else. I'm trying to think who at Jackson Hole has the most to lose."

Maile took her right hand and covered those of her boyfriend, "Or to gain."

It was the second time Ben had heard that. First Tobi, now Ellis's girlfriend. He said it to himself— *Who has the most to gain? Who?*

In Buzz's car, which was equipped with a cellular phone, Ben called Hilo HQ. He didn't get Rodriguez, but he did reach Detective Kala. Ben asked him for an update. Kala said they had made no progress on the Lyman murder and there were no leads on the *kahuna*. Ben told him he needed another check of Missing Ps.

"No problem."

"Go back three years."

"All Islands."

"No, just Hawai'i. Start with Puna. First name, Edward. Age range … about sixteen to nineteen. I'll hold."

"That why we missed him before?"

"Uh huh."

"No last name?"

"No."

"Give me ten minutes."

"Okay, call me back. I'm on O'ahu with Patrolman Kahani." Ben pointed to the number. Buzz nodded. "Here's his car phone."

Fifteen minutes later, as they sat in H1's traffic, the phone chirped. Edward Palea had been reported missing by his sister. The last time she saw him was the day after a demonstration at the drilling site. He had been arrested and held for a few hours for chaining himself to the fence by the main gate with a pair of Krypto Lok bicycle locks. His folder said he had left a note to his sister that said he was going to the mainland to look for work. It was something he had talked about many times before. A notation in the file stated that his sister said the note resembled his handwriting but she didn't think it was his. Furthermore, she said he'd never leave without saying good-bye to her and to his aunt, who had raised them both. And there was still a few hundred dollars in his checking account.

The officer in charge of the complaint had written ' ... no foul play suspected. Case filed with Honolulu, and copies forwarded to Los Angeles and San Francisco PDs. ... '

"Where to now, Ben?"

"Where's the Department of Land and Natural Resources."

"Right across from the Capitol."

"Hawaiian Home Lands in there?"

"Nope ... in the old Federal building... by the Post Office."

"Let's go."

Buzz raised his eyebrows, questioning.

"Just a hunch."

A half hour later, Ben had the background material he wanted. Hawaiian Home Lands was sort of a lottery system. Years before, the State had leased land—land that many argued rightfully belonged to Hawaiian families. As those leases expired, or in some cases, when the lands were foreclosed, the leases were to be offered back to native

Hawaiians. It was supposed to be an equitable way to return some of the land to the people. When Ben asked how it was decided who received what land, the clerk explained there were lists. An applicant had to be at least fifty percent Hawaiian. The pecking order was based on when you registered.

But, just as Skip the fisherman had said, the land offered applicants might be halfway across the Island, away from family and friends, away from the environment they had known all their lives. Away from their job or the forest that sustained their *'ohana*. In Skip's case, away from the place his *'ohana* had fished for generations. The man behind the drab desk said many people refused. Most didn't have the money.

When Ben asked the clerk what happened when someone turned down a parcel, the bureaucrat struggled with his answer.

"Is the parcel offered to the next person on the list?"

The clerk wasn't convincing when he told Ben that that was usually the case.

After Ben left, the clerk swallowed hard and went to pick up his phone. He nearly jumped out of his seat when it rang. The person he was going to call had beat him to it.

Chapter Nineteen

Having landed in Hilo, Ben found his Jeep with the interior soaked. He brushed off the seat with his hand, jumped in, wiped his hand on his pants, and headed for Jackson Hole's offices. He was there in ten minutes. He took the stairs two at a time, then slowed at the entrance to the suite to compose himself before he walked inside. He was promptly informed that both Geddes and Takehiro were in Wyoming attending a meeting.

"When will they be back?"

The receptionist shrugged. "Mr. Takehiro will be back tomorrow or the next day. Mr. Geddes usually stays a month before he returns. After all, he lives there."

"You tell ... " Ben cleared his throat. "Please tell Mr. Takehiro I'd like to have a word with him as soon as he returns." Ben handed her his card. This wasn't something he wanted to pursue over the phone. "As soon as he returns."

She nodded curtly.

On the other hand, he couldn't wait a month to talk with Geddes. Could the Wyoming police question him effectively? He guessed not. Too much of the local environment influenced the case. He wondered what Wyoming was like in the middle of October.

He drove back to Hilo HQ. Rodriguez and Kala were at their desks, pecking thoughtfully on keyboards, mugs of coffee near their left hands, perturbed expressions wedged into their faces.

Rodriguez looked up and pointed to a manila folder on the empty desk by the window. Ben headed for the desk. Against the background noise of clacking keys, he read the MP report on Edward Palea.

His sister had filed the report. Her statement indicated that he had last been seen sitting on the steps of the Civic Auditorium in Ho'olulu Park a half hour after being released. They lived together, sharing the family house. There had been a note in his room, but his sister insisted that it wasn't his handwriting. Their parents were deceased, and there were no other relatives on the Island except the aunt who had raised them both. She knew nothing. Relatives on Moloka'i had been checked out. They hadn't seen or heard from Edward. The notation at the bottom of the form burned in Ben's mind. 'No foul play suspected. Case filed with … '

Kala got up and left.

Ben watched him leave, then shifted his glance toward Rodriguez who was staring intently at his screen. He typed for a few seconds, stopped, gave the computer display a satisfied look, hit one last key to save his document, and leaned back in his chair.

Ben asked, "You read this?"

Rodriguez looked up. "Uh huh."

"What do you think?"

"That part about the demonstration bothers me."

"You starting to believe my theory?"

"Yeah, but who?"

Ben closed the file folder. "Right now I'm thinking it's Geddes or someone in the Foldagger clan."

"You're kidding?"

"Geddes hired the students and he has control over most of the people. Maybe he's got something on somebody."

"Blackmail?" asked Rodriguez.

Ben shrugged.

"What about the Foldaggers?"

Ben thought a moment. "Maybe."

"Have you investigated any of them?"

"No ... first I need to establish the identities of the victims. I think I know who they are ... but I have to be sure."

"The two you told me about before and this one?" He pointed to the manila folder.

Ben nodded.

"What about the *kahuna*?"

"It's not the *kahuna*. He was out there praying ... doing what his family has done in that forest for generations. He belongs to Pele. He was probably asking for her help."

"Think she caused the explosion?"

Ben snorted at Rodriguez's remark.

"Seriously, that's the one thing that doesn't fit," Rodriguez said, tapping his fingers on the side of the computer. "If someone's trying to frame the activists, why destroy the project site?"

"I've been thinking about that. Two things. The person who used the dynamite wasn't experienced. Why no electronic detonators? Why risk failure with old-style fuses?"

Rodriguez shrugged his shoulders and said, "It worked."

"Yeah, but the second thing is the charges were set around the main holding pond. Why not the well? I think whoever it was was trying to do something dramatic, something that wouldn't interfere with the drilling operation. Hell, a new pond can be dug in a day or two. I think the explosion got out of hand. I think the force of the blast and maybe some of the seismic activity it set off toppled the rig. I bet whoever did it is pissed. He had no idea what that many sticks would do."

"But they're already starting a new site."

"I know." Frustration filled Ben's sigh. "Okay ... what if the well no longer mattered?"

Rodriguez frowned. "Huh?"

Ben pursed his lips. "I mean, what if it wasn't going to produce. What if they were going to abandon it anyway?"

"Can you find out?"

"Henry Helenihi would know."

"He's talking to you?" Rodriguez raised an eyebrow.

Ben didn't answer.

Rodriguez took a sip of coffee. "It could be dangerous for him to talk."

"He knows that. He's being careful. So am I ... so are you ... starting right now."

"Don't worry about me. What next?"

"I want to talk with ... " he opened the file, "Mary Palea, Edward's sister. Maybe she can give me something that will ID the remains."

Detective Kala returned.

Ben wasn't sure why, but there was something about Kala he didn't like. He knew he wasn't ready to trust him. Ben sent a look to Rodriguez that put a halt to the conversation. Rodriguez furrowed his brow.

Kala's expression looked sour as well. "There's a demonstration starting at the new well site."

"Shit," said Rodriguez. "We assigned?"

"No, just patrol, but I think we should go watch for awhile. Konanui seems to be leading it. There are hundreds of people there already."

Ben asked, "I thought these things were publicized well in advance. I thought ... "

"Not this one," Kala answered. "The new well has really gotten some folks bent out of shape."

"Let's go," said Rodriguez. "Coming, Ben?"

"Later, I'm going to see Palea's sister first."

Rodriguez signed off of his computer.

Kala left to bring the car around.

After Kala was gone, Ben asked, "Ernie, how come there's nothing new on the Lyman homicide?"

Rodriguez gave him a dumb look. "You tell me I'm wasting my time with the *kahuna*. You insist it's not Konanui. Where would you like me to look?"

"What about going after Jackson Hole."

"Jackson Hole?"

"Let's put all of their employees through the computer. Maybe someone will come with a record."

"Like Geddes?"

"No, I don't think so. Maybe someone who's working for Geddes. Someone who's worked with him before ... might have done his dirty work before."

"Soon as I get back from the demonstration."

"Mahalo."

Mary Palea lived in Mountain View, twenty minutes from Hilo toward the volcano, just off Highway 11. She and her brother had inherited a small farm. Now it was hers alone. She grew papayas and some vegetables, and Ben found her sitting on her front porch, sorting papayas by size.

As Ben got out of his Jeep, he noticed a black rottweiler rising to its feet, ears up, tongue out, fur bristled. It seemed more than curious.

"Sidney ... sit."

The dog sat. Ears still peaked, tongue still out, but at least its fur was flat.

Ben approached. He waved. The woman stared intently at the portable blue strobe attached to the Jeep's roll bar.

"Mary Palea?"

"Yes," she answered, warily.

Ben hadn't met many Hawaiians who were so outwardly suspicious. He wondered if it had something to do with her brother's disappearance. "Detective McMillen. I'm with the Kona district."

"Kona?"

"I'm helping out on a case. Can we talk?"

Solemnly, "This is about my brother, isn't it?"

"It might be."

Mary Palea pushed aside a box of papayas and gestured for Ben to sit on the *lānai*.

Sitting, he said softly, "I know this will be difficult for you ... "

"Have you found him? Is he ... ?"

"We have found the remains of three men. We can't positively ID any of them just yet, but we did find them near the geothermal project."

Mary's eyes shifted from Ben to the fields across the road, south toward the Wao Kele O Puna. He gave her a few moments before he continued. "Did you know Ray Kamakani?"

"Did?"

"He's also missing."

"Oh, my god! You mean they killed people protesting the well?"

"They both were activists?"

"They were best friends while Ray was here. I thought he went back home."

"Can you tell me more about Edward?"

"Oh, no!" It hit her. Her mouth was open and her head was shaking.

"Mary, please, I need your help."

After a few moments, and after she closed her mouth and took a deep breath, she asked, "Like what?"

"Well ... things that would help someone identify him."

"Like scars?"

"No… " Ben hesitated, "I mean broken bones, deformities … "

Shaking, Mary stood and ran into the house.

Ben waited a few minutes. Just as he was about to go after her, she came back out. She was carrying a picture frame. She marched to the end of the *lānai* and stared out into the fields. The wind caught her hair and it fell over her forehead. She left it there.

"I never got his dental records like they said. It was like admitting … "

"It's understandable."

She handed Ben the photograph. "That's him on the left. The one in the middle's Ray. I don't know the guy on the right."

Ben took the picture and studied it for a few seconds. He recognized Loy Ellis as the person on the right. Ray and Ellis appeared to be about the same height, but Ray was much thinner. Edward was a few inches taller, handsome, but it was evident there was an angry young man behind his smile. "Mary, I don't think this will help us."

"Look closely. Look at his left hand."

Edward's left hand was around the shoulder of Ray Kamakani. Ben stepped off the *lānai* and held the photo up to the light. He stared at Edward's left hand. Then he looked at Mary. "His middle finger."

Mary nodded. "He sliced off the tip with a power saw when he was thirteen."

Ben examined the photograph again. "When was this taken?"

Mary let out a deep, slow breath. "Just a week before he disappeared."

He tried to give Mary a comforting smile. "I hope each of the remains has a left middle finger, then … "

She raised her head. "You mean you don't know?"

"No, I don't have the lab report with me, but I can check it out quickly. Can I use your phone?"

Mary stared at him and didn't move. "Do you really?"

"Huh?"

"Do you really hope they have all their fingers?"

"Of course," he said. And really, he did.

Ken Asumura answered the phone right away. Ben explained what he had found. Ken put him on HOLD. Ben gave Mary a weak smile. Her face was expressionless. Ken came back on. Ben listened, then said 'goodbye,' and hung up.

"Of the three sets of remains, two are missing the last bone on the left middle finger, but," he added quickly, "there are quite a few small finger bones missing. This only proves that it could be your brother, not that it is."

"It's him." Tears welled up in her eyes. "Please go, but call when you know for sure."

Ben extended his hand. Mary finally took it. Then she slipped into his arms. He held her for a few moments. Then she broke away and said she was sorry. He left still hearing her sobs.

Outside, to Ben's surprise, was a tall man dressed in combat fatigues, looking inside his Jeep. Crew cut, deeply tanned, he wore a faded red-and-white bandanna around his head. He turned slowly toward Ben as Ben stepped down from the *lānai*.

"You the police?" he asked gruffly.

"Detective McMillen. And you … "

The man walked away, headed for a grove of papayas that grew between the house and the driveway.

"Hold on."

The man kept walking.

Ben heard the door open behind him. He turned and saw Mary. She was watching the man.

"You know him?"

"He's lives with me."

Ben didn't like it. But it wasn't his place to comment. Now he knew why Mary had been so distant when he first arrived. The man was an ex-soldier, one of the hundred or so who had made the Puna and Ka'ū districts their home. They grew marijuana. Some stockpiled weapons. They thought of themselves as survivors—they trusted only each other. The war still festered in their souls.

Ben bit his lip and then headed for the Jeep, watching the man again as he disappeared into the forest beyond the papaya trees. Before he turned on the ignition, Ben looked hard at Mary. She held his stare defiantly.

His expression said— 'You're asking for trouble.'

Hers had a dual meaning— 'Mind your own business ... find my brother.'

Chapter Twenty

HALFWAY THROUGH THE SUGARCANE FIELD behind Pāhoa High, Ben came upon a parked car. Around the next bend in the dirt road were several more. Soon cars and four-wheel vehicles lined both sides of the road, tires caked with mud, windshields so dirty it was impossible to see inside. There wasn't much clearance, so Ben downshifted into second and sat forward in his seat so he could see better. It had rained hard within the last few hours—large muddy puddles appeared wax-coated in the sunshine. Ben passed a few people walking toward the drilling site. Some waved, others showed him a raised thumb and pinkie finger—hang loose. They wouldn't have been so friendly if he hadn't detached his blue strobe and put it on the floor behind his seat.

After another quarter mile, he stopped. Too many vehicles choked the dirt road. He pulled off into the fringe of the cane field and headed back a short distance until he was near the intersection of two roads. He maneuvered his Jeep so it was pointed toward the intersection in between two parked cars, with just enough space for him to exit, and none for any vehicle to block his path. He shut off the ignition, hopped out, and started walking.

Many of the people who joined him for the last half mile were chanting. The majority of the them were barefoot. Ti leaf leis hung from their necks. There were friendly smiles on their faces, but serious looks in their eyes. Some held hands. Some small children were perched on their father's shoulders. It seemed uncanny, but even the little ones looked as if they understood that the purpose of this gathering wasn't recreational. The cane thinned out. The roadway widened, although it was clogged with cars, pickup trucks, and 4x4s. The chanting grew louder.

Ben couldn't believe how many people had assembled. There were Hawaiians of all ages, a surprisingly large number of *haole* residents, two Honolulu TV crews complete with mini-cams, several newspaper reporters, and enough Hilo patrolmen to staff two shifts. The police officers stood inside the gate, forming a line across the asphalt access road. They stood 'at ease,' hands folded behind their backs. Although wooden batons and service revolvers hung from their belts, they seemed more amused than anxious. They were talking, ignoring the crowd. Ben checked his watch. It was ten minutes before noon. From the looks of things Ben guessed the demonstration had been set to commence at midday.

He scanned the area near the line of patrolmen for Rodriguez. The detective didn't seem to be inside the gate. Ben wondered if he was among the crowd of protesters, looking for the elusive *kahuna*, or picking up the undercurrent of conversation, trying to decide if the demonstrators might become unruly. To date, each protest had been peaceful with the exception of the few scuffles that had broken out when the demonstrators refused to disperse and police officers started making arrests. The tone of the crowd didn't seem threatening to Ben.

He made his way forward, looking for Rodriguez. Instead, he bumped into Nohea.

"Whose side will it be today, Ben?"

Ben smiled. "I'm on yours more than ever. Where have you been anyway? I have some things I want to discuss with you ... like Hawaiian Homes and the identity of the remains."

"If they don't lock me up, I'll be home around five." Big grin. Then Nohea introduced Ben to the people he had been talking with. A woman from San Francisco, who was head of the Hawaiian Campaign of the Rain Forest Action Network. Also, another PDF official— a doctor from Moloka'i, as well as the spokesperson of the local chapter of the Sierra Club, and a couple from the Big Island Rain Forest Action Group. Ben shook hands. He sensed some curiosity about his presence.

Nohea laughed and addressed the group. "Don't worry, Ben's on our side ... at least I think he is. He's a fraternity brother from USC. He's also the person I told you about ... the one I took into the forest. The one who was with me when I found Curtis Lyman." Nohea turned to Ben. "See, I protected your identity, at least up 'till now."

The members of Nohea's group—showing a different kind of curiosity on their faces now—gave Ben nods and smiles. The Sierra Club spokesperson said, "You know, Ben, it would be kinda unique if no one was arrested. Think you could pass the word along?"

"Getting tired of the cuisine?"

They laughed.

Ben asked Nohea if he was speaking.

Nohea answered that they all were. "It's time we really got the message across. The second well, unless we stop it now, will allow Jackson Hole to take over the entire forest. This may be our last shot."

"Well, good luck. Good luck to all of you. I've got to find someone. See you later at your place." Ben walked away. He was nervous.

Rodriguez found *him*. "Any luck with the Missing P in Mountain View?"

"Maybe. There's reason to believe the three could have spent time together ... two of them were good friends... and they all might have had reasons to want the drilling stopped. They belonged to PDF."

"Interesting."

"Catch your *kahuna* in the crowd?"

Rodriguez gave Ben a frown. "You think it's funny, don't you?"

"The *kahuna* angle … the guy we caught… yeah."

"You know him, don't you?"

"I think so."

"Then why was he there?"

"Because he had a right to be there. Because he believes. Because he was brought up to respect the land."

"You're withholding evidence. If he's innocent, why not have him come forward?"

"I said I *think* I know him. You don't want to get into a civil suit if I'm wrong."

"You're not wrong."

Ben decided to change the topic. "What's the plan for the protest?"

Rodriguez relaxed his stance, leaned against the fence, and scratched his ear. "They have some speakers scheduled. I think the main thing was to get the media here at the site. I don't expect any trouble."

"What if they refuse to leave?"

"You withholding something else?" asked Rodriguez.

"No, Ernie. I just wanted to know."

"As long as they stay on this side of the fence and don't chain themselves to it, we shouldn't have any problems. They can stay all night for all I care. Besides, it's supposed to pour like crazy later on. How are you going to get positive IDs?"

Ben ran his fingers through his hair. "There must be something. Something small that none of the families have thought about. All we need is one. I think that will be enough."

"Geddes and Takehiro will say it doesn't prove anything."

Ben raised his eyebrows and shrugged. "We'll see. Somebody will slip up. They always do."

"I've got some things to take care of. See you later."

"Ernie." Ben pursed his lips. "No arrests unless you really have to."

Detective Rodriguez placed his hands on his hips and studied Ben's expression. Slowly he smiled. "No arrests, partner."

"Thanks. Let's go over everything tomorrow morning."

"Fine," said Rodriguez. "I'll meet you at the station at eight."

"Alooo-Ha."

The crowd responded to Nohea in unison, their voices loud and strong. They chanted— "... *ua mau ke ea o ka 'āina i ka pono... ua mau ke ea o ka 'āina i ka pono ... ua mau ke ea o ka 'āina i ka pono ...* "

Nohea wet his lips as he scanned the crowd. He was pleased at the turnout. He raised his hands. The chanting died down. Some people who had been sitting stood and edged closer.

"Today," he began, "we must show much unity." There was a chorus of cheers. Nohea needed to raise his hands again to quiet the crowd. He was standing on a rough wooden platform, microphone in hand, which was connected to an amplifier and two speakers that were secured to the chain fence that blocked entrance to the drilling site. "First, let us hear from our Sierra Club brother, Darrin Ito."

There was applause and hooting. Even the patrolmen on the other side of the gate seemed interested.

"Mahalo, Nohea."

Darrin Ito, a young man of Japanese descent who wore wire-rimmed glasses, spoke for ten minutes. He described what the explosion had done to speed up the process of contaminating the water supply. He talked about the venting and of the dying hawks, the weeds and exotic grasses that were strangling the young *'ōhi'a*. He explained that the total extent of the damage would not be known for months. He added that Jackson Hole wasn't being very cooperative in the process. There were boos and catcalls. When he was finished, there was murmuring, not applause. The crowd was angry.

The uniform patrolmen shifted their stance, folding their arms across their chests. Tight lips had replaced bright, white smiles.

The woman from RAN was next. She told them of the media coverage. That the world was finally starting to understand the plight of the Wao Kele O Puna. It seemed to Ben that the gathered throng didn't really believe her.

One man shouted, "Where are the major networks? Where is CNN?"

Nohea stepped up onto the speaker's platform. He held his hands in the air. "Please, please … " He glared at the man who had disrupted the proceedings. "When we doubt one another and there is no trust, we are no better than the drilling company that destroys our forest and defiles our goddess. These things take time. Look around, there are many more people here today than before. More media people. More of you. It will happen. It will happen soon." He stepped down to applause and whistles.

The woman continued. She talked about the money that had been raised. She told them that a specialist in environmental law had volunteered his services. Someone shouted, " … as long as it isn't Takehiro." There was laughter, then cheers and more catcalls.

"I assure you," she said, "this man we have has never spent a day on industry's payroll."

The assemblage applauded her. She stepped down.

Albert James, representing BIRAG, spoke as well. When he said Curtis Lyman's name, Ben leaned forward and listened more intently.

"Let's not forget that a man was murdered not too far from here. We know in our hearts that the killer was not anyone connected with us or our cause. So we can only assume that Curtis Lyman was our friend. They found him with a dead hawk in his hand. I think he found it. I think he was going to return it to the sea. I think he was tired of misleading the people who had become his friends. I think he was fed up with his job, with the lies. I think it was they," he pointed toward the drilling platform, "who ended Curtis Lyman's life."

The crowd was stunned. The man from BIRAG had focused on something none of them was prepared for. But Ben thought about what he had said. Ben believed it. The dynamite in Lyman's truck wasn't planted. He had come to blow up the well. He had come to sacrifice everything he had. But he'd been found out. And then Ben thought of something else. Maybe Lyman had a partner, or a compatriot. Maybe *he* was the one who blew up the well. Somber applause broke Ben away from his thoughts. James stepped down. Ben had missed the man's closing remarks.

There was much talking among the crowd. The policemen closed their ranks a bit. Ben saw Rodriguez talking with Detective Kala. It appeared as if they were arguing. Finally, Kala nodded and hurried away. Rodriguez disappeared into the crowd.

Nohea stepped onto the makeshift platform for the final time and Ben had this ominous feeling that something was about to go wrong. He envisioned a sniper and frantically scanned the area. With so many trees and the large cane fields still within rifle distance, it would be impossible to spot someone hiding. Ben walked forward. His dark feeling darkened. Visions of the assassinations of the '60s bombarded his brain. Instinctively, he reached for his gun. He caught himself, remembering it was locked in his Jeep. His heart was in his throat. What if Lyman's killer was in the crowd? Would a spear end Nohea's life? Ben hurried through the crowd, eyes darting left and right.

"Brothers and sisters, I am not here to talk about specific actions."

The murmur in the crowd peaked, then it became eerily quiet. Even the forest creatures seemed to sense that something special was about to happen.

"I want you to think about something. I want you to really concentrate on it. I don't want you to cheer or shout, I want you to take a deep breath and really think about why you are here. Then think about those who are not here and ask yourself why?"

No one so much as shuffled a foot. Ben felt goosebumps on his arms despite the heat and humidity. He scanned the crowd nervously, the image of a sniper, though faded, still bothered him.

"In America we have three indigenous people. The Indians, the Eskimos, and the Hawaiians. And all of us are becoming shrinking minorities. Like these other Native Americans, we have our customs, our religion, our beliefs, our gods and goddesses of nature. We have our myths and legends and folklore. Our ancestors came here many years ago. They are part of the land. They are not buried in the fields of Europe or the plateaus of Asia. They lived here. They died here. You came here today for different reasons. Some are concerned about the environment. Some are concerned about the value of their property. Some the health hazards. Some are here just to be part of this happening. A few have religious beliefs and are angry about the defilement of our goddess and provider, Pele. But too few really understand what the rain forest means to us Hawaiians.

"I ask you today to unite in your beliefs. To focus on what this is really about. What we must all focus on is the land. It is what we have the least of. It is what should be most important to us. The land and our traditions. That is what Pele stands for. You see, most Americans live in a place foreign to them. Their ancestors and customs and traditions … their land, their beliefs, the mythology that makes it all seem so mysterious and yet at the same time so wonderful, is many miles away from them. They are not living where they were spiritually born. But we are different. We are here … here with our ancestors in *our* homeland. We should understand the importance of the sea, of the rich soil, of the birds and the animals. We cannot let anyone pollute the air and the water. We cannot let another single species become extinct. If it happens by natural selection, that is one thing, but to alter nature, that is dangerous.

"So I ask you to think about the people you know who are *not* here. Seek them out. Explain to them how important this is. Be relentless. Never give up. Remember … you only have them when they believe strongly enough to recruit someone else. And please understand ... this is not just about the geothermal project. It is about much more. It is about our heritage.

"Go to Ka Lae. Stand on the cliffs and look out toward the sea. Envision our ancestors who struggled so to get here. Think about the feeling of elation when they first saw these great islands. Think about how they respected the land. Think of their commitment. Think how sacred nature was to them. But most important, think about your obligation. To pass all of this on. Your obligation is to preserve the land ... to become an ancestor yourself. For if you do not ... our people have no future."

The assemblage stood silent. There were quivering lips. There were tears. And then there was a deafening roar. The kind that thousands of committed people make.

Ben swallowed and wiped his eyes. He looked up to his friend. Nohea winked. A wide grin filled his face. The sniper in Ben's mind had disappeared.

And then, suddenly, the camera crews jumped into action. But they weren't focused on Nohea, they were filming the cheering, teary-eyed crowd ... and the applauding, teary-eyed policemen.

Nohea looked exhausted as he sat with his back against his 'ōhi'a tree. It seemed as if his speech had made an impression on him as well.

"How do you feel?" asked Ben.

"Tired."

"You had them today."

Nohea shrugged, then moved his shoulders in a small circle, letting the tension escape. "But will the drilling ever end? There's so much money at stake. I wonder if our efforts really mean anything. We need much more support. We have to make the politicians worry about being re-elected. The trouble is there are so many politicians. Sometimes I think there are more of them then us."

Nohea's words frustrated Ben. "Let me tell you what I was thinking about after you spoke. I was thinking about a movie I saw once called *The Candidate*. Robert Redford was in it. He was running for the California Senate against a real politician, a smooth-talking, do-nothing shit who had the system wrapped around his finger. Redford had spoken honestly about the issues ... party lines were no barrier to his rhetoric. At first, he struggled, hardly attracting attention. But he didn't give up. He believed in what he was doing. He started closing the gap in the polls. And one day, near election day, he gave a speech in a large shopping mall. It was great. When he finished, people's eyes glazed. They had tears in their eyes. And to this day I believe the director didn't have to tell them to cry. In fact, I'm sure that it wasn't even in the script. The people in the scene did that on their own ... they were moved by the sincerity in his words. They actually forgot they were in a movie. I don't think that happens often. But I think it happened today. People won't forget what happened in the Wao Kele O Puna this day. What you said and how you said it ... it made a difference. Take the night off if you wish, but come back strong in the morning. You're closer than you think."

Nohea looked up and sighed. His smile broadened but it seemed forced.

Ben winked at his friend. "You saw me."

Nohea's eyes glazed.

"I wasn't acting."

"Thanks, Ben"

"Hey ... thank *you*."

Nohea got up. So did Ben. They shook hands. They hugged. Nohea's strength seemed restored, yet Ben could still sense his friend's frustration. His thoughts, Ben guessed, were miles away. Maybe not miles away, maybe in a different time period. Like when their forefathers first landed. He could tell that Nohea just wanted to start fresh.

"You hungry?" asked Ben. "I'll cook."

Dinner was makeshift, but good. Afterward, they went back outside and sat on the *pili* grass near the base of the *'ōhi'a*. Nohea still had a faraway look in his eyes. Ben felt lost. The exhilaration of that afternoon had worn off, partly because of his friend's mood, partly from the thoughts of the three men who had met their deaths in the rain forest. And also there was Curtis Lyman, whom Ben was now sure was killed for the same reason as the other three. They all opposed the drilling project. Three years ago the killer hid the remains, careful to make identification nearly impossible. But last week, he had had a new idea—frame the activists. And it wasn't just the drilling project. There was something else at stake as well. Something connected. Like Hawaiian Home Lands.

"Nohea." No response. "Hey, Nohea." Ben nudged his friend. Absentmindedly, "Yeah."

"Tell me about Hawaiian Home Lands."

Nohea seemed to be having trouble concentrating on their conversation. He seemed isolated in thought, alone in the great forest, like he was weighing the risks of some plan. "Hawaiian Homes?"

"Yeah. Tell me exactly how it works here." Ben watched his friend closely.

"How it works ... it doesn't work."

"How about a little more," Ben urged with a smile.

Nohea rested his chin in his palm.

"What about the lists themselves?"

"You have to be fifty percent pure."

"No, I mean, how do people cheat?"

"The real cheaters are the ones who control the lists."

"Meaning?"

Nohea made an angry face. "Meaning you can't be sure what really happens with the names, the order, bribes ... who gets the good parcels. Who knows?"

"Nohea. I did a little checking the other day. I was thinking about the drilling project ... the entire project... and I got to wondering about the transmission towers that will have to cross the Big Island ... that the land will become valuable. Any idea who owns it?"

"The State or the County ... at least the part that is planned to go along the Saddle Road."

"But what about the land near Waimea and Kawaihae? The towers are supposed to go through there."

Nohea shrugged.

"I think someone is acquiring the lease rights from people who don't want to move there."

The activist stared at Ben. "What do you mean from the people? If you refuse, the option is supposed to go to the next person."

"What if someone who controls the lists has a list of his own? A list of properties that someone wants. When those parcels are refused, he slips the other person's name in, someone fifty percent pure who's fronting for an individual, or a partnership, or even some company. Then in five years when the transmission system is needed, they'll sublease it to Jackson Hole or the Foldagger family ... or better yet, keep it and charge a fee, like a royalty."

Ben expected shock, but instead Nohea's expression was sullen, disconsolate. The tired look of defeat in his face.

But Ben felt differently. Find the leaseholders of the land, and maybe you find the murderer. "What are you thinking about?"

"About the Foldagger family." Now a child's wishful expression filled Nohea's face. "I have this dream ... something I think about all the time."

"Go on."

"The Foldaggers used to be friends of my grandmother. There was one woman, Catherine Foldagger, she seemed like a nice lady. She was my grandmother's age. I met her once when I was fifteen or so. She gave me the impression that she really cared about the land ... about the Hawaiian people. My grandmother said once that she was the only *haole* she had ever met with a Hawaiian heart." He paused as if a sharp vision filled his brain. "Catherine Foldagger hasn't been seen in public in a long time. I can't help believing that this geothermal mess has been hidden from her. I don't think she'd stand for it. My dream is that I sneak into her house and tell her everything … " Water rimmed Nohea's eyes. "She's furious and she puts an end to it." He snorted. "Some dream, huh, bruddah?"

"Where's she live?"

"O'ahu … windward side."

"Why would you have to sneak in to see her?"

"I think they keep her under lock and key. It wouldn't surprise me if they kept her under a mild sedative all the time. I read that they've taken all her power. Someone else votes her shares. I don't think she knows a thing. I think it's been so long, she's probably convinced that she *is* a bit senile." He shook his head. "Not the woman my grandmother described to me."

"Why not try to talk to her?"

"I'd never get close … I'd be jailed for sure. Then how would I fight the battle?" Nohea stood. "I must go for a walk in the forest."

"I'll go with you."

"No, I must go alone. I must be alone with Pele. She will tell me what I must do next."

And he was gone.

Inside, Ben cleaned up the dinner plates—stacking the dishes in the cupboard, rinsing the pots, drying them, leaving them on the stove. Then he poured himself a cup of coffee, took a sip, added raw sugar, found no milk, but did find a quart of vanilla ice cream. He took a spoonful and added it to his coffee. Sitting by the fireplace, he thought about what Nohea had said that afternoon. About everyone's responsibility to become an ancestor. That meant something else as well. It meant marriage and children. For the first time the idea really appealed to him. He guessed that if Lisa had been standing next to him as Nohea delivered his speech, he might have asked her to marry him. He shook his head and smiled.

Then he thought about the movie again. He thought about the ending, the part he had purposefully left out. When after Robert Redford won the election, he was in his hotel room, minutes before he was to address his supporters, standing with his campaign manager, feeling the enormity of the task at hand, and asking Peter Boyle, "What do we do now?"

Scary. Scary for the candidate. Scary, now, for Nohea Konanui.

Ben got up and paced. After a while, he found himself confronted with the door to Nohea's dark room. He wondered what it looked like. He was pretty sure that Nohea hadn't been taking photos recently, so he wouldn't be disturbing the developing process. He tried the door handle. The latch opened easily. He stepped inside and flipped on the light. An eerie red glow filled the room. He spotted a large bottle of chemicals sitting on a sturdy-looking shelf with built-in slots for photographic paper. Paper neatly categorized as to size and texture. Trays for solution.

He tripped over a coil of wire. Bending to stuff it back under the workbench, he noticed that it had spilled out of a large, heavy-duty cardboard box. The wire looked familiar. He slid out the box. Newspaper covered it. He peeked inside. His heart stopped as if he had seen a coiled cobra.

Dynamite! He counted, but he knew how many sticks he'd find. He finished and slowly rose to his feet. His heart started once more. Faster than normal—as fast as it beat during the last mile of the triathlon.

Thirty-two sticks. Red ones. *Texas Blasters.*

Chapter Twenty-one

Hiki aku la i nā 'Ole—it has reached the *'Ole* nights. The time of the month when the phase of the moon was not good for fishing and planting. The expression was used when you were facing a bad time. Ben was facing such a time.

He wanted to believe that the dynamite had been planted in Nohea's dark room. It could have happened that way. Nohea certainly didn't lock his house. He hadn't been home much. The opportunity was there. But what about Nohea's sullen mood? Just hours before he had given Ben the impression that he felt the situation was hopeless, his moving oratory of the afternoon notwithstanding. Had he felt that way before? For how long? Nohea was smart. Smart enough to make Ben believe that the Lyman homicide was a frame-up.

Point the finger at yourself. Do it so simply that people believe that you've been framed.

Sitting outside behind the clouded mask of the descending moon, Ben heard the flapping of an owl as it hunted field mice at the edge of the forest. He could smell the damp, cool air. He saw glowing lime-green eyes close to the ground. They watched him, then disappeared into the forest when he shifted. He picked a few blades of *pili* grass and placed them between his palms, rolling his hands back and forth until the grass twisted and broke apart. Ben reached for some small stones near his feet. He flicked them one by one into the dense forest, hardly hearing them as they landed on the moss.

Waiting for Nohea's footsteps. Wondering if he was going to come back.

Ben glanced at the luminescent dial of his watch. It was past midnight. He was determined to spend the night if he had to. If Nohea showed up, they'd talk. Then he'd take him to Hilo. If he didn't show by first light, he'd go to Hilo himself, taking the box of dynamite with him. He'd explain everything to Rodriguez.

A Jackson Hole employee framing Nohea? Or Nohea making it look that way?

What would Nohea say?— 'Ben, after all we've been through, you still don't trust me? Fine, then turn me in.'

The stars were out in force. Ben tried to pass time by constructing the constellations. He got nowhere. He wondered how his ancestors had navigated across the Pacific. Then he picked up a stick and started drawing his version of the petroglyphs. He drew the forest and Nohea in the middle of a clearing. The well. A dying hawk overhead. The volcano in the background. Madame Pele watching. He heard footsteps. Nohea came out of the forest.

"Why are you out here?" Nohea asked.

Ben didn't answer. He stood. He said, "Come with me."

They marched into the house without a word. Ben walked directly to the darkroom door. As his hand found the latch, he turned and watched Nohea's face. Nohea looked puzzled, not alarmed.

"Go in if you want," he said.

Ben opened the door. He had left the box of dynamite and the long coil of fuse on top of the work bench. Ben pointed. Nohea's brow furrowed as he stepped forward to take a closer look. Then he turned and said exactly what Ben had thought he would say.

Ben took a deep breath. "I do trust you. But you have to understand my position, I just can't question you and turn you loose. Someone else has to see this. We should go into Hilo. I have no choice. You just tell them it was planted."

Nohea folded his arms across his chest. He looked disappointed, not angry or worried. Ben guessed it had nothing to do with the dynamite. Nohea was disappointed with him.

To show how ridiculous it was, Nohea insisted on helping Ben carry the box of explosives to the Jeep. They got in, Ben made a wide circular turn, and they headed for Pāhoa. Soon they were surrounded by the cane fields. The wind picked up and the cane leaves rustled in the darkness. The going was slow. Between the cloud cover and the mud on Ben's headlights, it was hard to see. Ben leaned forward and squinted.

"Want me to wipe them off?"

"No."

Ben hesitated at a fork.

"Left."

Ben angled left. They crossed two dirt roads Ben didn't remember. The moon disappeared completely just as they headed into a big bend in the old road.

Nohea yelled, "Look out!"

Ben braked abruptly. Nohea jumped out, shouted "See ya, bruddah," and disappeared into the sugarcane. Ben leaped out and ran after him. But in the darkness it was useless. The noise of the breaking cane faded—all he could hear was the wind. An owl hooted at him. He wondered if the *pueo* was leading Nohea away—or was it mocking *him*? Air sputtered through his lips. Then he cursed.

This is going to be fun to explain. First the kahuna, now Nohea.

In frustration he called out to his friend. "Good luck, bruddah."

Rodriguez sat behind his desk with an amused look on his face. "Say something."

Rodriguez raised his eyebrows, his silly grin puffed out his cheeks. "Tell me more."

"More? He escaped." How was I supposed to find him in a cane field that he knows, in the dark, when … "

"I guess it might have been easier if he had been handcuffed."

"I didn't think he'd … "

"If he wasn't your friend, you'd have handcuffed him." Rodriguez got up and pushed his chair away. "Konanui used you."

Ben bit his lip. He stopped short of snarling.

"C'mon … let's have a look at the dynamite."

"I think it was planted." *Is he really using me? Did he make it easy to find so I'd think it was planted? Nohea's clever …*

Rodriguez folded his arms across his chest. "Then why'd he run away?"

"Under the circumstances, you'd have done the same thing."

Rodriguez ignored his comment. "I told you I thought your theory had merit. I told you I hoped you were right. But we have a homicide here … maybe four. I think the time for hunches and friendships and save the rain forest has passed."

No question. The explosives were those stolen from Classic Structures.

After completing his report, Ben decided it was time to go back to Kona and talk with Tobi. Detective Rodriguez decided it would be a waste of time to hunt for Nohea. Instead, he had two patrolmen assigned to watch Nohea's house. There was another positioned a short distance from PDF's offices, and Detective Kala and another patrolman resumed a stakeout of the drilling site, this time a few hundred yards deeper into the forest where preparation work for the new well was under way. Ben sensed that Rodriguez was beginning to believe that the reason they had made no progress on the Lyman homicide was directly related to eliminating Nohea as a prime suspect. Ben started wondering about that, too. It began to torment him. What if Nohea had outsmarted him all along? He didn't want to believe it.

He decided to take the Saddle Road back to Kona. As he climbed through the lower elevations above Hilo, he kept picturing Nohea's face when he had confronted him with the dynamite. Ben couldn't find a clue there. He had to make a choice. Either Nohea was a murderer, or he had been framed. Ben's right hand drummed the steering wheel. He accidentally hit the horn. The noise jarred him into a decision. "Framed," he said. "Framed."

Just out of Hilo the roadway began its climb up the broad slope where the two volcanoes met. Both sides of the road were covered with stunted *'ōhi'a*, large ferns, and a few patches of ginger. There were small, bright houses, with gardens of orchids and hibiscus. And in Ben's rear-view mirror, a splendid view of Hilo Bay.

Soon, most of the greenery turned brown, and the flowering bushes gave way to scrub trees, browned *pili* grass, and lava rock protruding out of the embankments. This portion of the Saddle Road had recently been repaved. The bright yellow lines at the edges of the road gave stark contrast to the fresh black asphalt. For the most part, the white center line was solid. Passing zones were at a premium.

It wasn't long before the shrubs disappeared entirely and frozen rivers of lava covered the landscape. There was a distinct difference in the texture and color of the flows. Some were pure black, smooth. Others had a brownish orange coloring and sharper features. From time to time, as Ben crossed the saddle, huge cinder cones appeared, several hundred feet high, random reminders that nature was not predictable.

... and neither are people.

"Howdy, stranger," said Joyce.

Ben smiled. "You look like your love life is back in order."

"It is."

"Good. Any messages?"

"Plenty. "Ken Asumura called twice. Lisa. Danny Mitchell. Your bank."

"What did they want?"

"Banks leave numbers, not messages. You overdrawn?"

"I haven't seen my checkbook in weeks … or my ATM card for that matter. How could I be overdrawn?"

"Maybe somebody else found them."

Ben gave her a wry look.

Joyce scanned the list of messages again. "And … Andrew Takehiro called. Very polite."

"When?"

"Yesterday … just after five. He left a number on the mainland." She handed Ben the stack of pink telephone slips. Takehiro's was on top. The area code was 307. "Who is he?"

"Jackson Hole's attorney. Anything else?"

"That's it."

"Tobi in?"

"He's been expecting you."

"I didn't call."

"He usually can sense when one of his detectives is stuck."

"Well, I'm stuck all right."

"I think he's back talking with Vice. Go on, I'll get you some coffee."

"Mahalo."

Tobi was leaning against the door frame. His arms were crossed and he had the uncharacteristic look of someone plotting revenge. Sitting a few feet away, in his office, was Lieutenant Hector Dzura, the man in charge of Vice. Everyone called him 'Dizzy,' except Tobi.

Ben greeted them both.

Tobi said to the Vice Lieutenant, "Let me think about it some. It is risky. I want to talk to the Major."

"That's fine, Tobi. But we don't have much time if my information is accurate."

Tobi rubbed his wispy beard and nodded. He turned to his detective, "Been expecting you." Then he turned back, "Talk to you later, Hector."

On the way back to CIS, Ben asked what they had been talking about.

"Hector has one of his men undercover. Apparently there is a meet set up for tonight in South Kona. From what he can tell, two major dealers from O'ahu are coming. He wants to put a wire on Benes ... "

"Risky."

"I know. These are big players. I wish we had more time to set it up. Enough of that ... my problem, not yours." They had reached CIS. Tobi extended his hand. Ben walked inside and headed for Tobi's office. Joyce handed him a cup of coffee. "There's a fresh pot of tea on your credenza," she said to Tobi. He bowed to her. Ben didn't know anyone more polite than Tobi.

When they were seated, Ben eyed the phone while Tobi poured tea. "Maybe I should call Ken before we start. He might have something positive on the IDs. So far, all I have is a theory and three people who logically fit."

Tobi pointed toward the phone. Ben dialed the hospital and asked for pathology. Ken was on the line ten seconds later. Ben listened intently. He asked no questions. Then he handed the phone back to Tobi who hung up.

"Honolulu established the races. They match my three pretty well."

"You need something positive. Even if it is just for one."

"I know. But with no teeth ... "

"There is nothing on the Lyman homicide?" Tobi asked.

"Not a thing."

"Tell me what you think about your remains."

Ben told Tobi about Henry Helenihi and the list. "Two worked at Jackson Hole ... the third was a friend of one of the other two. Their nationalities, heights, and time of disappearance match up with what Ken has given me."

"Pretty conclusive for you and me."

"... but not for a jury."

"Convenient for Jackson Hole. They will tell you it was an oversight since the two were university interns, not regular employees. And they will say the students were finished with the work-study program and went back to the university."

"Tobi, it's somebody connected with the drilling company. Let's assume that it's someone with a lot to gain ... just like you said. I think there is somebody on the periphery, who hasn't got a lot of money, but knows what's going on. He's figured out some way to cash in, but only if the project goes through."

"Good theory."

Ben paused a second to inhale Tobi's praise.

Tobi added, "Maybe a county or state official?"

"Maybe. Here's the angle." Ben asked Tobi if he knew about Hawaiian Home Lands.

Tobi smiled and nodded.

Ben frowned. *Dumb question.* "Okay ... there are two other components of the drilling project ... the transmission facilities ... the undersea cable and the transmission towers. I guess the state or the federal government owns the undersea rights, and most of the transmission lines go across State land, but there are quite a few points where they don't. One of them is between Waimea and Kawaihae ... one of the major Hawaiian Home Land parcels." Then he explained meeting Skip, the Ka'ū fisherman and how he had refused the land at Pu'u Huluhulu, thinking a friend, next on the list, would get the parcel. "But he didn't. Someone else did. They slipped in someone else ahead of him."

"Who?"

"I don't know yet." Ben explained his theory about someone in the DLNR with a second list.

Tobi looked at his watch. "Must leave."

"No advice?"

Tobi flicked at the wisps of hair that floated around his ears. "It seems to me that you are waiting for something to happen. You have a theory ... check it out."

Ben called the number Takehiro had left. There was no answer.

He raced home for clean clothes, looked around for his checkbook, couldn't find it, debated calling the bank, didn't, and left, wishing it wasn't two hours back to Hilo. He'd have to hurry to make it before the State's offices closed.

———————

The Department of Land and Natural Resources, Land Management Division, was on the second floor, third door on the right.

The young, dark-haired woman seated behind an ancient koa desk was on the phone. She held the receiver a few inches from her ear. Ben could hear the caller—a woman shouting her complaint. It went on for another thirty seconds.

When she hung up, the woman looked up at Ben.

"Another satisfied taxpayer?"

"I wouldn't mind if they realized that I'm not their problem," she said. "I didn't make the law. I'm trying to help."

"Ben McMillen ... Kona police."

"What brings you over here?"

"I need some information on the Hawaiian Home Lands transactions for the last few years."

"Sure. The records are down the hall. The room's marked," she smiled, "Records. Paul Sumida can help you, but be patient, he's new."

Ben glanced outside. It had started to rain lightly. "Mahalo."

The room was surprisingly airy. All the windows were open, and since it was a corner room, there was good ventilation. A young man popped his head around a bank of file cabinets. "Oh, hi. Be with you in a minute." He went to the street side of the room to check if rain was coming in. It wasn't. "Now, what can I do for you?"

"Paul Sumida?"

The man nodded and extended his hand. Ben took it and identified himself.

"What do you need?" Paul asked eagerly, as if he were beginning to taste a hint of intrigue.

"I want to look at the Hawaiian Homes transactions going back ... say, three years."

"Not a problem."

"What I really need is people who refused the land when it was their turn."

Paul Sumida's grin disappeared and he shook his head. "Sorry. They're taken off."

"Thought so." Then Ben opened the map he had found in Curtis Lyman's pickup. Before coming to the DLNR, he'd been to Hilo HQ and checked out the map from the evidence locker. Spreading it out on the table next to Paul's computer terminal, Ben pointed. "Can you look up this parcel? He was pointing to the spot marked in red near the cinder cone named Pu'u Huluhulu.

"Not good enough. The map's too small. There might be a dozen parcels the touch that spot."

Ben was stuck.

"Wait a minute. Give me the name ... I just thought of something."

"Skip ... I mean ... Peleki Alu."

Paul sat down at his desk, then gestured for Ben to pull up a chair. The records clerk eased his glasses from the top of his head down onto his face. His fingers whizzed across the keyboard. Soon the orange monochrome screen welcomed them to the HHL data base. More typing. He frowned, looked at the ceiling, then seemed to have thought of something else, and typed some more.

Ben had trouble sitting still.   .

A minute later Paul smiled, clasped his hands on top of his head, and gestured by nodding to the screen. "There it is."

"I thought it was gone."

"Technically, it is. But when computers delete stuff ... well, let me make this easy. Every entry has an index. When something is deleted, what really goes away is the index, not the data. I used a utility program to search for your Alu. There he is. Not formatted real pretty, but you can read the sector and lot. That's what you wanted, right?"

Ben looked over his shoulder in the direction of the lobby. *Be patient ... he's new.* "You got it."

"Peleki Alu ... the parcel's in the town of Waimea—Sector 53, Lot 127. You need the degrees and minutes for the four boundaries?"

"No. But can you find out who leased that parcel?"

"Simple," said Paul. "We take the property information, log into the landholder data base."

Thirty seconds later, the orange letters appeared on the screen. Ben said out loud, "John Kekoa."

"Know him?"

"Didn't expect to."

Paul seemed puzzled. "What now?"

"I need a few more names of people who did the same thing. I mean people who leased property near one of theses red marks on the map, but only after someone else refused it."

"And you don't have anymore names, right?"

"Right."

Paul Sumida got up and paced, but only for a few moments. He spun around and said to Ben, "It'll take some time but here's what we can do." He explained that the sector and lot numbers were in numerical order in a grid. "We can probably guess a sector and lot number pretty close to the red marks ... what are they anyhow?"

"Sites for the geothermal transmission towers."

Paul Sumida's eyebrows raised.

Ben could tell he'd figured it right away.

"Okay, we pick some numbers, use the utility program to see if there's a deleted record. Eventually, we'll find them."

It took forty-five minutes, but Paul was right. They found three more situations the same as Skip's.

Ben looked at the names. "Now the hard part. We have to find some common denominator."

"No offense, Detective McMillen, but I may be a bit ahead of you. You see, the rest of data has some of their application information. Like where they work. I've noticed each of them works for HLC."

Ben was beaming, thrilled. He knew he was lucky, too. "You should be my partner."

"Thanks." Paul cleared his throat. "I've seen those initials before. They stand for the Hawai'i Land Company. Want to look them up? Probably a holding company."

Ben pointed to the computer. "On here?"

"Let my fingers do the walking."

Ben patted him on the back.

"We can get to the Corporations and Partnerships database. But let me tell you ... just like in the movies ... we'll have a tough time tracking them down. If there's something fishy about this, you're gonna find holding companies of holding companies. It'll take a lot of searching."

HLC listed Foldaggers as two of their directors. After going through ten computer screens of information, they found out that HLC was a subsidiary of M.V., Ltd.

The rest turned out to be easier than they thought. Within fifteen minutes they discovered that M.V., Ltd. was a subsidiary of Makaha Valley Investment Company and the same two Foldaggers were directors. Makaha Valley Investment was a division of Hawai'i Sugar Express, and the 'Express' motored right into the Foldagger Foundation. The Foundation head was Robert Foldagger. The majority shareholder was his aunt, Catherine Foldagger.

Ben pounded his fist into his palm. "Got them!"

"Mind telling me what they did?" asked Paul.

"Something no Hawaiian would ever do. I've got to get going … sorry I can't tell you more right now. But I'll tell you this. There's no way I'd have gotten this far without you. And I'll make it up to you sometime, but I've got to run now."

Ben shook Paul's hand and hurried out.

Yes!

After two hours in the Hilo Public Library, researching the Foldagger family, person by person, Ben sat back and thought. He wondered about Catherine Foldagger, remembering how Nohea had described her. He had trouble picturing her as playing a part. The newspaper articles, though vague in parts, seemed to support Nohea's contention that someone had made her a prisoner in her own home. Robert Foldagger, on the other hand, seemed to fit the role of a villain. Over the last ten years, stories of affairs, drunk driving, and the hint of a drug habit had popped up from time to time in the O'ahu papers.

So Ben came up with a plan. A way to lure the killer into a trap. That was, if Catherine Foldagger would listen. If she'd believe him. If she'd talk to the press. Hell, he had to find her first!

But what if he was wrong? He had a feeling that she was much smarter than her nephew, Robert. What if she was the mastermind?

Ben prayed that he was right, because on the surface, the idea seemed a little strange. He doubted Tobi would approve of his plan.

He drove home, not getting there until nine-thirty. He skipped dinner and dropped into bed, exhausted, but hopeful.

In the morning he wouldn't be able to remember any of his dreams. There'd be too many.

Chapter Twenty-two

T HERE HAD BEEN ANOTHER power failure. This time the South Kona District was out for a couple of hours. So Ben's alarm didn't work—it just flashed luminescent green, and he slept until nine-thirty. Unshaven, he made it out of the house by ten.

He decided not to tell anyone where he was going. If his suspicions were correct, then he was putting Catherine Foldagger, the matriarch of the family, in danger. He worried. What could she really do? She was eighty-three and not in good health. What if he found her in a wheelchair? What if she was senile? What about Alzheimer's? Visions of a decrepit old lady who had little control over her mind, let alone the complex functions of the Foldagger Foundation, kept creeping into his head.

He left from Keāhole at eleven. The Aloha inter-island flight stopped in Kahului before continuing on to Honolulu. There, he rented a car and headed for Makaha on the leeward side, taking H1 west, then 93, then heading into the foothills on Makaha Valley Road. Toward the mountains, past the manicured Sheraton Resort to Maunaolu Street. At the end, overlooking the Pacific, was the

Foldagger Estate, over a hundred acres of forest and mountain streams, an idyllic setting where one of the biggest landholding families—owners of thousands of prime acres, industrial parks, old sugarcane plantations, partners in the geothermal project—had once basked in paradise. Now only Catherine Foldagger and her attendants—nurse, cook, housekeeper, and gardener—lived there. Family members visited from time to time, and there were parties each month, but the other family members preferred to be closer to Honolulu and their business interests.

As Ben expected, there were no other cars on the road, so he drove close by the estate once, surveyed the garden fortress, then turned around and headed back toward the Sheraton. His assumption that there would be a guard at the front gate had been confirmed. The burly dark-haired man had looked up both times when Ben passed the entrance.

Near the back of the Sheraton, Ben parked in the shade of several monkeypod trees and began to walk through the woods. He felt a little foolish, thinking he might have driven up and simply announced himself. Chances were they would have let him in. But then, he wouldn't have been able to talk with Catherine Foldagger alone. He couldn't be candid. On the other hand, the front gate reminded him of a Mafia family compound. Announced, he might get in. But would he get out?

He'd chosen his running clothes to wear so he'd look like a jogger. For awhile he followed a trail just beyond the golf course. He saw golfers through the trees, but no one paid him any attention. Soon, he came to a spot where the forest was much thicker. After a quick glance over his shoulder, he headed into the dense growth, leaving the golf course behind. He figured he had another mile to go.

Ben met no one as he tramped through the forest. It was only slightly uphill, a grade of no more than a few degrees, and the heavy foliage blocked the heat of the sun. It was wet in spots—near the base of several large trees were puddles. He could hear a running stream not far away, to his left. He came to a narrow paved road, Alahele Street, which he had passed before. Looking both ways, taking his time before committing himself, he watched and waited. Finally, he dashed quietly across the road and disappeared into the forest once again. A few hundred yards farther, he saw a wrought iron fence melting into the foliage that had grown on either side. He stopped and listened. No sounds except a few birds. No watch dogs. He wondered if he was being too melodramatic.

Scaling the fence was simple, although the barrier was at least eight feet high. He guessed trespassers really weren't on the minds of the estate members; making a statement of their holdings was probably more important. Maybe years ago there were guard dogs.

Ben carefully went forward. For the first hundred yards there was nothing to indicate that he wasn't just in some part of the State forest. He knew he was quite a distance west of the main entrance. He angled northeast. After another hundred yards he came upon a gazebo. It was badly in need of repair. To the west the view was clear to the ocean. He stood by the gazebo for awhile, picturing a young Catherine serving tea or reading as she watched the glimmering Pacific far below. There were trees to the south. But they were smaller than the others. New trees, for once the entire area had been cleared to afford a clear view of the ocean. The sound of the stream was louder.

There was a path, now starting to fill with weeds, leading from the rear of the gazebo. Ben followed it. After another hundred yards, he saw the house, a huge white Victorian with a green roof. Brown pine needles covered most of the roof. He imagined it contained at least two dozen rooms. Ben checked his watch. It was one-thirty. He wanted to talk with Catherine right after lunch when he guessed she'd be alone, resting in her room. His eyes scanned the driveway. There were no cars in sight. What about servants? Could any be trusted?

Ben approached the wide veranda that ran along the rear of the house. He saw no one. Quietly, he stepped onto the long porch and tiptoed to the window. Peering inside, he looked into the kitchen and spotted a young woman who was deboning a chicken. Looking around, Ben determined that she had just started preparing dinner.

To his left was the back door. He walked to it, careful to stay close to the house where the floorboards would be nailed and be less likely to squeak. Opening the screen door slowly, he looked toward the kitchen. He could see the young woman's back. How do I explain myself if I'm caught? Kona detective. Wrong Island. No warrant. Sneaking around in the home of one of Hawai'i's wealthiest families. How about lost jogger? He supposed if it came to that, the truth would have to do.

Where would she be this time of day? Napping or reading in her room? And where would that be? If she was handicapped like the articles about her led you to believe, then maybe she'd be on the first floor. But if someone really wanted her to remain as invisible as possible, then perhaps she'd be upstairs. Second floor, not third. He went with his hunch and tiptoed toward the front of the house and the stairs. Up the broad staircase—the setting reminded him of the mansion in *Gone with the Wind*. At the top was a hallway leading around three sides of the house. The number of doors was incredible. There must have more than a dozen. All were closed. He tried the first, the one directly across from the stairs. It was unlocked. Carefully, he peeked inside. An empty bedroom. He moved left. The next door was unlocked as well, another empty bedroom. He closed the door quietly. The next door was locked. Suddenly, he heard music. Then a man's voice, singing softly, playing a guitar. It came from the room at the end of the hallway, farther down in the same direction that he had been progressing. Stepping onto the Oriental runner, Ben followed the sounds. When he stopped in front of the room where the music was coming from, he felt his heart pounding and perspiration forming on his brow. He listened, concentrating, hoping to determine how many people were in the room. Then he heard the crackle of applause, which quickly died away. It was a recording. He touched the door handle. It was gold and the kind that you moved to one side to open. Carefully, he pushed the handle right. It was unlocked. He inched the door open. The light in the room was muted, the curtains were closed, although they fluttered a bit in the breeze. There was a phonograph spinning. The next song began. Then, as his eyes adjusted to the dim light, he saw a huge four-poster bed and a woman sitting on the edge, her attention focused on the record player. She was dressed simply, a long white skirt and a light pink blouse. Ben expected something from long ago, but the outfit seemed new, contemporary. He looked at her face. She looked much younger than he had imagined, making him think that this was not Catherine Foldagger, not a daughter, not that young, but maybe a younger sister. His mind sifted through the articles he had read the day before. He couldn't remember any mention of a sister. Her expression was sharp and alert. If he didn't know better he'd have guessed it was Catherine Hepburn, waiting for Spencer Tracy to escort her to dinner. Her voice startled him.

"Who the hell are you?"

Quickly, Ben stepped inside and shut the door.

"Mrs. Foldagger?"

"Who did you expect?"

"Is it you?"

"Who are you, young man? Be out with it, or I shall call for help."

Ben figured his badge might help. He took out his detective's shield and took a few steps forward. "Ben McMillen, Ma'am. I'm a detective with the Kona Police."

"The hell you are!" she shouted.

He shushed her and said, "Please." This woman had spunk.

"Don't tell me to be still! Who are you?"

Ben straightened. "I'm exactly who I said I was."

"What's a Kona detective doing on O'ahu?"

"I have to talk with you."

Then Ben saw the wheelchair in the opposite corner of the room.

He looked at her legs.

"I don't use the thing. I'm not old and sick like they make me out to be. They forget I used to run this family." Her voice softened and cracked. "Now they ... they won't let me go anywhere. They hear me when I go down the stairs. They've stopped me every time. If they didn't, I'd leave. Drive the car into town ... that would show them."

She seemed out of breath but Ben saw the determined look in her eyes. He liked her already.

She raised her voice again, but she was straining to do so. "Why are you here, dammit? How'd you get in without anyone seeing you?"

"Mrs. Foldagger, I came to ask your help. You're our only chance."

"Me? About what? What's this about?"

"Can I sit? Will you promise to listen? I have a lot to tell you and not much time."

"What could we possibly have to discuss?"

Ben decided to be blunt. "The destruction of Hawai'i."

"What! My Hawai'i! What are you talking about?"

Ben took a deep breath. For some reason, he suddenly became overwhelmed with the situation. He felt like he was fighting for the survival of his people. He felt the wetness in his eyes.

And that's what did it.

"Young man, you're crying."

"I'm sorry."

"Don't be sorry. Only men with character cry. The rest are worthless. I may sound like a tough old broad, but that's because all my life men have been trying to take advantage of me," softly with a glance to her window, "even now." Her tongue came out and wet her lips. She was quiet for a few seconds and very still. "Tell me why you sneaked in here."

"I wasn't sure it was safe for either of us to have someone know that I was coming." Ben saw her puzzled look. "Let me explain."

"Sit and be quiet, my hearing's fine. Problem is, so is everybody else's in this damn house." She looked at him quizzically for a few seconds. "You know … you need a shave."

Ben grinned and nodded. Then he blew out a short breath. "Who else is here besides the man at the front gate?"

"Now, just the cook. But my nephew will be here in an hour. He comes every Wednesday afternoon. Says he wants to see how I'm doing. I think he comes to see if I've died yet. Excuse my French, but he can go play with himself."

Ben wiped away a tear that had trickled down his cheek. He gave Catherine Foldagger a big smile. Then he sighed deeply. "Here goes."

Right off, he asked her if she'd heard about the geothermal drilling project. She hadn't. Ben started slowly, not sure if she could keep up. He told her about the original well and Kīlauea's eruption. Then he explained the land swap. Her eyebrows raised quite noticeably upon hearing that. Ben increased the pace of the conversation.

"Those lands were ceded in perpetuity to the Hawaiian people. Now they can't even enter *their* forest, not to mention hunt, plant food, gather medicinal plants … and they cannot partake in religious ceremonies. To this day, many believe in Pele."

"Count me in that group, young man. Hawai'i has wonderful legends."

Ben smiled. "The wells vent toxic hydrogen sulfide gas. The animals are dying. I buried a dead hawk. Hawks are endangered. The high concentrations of silica and other chemicals … like arsenic … have gotten into the water table."

Then he explained the economics of the geothermal project—that is—the lack of economics. The towers, the cables in the channels, the interference of the marine life. He sped on, like a man possessed.

Catherine Foldagger had hardly blinked. Ben could see she was absorbing all of it. He saw anger in her eyes.

"And … Mrs. Foldagger … "

"Catherine, Ben. My mother," she laughed, "my mother is … actually she wasn't, she was Mrs. Davis." She tried to cover her smile with her hand.

Ben laughed. But then he shrank a bit and sighed. He felt he had to drive his argument home. "Catherine ... there've been four murders."

"Oh, my God!"

"Haven't you heard about any of this?"

"I don't watch television and I never saw anything about it in the newspaper." She pointed to a neat stack of papers on her desk.

Ben guessed they censored what she read. "One of Jackson Hole's supervisors ... just last week. Three others, hidden until now in a burial cave with ancient remains, were recently unearthed during the explosion."

"Explosion?"

He had forgotten the dynamiting. Ben described it.

Catherine leaned back on her bed, her thin arms bracing her body. Ben thought she was shivering.

"Are you okay?"

She nodded curtly. "*I* am fine."

"That's it."

"Could there possibly be more?" she asked, giving him an incredulous look. "What do you want me to do?"

Here we go. He explained his theory about the murderer and the connection to Hawaiian Home Lands. As her face wrinkled up, he starting explaining Hawaiian Home Lands. She nodded. Ben continued.

When he was done, she said, "A fine mess."

"I checked some of the transactions. Your name, indirectly, is on them."

"Mine?"

"Who has power of attorney for you?"

"My nephew."

"Robert?"

A soft 'yes.'

"And he's coming here in an hour?"

This time her voice was loud and angry. "YES!"

They waited until three.
"He's never late," she said when Ben told her the time.
They waited another half hour.

Ben was standing by the window.
"Let's go," she said.
He turned. "Where?"
"I want to see it for myself."
"The drilling site?"
"Yes ... and ... and the forest my family has ruined ... the ani-
mals ... and the birds ... " Her voice trailed off as she stared outside,
crying.
Ben waited for a few moments. Then he said, "Today? Now?"
"Absolutely."
"I had hoped you and I could talk with the press."
"After I see it for myself, young man!"
"Can you travel?"
"I will make myself make it. You pack me some things. I'll tell
you were they are. And be quiet."
"My car's not in the driveway ... it's two miles away."
"You look strong ... carry me."
"There's an eight-foot fence."
"There's also a side gate."
Ben hadn't counted on this. But he felt he owed this to her. It was
like this woman was his grandmother. He didn't know why that
feeling came to him. He just knew it was there, and her wish was
something he couldn't refuse.

They left the bedroom ten minutes later and the man who had
been watching them through binoculars pounded his fist against the
trunk of a tree. Although he must have felt the pain from the rough

bark, he gave no evidence of it. When he saw Ben carrying Catherine Foldagger through the woods, passing within a hundred feet of his hiding place, he didn't know what to make of it.

He cursed. Then he followed. And soon, his expression changed. He realized he had been lucky. Trailing McMillen hadn't been such a bad idea after all. Maybe this was his day to kill two birds with one … spear.

Chapter Twenty-three

I T WAS AN HOUR BEFORE DARK when they reached the gate to the new entrance. By then, Ben felt as if they were old friends. Catherine Foldagger was like a scholar who had been locked in a time vault. She had questions. But also she had answers. She had a life story that kept Ben spellbound.

She told him of her earliest memories of the Islands. When downtown Honolulu had dirt roads. When twenty people on Waikīkī Beach was considered a crowd. When the Islanders used to marvel at approaching Pan Am Clippers as they droned laboriously over the final stretches of the Pacific before banking right and landing just beyond the military fields at the newly constructed commercial airport. When sugarcane was king and her family controlled the trade.

She hadn't always lived in the Makaha mansion. For a time the family lived on the leeward side of Maui, near Honolua. He asked her about school and found that school had come to her in a steady stream of teachers and tutors that the family hired for her and her younger brother.

Hawaiiana had always fascinated her. She knew a lot of the language. She liked the customs, the folklore, the mythology. She liked the Hawaiian reverence for children and parents. She said it took the focus away from the individual.

"Too many people think only of themselves. And too many people regard caring for their parents and their children as an obligation instead of an honor."

When she was reminded of her first husband, tears filled her eyes, and she had been either too proud or too stubborn to wipe them. He had drowned near Diamond Head just a few years after they married. She held onto the details, but told of her regret that there had been not enough time to start a family. When she had talked about that, Ben noticed she seemed filled with longing just from the memory. The expression was quickly replaced with disdain when Ben asked if she had remarried.

"Yes," she said curtly. "And our Hawai'i would be a much better place today, if not for people like Devon." She added, "Unfortunately, there was one like him in every major landholding family." She had referred to them as 'greedy bastards.'

He liked her a lot. He was glad she would see the forest first-hand. But he worried that bringing her to the press would put her in danger. It had been his plan to use that meeting to draw out the murderer, but that was before he had met her. Before, she had just been a name. Now, she was a friend of his people.

Ben showed his badge to the gatekeeper. He let them through.

The new road skirted the old road. Much of the debris from the explosion had been removed, but the stark reality of the blast still remained. As they passed clearing painted with silica crystals, Ben could see the look of horror pressed into Catherine's face.

"Where was the well?" she asked.

Ben pointed and said, "Over there."

Catherine nodded. "This white stuff is the silica?"

"Uh huh. And sometimes, in the air, there's huge invisible clouds of hydrogen sulfide gas. It's what killed the hawk I told you about."

Her lips quivered for a few seconds.

"They started a new well just days after the old one was blown."

There was no comment from her this time, no indication she had even heard him. "The forest is beautiful." She pointed up, beyond the new drilling site where the great canopy started.

"On the surface. But look down … see how brown and thin the trees at the edge of the clearing are?"

No answer. He could tell she was deep in thought. Ben shifted into third and the Jeep lurched forward.

A quarter mile ahead they reached the end of the new dirt road. Farther in, he felt it would be too bumpy for her, so he stopped the Jeep. Again he became worried. His plan didn't seem so clever any more. Drawing the killer out into the open at Catherine Foldagger's expense seemed foolish. Why had he thought that the killer wouldn't harm an old woman? What made him think that he alone could protect her? He needed Rodriguez's help. And then something else occurred to him. All along, he had felt that the murderer would try to intervene with their contacting the press. But here they were, right in the middle of the killer's hunting ground. What if … ?

No. We had an hour's head start. No one saw us leave. We were in the air before Catherine's disappearance could have been discovered. No one would expect her to come here. Hell, why would they even connect her disappearance with the geothermal project?

He felt better. *Tomorrow, when we talk with the press … no after … after is when something will happen. I'll call Rodriguez tonight.*

He turned and looked at her. Catherine's eyes were closed. He wondered if the plane trip and the drive might prove to be too much for her. By her own admission, her recent travel had been confined to slow walks to the gazebo and back. The last thing he needed was for her to collapse—they weren't close to a hospital. He looked at her, staring for a long time as they sat there surrounded by the Wao Kele O Puna. She looked fine. Her cheeks were reddish, but it seemed to be good color, not signs of increased blood pressure. They remained silent. The only sound was the uneven whine of the Jeep's engine.

With uncanny timing, she said, "Turn it off."

He twisted the key. They sat for a few minutes. Neither spoke. Then she asked him to help her get out.

"Are you sure?"

"Young man, we're going for a hike." She reached for the door handle. She seemed in a hurry.

Ben jumped out and ran to the passenger's side. He opened the door for her and helped her out. The earth was fresh and soft. He tried to hold her hand, but she jerked it loose. Then she bent and scooped up a handful of volcanic soil and brought it to her nose. Inhaling deeply, smiling. Saying, "This reminds me of the pineapple fields of Honolua. When my brother and I used to run through the fields between what seemed like endless rows of pineapple crowns. We'd fly kites up there on the hills. It would be nice to go back and visit there, too."

Ben said, "It's getting late. It'll be dark in less than an hour."

Catherine said, "Then we better get going."

Ben expected her to turn for the Jeep. Catherine marched off toward the forest. She seemed much stronger now, as if the raw earth and forest air was just the elixir she needed. Ben shook his head and caught up. "Let me hold your arm, please."

This time she smiled and offered it as if he had asked to escort her onto the dance floor. They walked for five minutes until they heard the screeching of a hawk. Both looked up. Catherine spoke, a hint of fear in her voice, "My mother used to say that when you hear 'io screech, he's warning you to go back."

"That's funny," Ben said, "my grandmother told me it meant he was trying to teach you the language of the land."

"I like that one better." After a few more paces, Catherine stopped and looked at him. "Tell me, Ben, are you married?"

Ben smiled, "This is only our first date ... but I accept."

She hit him on the arm. "Don't tease me, you fool." She laughed.

"Not married ... a shame. A man like you should have a family. I wouldn't wait."

"I have a very close friend. I think we're getting closer."

Catherine locked onto his arm once more. "Tell me about her."

Up ahead, the *kahuna* knelt before an angry idol. The *ki'i akua* seemed to be snarling through its big carved teeth and flaring nostrils, setting a spell with wide eyes, a tongue poised to lash out at his enemies.

This was the first time the *kahuna* had come during the day. He couldn't wait any longer. It had been almost a week since his last visit. The murder had scared him off, but now they were starting a new well. It was his responsibility to pray for the destruction of this new one. He had a special *mele* for this occasion. A chant for Pele. One that was so sacred only true descendants of the royalty of Puna knew it. He closed his eyes, readying himself. It was a long chant and his great-grandmother had told him once you started it, you must not stop until the end. He breathed slowly, concentrating, getting ready. Then his head snapped up. He thought he heard voices. He listened intently, and hearing nothing except the sounds of the forest, returned to his prayer—the prayer his great-grandmother had told him should never be interrupted.

The man dressed as a *kahuna* cat-walked through the forest. His eyes shifted back and forth. He had lost their voices. He was nervous. He tightened his grip on his spear.

Ben and Catherine stopped at the edge of the forest. Neither spoke. The hawk had gone, soared inland, high above the canopy of *'ōhi'a*, until it was a tiny speck in the darkening sky.

"It's peaceful here," whispered Catherine. "Like how I remember the slopes of Haleakalā near Kula. We had a summer home there. High up where it was cool. We had horses. I used to ride mine almost every day. I named her Kula. Pretty original, don't you think? I was only ten." Catherine grinned. "I remember a very funny thing. You see, I learned that she was a mare. One night there were people for dinner. Many people and I was the center of attention." She made a sour face. "My brother had misbehaved and was in his room. My father asked me to tell everyone about my horse. I told them she was the mayor of Kula. They all laughed." She sighed. "It's funny what you remember when you get older."

A roll of thunder echoed behind them. Ben turned.

"What was that?" she asked.

"Just thunder. This is the month of thunder and rain, big surf, and much wind. *'Ikuwā.*"

"I remember that. Should we be getting back?"

Looking skyward, "I don't think it's going to rain. But it'll be dark soon … we should go. Have you seen enough?"

"I see what more drilling will do. I understand how impractical the transmission towers would be. I can see how our friend *'io* will disappear forever. I guess I have seen enough."

"Do you have any idea who might have committed the murders?"

"No. But I believe we can find out."

"How?"

"I still have a few old friends. They are powerful people. They will help us."

"What if they're involved?"

"Not these people … trust me. You see, there is a generation of us … older people who still own majority interests in a lot of what you see around you. But our voices were taken from us. It's called power of attorney. We were lied to. You have shown me the truth. I will tell them. Perhaps they will want to come here, too."

Just then, Ben heard a humming sound. He grabbed Catherine's arm and they stopped. He put a finger to his lips. They both listened. Someone was chanting. Abruptly, it stopped. Ben's eyes searched for the source of the prayer. Seconds later he spotted the *kahuna* watching them from behind a small patch of taro. "Stay here. Don't go anywhere, understand?" He didn't wait for an answer. He started walking toward the *kahuna*. Immediately, the man started running. His speed didn't surprise Ben. But the fact that he had returned did. It was time to find out why. Ben took off after him.

After dashing fifty yards, he came to the end of the new clearing. He glanced back over his shoulder. Catherine was still there. He turned, ducked between two *'ōhi'a*, and pursued.

The forest was thick and the fleeing *kahuna* was nowhere in sight. Ben was slowed by the dense undergrowth, fallen logs, and patches of exposed lava. He remembered Nohea's warning about invisible fissures. Crevices that could open up just inches below the surface and swallow a man. So he ran, but carefully, shifting his eyes from the ground to the forest ahead, hoping to catch a glance of the *kahuna*, praying that he wouldn't be looking up when he should be looking down.

Finally, he stopped. He heard running steps maybe fifty yards ahead. The *kahuna* seemed to know where he was going. And even though he was close, he was invisible, completely enveloped by Pele's forest. Ben cupped his hands around his mouth and shouted. "Ken! Ken!"

The footsteps stopped immediately.

"How did you know?"
They stood a few paces apart. Ken Asumura was breathing hard. Ben's breath was more under control.

"When the Hilo detectives and I watched you chant, it seemed real … I mean sincere. Right then I had trouble envisioning whomever we were watching as Curtis Lyman's murderer. By the way, your disguise is great."

"If it's so great then how come you knew it was me?" Ken asked.

"Funny, but there was something about your eyes that got me thinking. I didn't place it until a couple of days later when I was out with Danny looking for a stolen charter. We found it abandoned in a cove near Miloli'i. There was a marlin on the back rail. The birds and sharks had done a number on it, but something about its eyes held my attention. You see, there was blood all around, but one of its eyes was more bloodshot than bloody. It had a broken blood vessel, just like the right eye of a Kona pathologist I know. Just like the *kahuna* we captured. I guessed it was you. I wasn't positive, although I told Tobi not to pursue it. I think I convinced Rodriguez the old *kahuna* wasn't the perpetrator. Anyway, I separated myself from you and Lyman's case. Rodriguez and Kala had that one. I knew they wouldn't find you unless you came back."

They exchanged stupid grins.

"I concentrated on the remains. That way I really wasn't with-holding anything. Anyway, a broken blood vessel on a marlin is hardly evidence."

Ken worked his hands through his hair. "Mahalo, Ben. This is something my *'ohana* feels strongly about. I had been coming here to pray long before the geothermal project."

"I kind of remembered that, too, but I wasn't sure. But tell me, I'm dying to know how did you ... "

Catherine Foldagger's scream filled the forest. Ben froze for a second, then raced toward her. Seconds later, he heard Ken trip and fall. He didn't stop. As he ran, he hoped that was what had hap-pened to Catherine—that she had been trying to find him and fell. But there had been terror in her scream. Maybe she had fallen into a fissure. Ben's stomach knotted. Seconds later, when he emerged from the *'ōhi'a* forest, he saw Catherine Foldagger on the ground and a man running from the scene, heading for the forest to the west. The man glanced over his shoulder, and although dusk had settled in,

Ben recognized him. It was Nohea.

He sprinted to Catherine's side. There was blood on her head but she was alive, breathing and groaning, trying to push herself onto her fragile elbows.

Ben heard Ken scramble out of the forest.

"You go after him, I'll help her," Ken shouted.

Ben raced after Nohea.

Fuckin' Nohea. I trusted the sunnufabitch! You sunnufabitch ... I trusted you!

Ben caught a glimpse of Nohea about fifty yards ahead. In the growing darkness, under the canopy of *'ōhi'a*, it was hard to gauge the distance. Nohea had the advantage. He knew his way through the Wao Kele O Puna—knew where the fissures where, where the trails led. Ben realized it was a only a matter of time before he ducked into a lava tube and escaped in the network of underground passages.

Ferns and low branches slapped at his face, stinging his cheeks. One caught him directly in the left eye. The eye clouded with tears.

Night fell upon the forest like a stage curtain in free-fall. He had only sounds now and gray shadows to guide him. The only thing on Ben's side was his stamina. Nohea would soon be out of breath. Ben felt he could run forever as long as he didn't fall into the earth.

He heard Nohea running ahead, slower now, maybe because of the dark, maybe from fatigue. Or maybe because he was nearing his underground escape route. At the last second Ben saw the outline of a fallen tree. He jumped it, catching the bark on top, praying as he was about to land that there wasn't a huge hole waiting for him. He was lucky, there wasn't. He raced on, dodging ferns and low branches instinctively, using his hands to fend off the attackers. Suddenly, he realized the sound of running footsteps was far ahead. It seemed almost impossible. Nohea had doubled the distance between them. Then he tripped and fell. A hand reached out. Ben jumped back.

A panting voice. "It's ... me ... Ben."

"Nohea!"

"Get ... get him. He's getting away." Nohea pointed. "He's headed for our tree."

"Who is it?"

"Couldn't see. Hurry! And be careful ... he's got a spear."

For an instant, Ben wondered what to believe. He quickly decided he was with Nohea all the way. He jumped to his feet and took off, following the faint sounds ahead, but this time knowing where he was headed, to the old roadway, to the venerable *'ōhi'a* that he and Nohea had used to gain entrance to the forest. He veered left, moving quickly toward the old drilling site, hoping to reduce the distance between the man he was now chasing—the man he hoped Nohea had been chasing, not running with. Ben burst into the old clearing. It was lighter. Traces of silica were everywhere. The moon slipped from behind the clouds. Ben raced toward the old tree that marked the entrance of the lava tube. He could hear the other man running. The sounds were to his right, slightly ahead, making a parallel track to the tree. Ben tried to run quietly. Gravel crunched beneath his feet, but he assumed it would be hard to hear fifty yards away, especially when someone was running hard, and his breathing was heavy. Ben believed that if the man heard him cutting through the old drilling site, apparently knowing where he was headed, he'd change course and head deeper into the forest. Ben ran on the balls of his feet, gliding now. His eye cleared; he was feeling much better. In the back of his mind were visions of Nohea. He wondered why he still trusted him. It came to him again—what if the man he was chasing had been with Nohea? Then Ken and Catherine were in danger. He was tempted to abandon pursuit, but Tobi's voice echoed in his mind. 'People who second guess, come in second.'

The form of the large tree loomed ahead. When Ben was within fifty yards of it, his heart sank. He saw a shadowy figure reach the base of the tree, turn in his direction, and then disappear.

Ben reached the fissure and scrambled down the stone steps, concentrating on the layout of the tube, trying desperately to remember the direction he and Nohea had taken before. He tried to visualize the dimensions of the cavern. Some came back to him, at least for the section near the tree. After that he was guessing. Ben knew if the man knew his way, he had two choices. He could follow the correct path and put much distance between them. As soon as Ben could no longer hear his steps, the man would be free. But Ben realized that the man couldn't know who was following him, and moreover, he might suspect that whoever it was was just as familiar with the underground network as he. So the second choice would be to take a side route, find a hiding place, and sit tight for a few hours. Ben would pass him, the man would hear his footsteps, and then when the time was right, he could retrace his steps and come out in the forest again, and make his escape over land.

Ben walked briskly. He heard gravel and rocks ahead. The noise was faint, and getting fainter. Then it stopped. So did he.

And a new thought popped into his head. What if the man was waiting in ambush? He'd forgotten about Nohea's warning of a spear. And since it must be the same man who had killed Curtis Lyman, then the spear was definitely something to fear. Ben pictured himself being tossed down a fissure, falling hundreds of feet, pulling at the spear that protruded from his chest.

He slowed his pace. His eyes moved back and forth, but they weren't going to help him. It was black. He stopped and listened. He could hear running water. He remembered that from before. It also meant that he was near the large 'ōhi'a root that extended from the surface and touched the floor of the lava tube. He knew that when he was near it there would be some light. Not much, but remembering the position of the moon, he thought some moonshine would make its way down into the darkened shaft.

A few paces farther, the blackness turned only slightly lighter to dark gray. He could make out the faint form of the *'ōhi'a* root, a few feet wide, a mass of twisted fibers. He looked up toward the roof of the tube. The moonlight was there, but it cast its beam against one of the smooth walls, high above. It would provide some light as he worked his way farther into the cavern, but not for long as he remembered a bend just ahead. As his eyes adjusted a bit more, and as he started to walk around the ball of roots, he saw a glint of something shiny. It moved upward slowly, then ...

He ducked as he heard the man grunt. The gleaming steel tip turned black and Ben heard it whiz by his head. It crashed against the opposite wall and then clattered against the floor of the cavern. The man started to run. Ben lunged. He caught him by the ankles and the man fell hard to the ground. Ben was on top of him immediately, groping for the man's arms, hoping there was no other weapon. He made contact with a failing fist, grabbed the man's wrist, and broke it with one quick snap. The man screamed in pain. His other fist caught Ben on the side of the head. The blow was strong and totally unexpected. Ben tumbled left, his back hitting a jutting point of lava, bruising his shoulder blade. He reached out and caught the material around the man's waist. The texture of the clothing surprised him. They wrestled and twisted, but the man's broken wrist reduced him to fighting with one hand. Soon, Ben was on top of him again. He punched the man flush on the jaw and heard that break as well. The man's body relaxed. He was out.

The moon had disappeared behind a cloud. It was completely black. Ben stood and caught his breath. He was glad of one thing. He had his handcuffs tucked into the back of his pants. He secured them around the man's wrists, being careful with the broken one, for what reason, he did not know. Then on his hands and knees he searched for the spear. He found it shortly. The man was still unconscious. After sitting for a few minutes, gathering himself, he bent and hoisted the man onto his good shoulder, dipped to pick up the spear, and slowly made his way back out.

The man was light. Ben started thinking about who it was. He ruled out Geddes, his prime suspect. Geddes was six-two and weighed over two hundred. This man was much shorter and lighter. Finally, he reached the steps. A voice called out.

"Ben? It's me, Nohea."

Nohea limped down the stone stairs. Together they carried the unconscious man out of the lava tube.

"How's Mrs. Foldagger?"

"She's okay. A little woozy but okay. Here they come now."

Ben could see the Jeep's headlights. It pulled up next to them just as they placed the man on the ground. Ben ran over. "Are you okay, Catherine?"

"I'm fine. This is exciting, isn't it? We caught the murderer."

Ben smiled. "You're something else, Catherine," he said. "You're *really* something else."

"You haven't seen anything yet, young man."

"Holy shit!" It was Nohea shouting, staring down at the unconscious man whose face was bathed in headlights. "You'll never believe this!"

Ben walked closer, but before he could see the man, he said, "It's Takehiro, isn't it?"

"How'd you know?"

Ben drew closer. He bent and studied the man dressed as a *kahuna*. There had been two of them. One *kahuna*, and one dressed as a *kahuna*.

"How'd you know?" Nohea repeated.

"It just came to me. His size. And something Catherine said to me. It was a good pun actually and it got me thinking. That they'd taken away her voice. That someone had power of attorney. Here's your attorney and the power was geothermal. His motive? ... He's been using Foldagger employees as a screen to lease certain Hawaiian Home Lands after they've been refused. He has someone in the DLNR working with him, and my guess, Robert Foldagger is as well. The land's strategically located right where the transmission towers are supposed to go. Takehiro used to work closely with the Hawaiian Home Lands Commission when he was with the State. He'd know how to scam the system, who to bribe. Only a few people know the locations of the towers. In fact, I wouldn't be surprised if Takehiro helped pick the sites. You see, he's the only major player in this with no major source of income other than his job. I think he was one guy who really couldn't afford to have this thing fail."

Just then, Takehiro let out a primeval scream. He tried to get up. Ben put his foot on the attorney's chest and pushed him to the ground.

The bewildered attorney cried out, "Help me!"

Nohea glared at him defiantly. "Don't worry, Takehiro ... Pele will take care of you."

Chapter Twenty-four

Two months later—

Foldagger puts lid on Geothermal

By Dave Pali

Tribune-Herald Columnist

Today the elders of Hawaii's big landholding families spoke. And today the people of Hawaii received a new lease on life—life the way it used to be.

The Pele Defense Fund had scheduled a press conference for eleven a.m. By ten the street in front of the State Office Building, the scene of many geothermal vigils, was clogged. Many people were in traditional Hawaiian dress. Some brought blankets and gourds, and pockets of ritual hula erupted all along Aupuni Street. The scene resembled the final day of the Merrie Monarch Festival. By ten-thirty it was evident that the crowd expected a significant announcement concerning the controversial geothermal project in Pahoa. They were not disappointed.

Nohea Konanui, spokesperson for the Pele Defense Fund, introduced Catherine Foldagger, the matriarch of the Foldagger family, one of Hawaii's much-maligned landholders, to the assembled throng. At first, reaction was mixed, but when Foldagger explained how she and other heads of the large landholding families had been railroaded by members of their families and unscrupulous business associates of these family members, the crowd became intently interested and respectful. When she announced that Jackson Hole Geothermal, the company drilling in the Wao Kele O Puna rain forest, had been shut down for good, the crowd exploded in cheers and started chanting her name.

Ever since the first geothermal well was started, the people of Puna have protested. They cited environmental problems—the venting of toxic hydrogen sulfide gas into the air, and holding ponds of toxic silica, a by-product of the drilling, which contaminated the drinking water with high concentrations of arsenic and other dangerous minerals. They called for an Environmental Impact Statement. None was ever commissioned even though over $40 million in Federal funds had been committed to the geothermal project.

In 1985, when Kilauea covered Jackson Hole's original drilling site with over 300 feet of lava, the Foldagger Estate and the State of Hawai'i swapped land. The State received the lava covered Kahauale'a area in Kilauea's East Rift Zone,

while Foldagger received the lush Wao Kele O Puna, a rain forest that had been ceded to the people of Hawai'i in perpetuity. It soon became off limits and the site for a proposed series of wells and power plants that were to generate 500 megawatts by the mid-1990s.

The protests increased, focusing upon the endangered species and the rain forest itself. Many ohia and other native plant-life have died as the result of clearing the land coupled with the invasion of alien weeds and grasses that choke the native species. Plants and herbs that for centuries had been important medicinal cures were killed. Access for religious ceremonies was denied. Groups like PDF, the Sierra Club, the Rain forest Action Network, and BIRAG, the Big Island Rain Forest Action Group, have demonstrated and brought suit for years. Until now, all in vain.

Recent events—the murder of Jackson Hole's Chief Inspector, Curtis Lyman, the dynamiting of the well, which unearthed an ancient burial cave and the remains of additional murder victims, and the arrest of Andrew Takehiro, Jackson Hole's attorney—finally got the attention of Catherine Foldagger and her life-long friends, people who still remember Hawai'i as it was, people who knew nothing of the geothermal project—it had been hidden from them. And they came to the rescue. It is not clear how they were brought in, but sources point to a Kona detective, Ben McMillen, who had been assisting Hilo detectives with tracing the identity of the remains that were unearthed when the drilling rig was sabotaged last October. McMillen was not available for comment.

With regard to Andrew Takehiro, the list of crimes attributed to Jackson Hole's former attorney is mind-boggling. Hilo detectives suspect that Takehiro was responsible for dynamiting the well and possibly for the murders of the three mystery victims. Also, the Tribune-Herald learned yesterday that Takehiro allegedly attacked Catherine Foldagger when she visited the rain forest to inspect the environmental damage first-hand. Takehiro is also suspected of land fraud. (Please refer to the article on page 4 regarding Hawaiian Home Lands.) It is believed he was acquiring leases for land that was slated for use by the energy consortium. Land that was to house the overland transmission towers and the termination points of the undersea cables to Oahu. Speculation is that Curtis Lyman was about to expose Jackson Hole management for forcing him to falsify Environmental Protection Agency statistics. Under those circumstances, any stoppage of the drilling project might have meant financial ruin for Takehiro.

Takehiro's trial is scheduled to start right after New Year's. He is currently being held without bond in an undisclosed facility.

Finally, the Foldagger family set aside the remaining Jackson Hole's assets for assisting in the cleanup effort currently underway in the Wao Kele O Puna.

Hawaiian Homes gets Trust; warning from Foldagger

By Marsha Ho and Dave Pali
Tribune-Herald Columnists

In addition to the announcement of the geothermal shutdown, the Foldagger family and friends revealed plans for the formation of a People's Trust—a fund seeded with $50 million to assist native Hawaiians in acquiring land as provided for under the Hawaiian Home Lands Commission Act of 1952.

There has been much controversy over the years regarding Hawaiian Homes. Native Hawaiians argued that they shouldn't have to buy back what was rightfully theirs in the first place. Rumors of improprieties, of manipulation of the lists, of representatives of wealthy landowners subleasing properties from Hawaiians who knew nothing of the commercial plans for the land in the future. Some were directly associated with the geothermal project—lands on which the cross-Island transmission towers were to be built. Lands where the undersea cables would come ashore.

Acquisition of this land is postulated as the prime motive in Andrew Takehiro's, Jackson Hole's former attorney, alleged crimes of assault, murder, and dynamiting the drilling site. An Oahu DLNR official, William Gates, suspected of aiding Takehiro in the scam, has been arrested. Apparently, Takehiro arranged land leases for Hawaiians in the employ of Robert Foldagger's various business enterprises. Gates allegedly strategically placed these person's names on the Hawaiian Homes lists. The land was slated as sites for the geothermal transmission towers that Takehiro, himself, helped pick. Robert Foldagger, Catherine Foldagger's nephew, a man known to have made many bad investments, is missing. Hilo and Honolulu police suspect he was Takehiro's partner.

John Forester, head of the second largest of the major landholding families, who said his circumstances—being forced to assign power of attorney—were similar to that of Catherine Foldagger, was named to head People's Trust.

"For a long time, people who finally made it to the top of the lists were too often given an option of land that was many miles from where they lived, far from where their friends and families lived. And most

times the land was unsuitable for farming, for even building. There was no electricity, no water, no access. That will stop."

Forester added that, "the second problem is money. People simply can't afford to lease the land and work it. That's when greedy politicians and outsiders with other interests offer the cash to sublease the property. This has got to stop as well."

Forester said that the lease prices of the land will be set at whatever the person can afford. "If it's a hundred dollars a month, so be it."

And Catherine Foldagger warned that "if the politicians and appointed officials who control Hawai'i[an] Homes don't play by the rules, then we'll see that people are elected who will."

Nohea Konanui, spokesperson for PDF, said, "The closing of Jackson Hole is a victory for Madam Pele and for those with a life-long commitment to the land. The Hawaiian Homes Trust is [a] good compromise. We would rather have our land back free and clear, but this is fair."

When asked what was next for him, Konanui laughed and said it would be nice to think that the environmental movement in Hawaii was no longer necessary, but he said, "it would be foolish to believe that." When pressed, "So, what's next?", he responded, "The boat ramp at Ka Lae."

Chapter Twenty-five

One month later

THE COURTROOM CLERK, Circuit Court - Second Division, said in a loud voice, "All rise."

Judge Manalo entered the courtroom. He paused for a few seconds at the bench before he sat. Then so did everyone else—everyone except Andrew Takehiro. Finally, Takehiro's attorney reached up and put his hand on his client's shoulder, urging him to be seated. The judge watched with interest.

"Are you ready for sentencing, Mr. Kagawan?"

"We are, your honor," answered Takehiro's attorney.

"So be it."

The hush in the courtroom turned into whispers and then there was silence.

Takehiro and his attorney stood. Their chairs squeaked as they pushed them back.

"Mr. Takehiro, you have been found guilty of attempted murder and murder in the second degree." Feet shuffled in the courtroom. Someone sneezed. The judge raised his arms, allowing his flowing sleeves to fall back near his elbows. "State law mandates a prison term of not less than five years and no more than fifteen on the first charge, and twenty years to life for the second." The judge paused and stared at Takehiro. Then he continued. "I have given your sentence as much thought as any. I've considered not just what you've done, but what greed has done to our Islands. I've thought about the Wao Kele O Puna. What a remarkable place it is. A tropical rain forest that was so determined to grow that it took hold and sprouted time and time again after the devastation of countless lava flows for millions of years. I thought about the 'io and the honeycreeper, and of our ancestors who planted taro patches so they would have food in reserve during long hunting journeys into the forest. I thought about the Happy Face Spider. Why he's happy with men like you destroying his fragile foothold on life is beyond me. And I thought about people with ailments and a forest void of medicinal cures.

"Then there's Curtis Lyman, a man who decided that there'd been enough lying and cheating, and so what did he get? A spear in the heart. And poor Catherine Foldagger. Imagine, trying to kill an eighty-three-year-old woman. Imagine the type of person who can bring himself to do that."

Outside, a fine mist began to fall. Inside, the people in the courtroom seemed to be transporting themselves to the rain forest.

"Mr. Takehiro, what about three missing students? You won't speak about that. Three people whom we can't ID because someone … " He paused and gave Takehiro a fierce, chilling stare, "pulled their teeth and violated sacred burial grounds to cover up the crime. Think about the families of those three young men, Mr. Takehiro. Think about their anguish. Think about the pain they will have to live with forever. Let me tell you this, Mr. Takehiro, the pain of not knowing is worse than any other."

All the time, as Judge Manalo spoke, Takehiro's head remained bowed. His eyes were unblinking. Ben who was seated next to Nohea in the last row of seats, doubted if Takehiro felt shame or remorse.

He bet what he felt was self-pity.

"And so, Mr. Takehiro, we come to my duty to pass sentence. I asked myself as I was thinking about what you have done ... what will prison teach this man? Can it reform him? Quite frankly, I have trouble believing that. Nothing in your defense points to any remorse. Not once did you say you were sorry. Hollow as that might be ... not once did you apologize. I find that appalling. I thought about you in prison. I even visualized it. And do you know what I saw, Mr. Takehiro? I saw you preparing appeal after appeal, looking for a new trial, thinking only of yourself. Pretty sad statement, isn't it, Mr. Takehiro, if that was all that came to mind?"

The judge took a deep breath.

"So Mr. Takehiro, I've decided not to send you to prison."

The courtroom erupted. The judge banged his gavel, but he didn't seem angry. Ben studied his face. The judge seemed to be getting some delight out of the disorder. The Court Clerk looked at the judge. The judge waved him off.

Takehiro, for the first time, raised his head. Ben thought he saw a glimmer of a smile in the defendant's face. Ben felt like getting up and punching him.

Finally, the noise settled down.

"So what have I come up with, you wonder? I will tell you, Mr. Takehiro. It's simple. It's called community service."

The State's prosecutor jumped to his feet. His protest was drowned by the shouts echoing throughout the courtroom. This time, as the judge slapped his gavel to the bench, there was a scowl on his face. But it wasn't for the unruly people, it was directed solely at Andrew Takehiro.

Quiet was restored once again.

"Yes, community service, Mr. Takehiro ... You smile. Maybe a bit prematurely."

Takehiro stopped smiling.

"Your sentence, Mr. Takehiro, is to work for the County of Hawai'i.

You will be paid minimum wage. You will work a standard shift Monday through Friday. Saturday and Sunday you will be confined to the minimum security facility here in Hilo. Your job will be to help those who are cleaning up the Wao Kele O Puna."

A few people started to applaud, but quickly stopped when Judge Manalo looked their way.

"When that is done, you will help those in the Puna District who acquire new homes through Hawaiian Home Lands. You will help build houses, help them plant crops, help them feed their animals. Mr. Takehiro, your community service will be whatever the people of Puna ask of you. Your fate is in their hands."

All eyes shifted to the convicted murderer. Takehiro seemed to be weighing what all this meant. At first he didn't seem to know how to respond. Then his eyebrows raised as if he had missed the obvious. As if the sentence might contain a loophole for him. Immediately he changed his expression. His expression became sullen, as if his sentence was a tremendous burden. Then he bowed to the judge.

Ben watched the interaction between the two. To Ben it seemed as if the judge had something else planned, but yet he said nothing. Obviously, it was either Takehiro's turn to speak, or to remain silent. Ben's first thought was that Takehiro had gotten off easy. But there was something in the judge's eye that told him there was more. That the judge seemed to be waiting for something to happen.

Just then, it did.

"Your Honor." Takehiro cleared his throat a few times.

The sound of his voice seemed to startle the people in the court-room.

"One question."

Judge Manalo nodded.

It hit Ben then—how long?

"If I may ask, Your Honor, how long is my sentence? How many hours?"

"You see, Mr. Takehiro, I honestly don't know."

286

There was a murmur in the courtroom. Takehiro's mouth asked 'What?' but nothing came out. He wet his lips. "I beg your pardon, Your Honor?"

The judge sighed. He clasped his hands and rested his elbows on the bench. "You must understand, Mr. Takehiro, it would hardly be fair for me to determine that. Not after what you have done to the people of Hawai'i."

Takehiro was speechless, his expression puzzled and fearful at the same time.

The judge stood, beaming, and bowed back to Andrew Takehiro. Then his eyes shifted to the window, toward the volcanoes. Everyone followed his gaze, including Ben and Nohea.

The judge's head lifted. He faced Takehiro. "Your sentence is up to her ... Madam Pele will tell you when you have served your time."